Cottage Cove Homecoming

A Cottage Cove Sweet Romance

Merri Maywether

This book is a work of fiction. The characters, incidents, and dialogue are from the author's imagination and are not to be construed as real. Any resemblance to actual events or persons, living or dead, is entirely coincidental.

Merri Maywether

P.O. Box 109

Sweet Grass, MT 59484

merrimaywether@gmail.com

979 885-4112-178

Living a life full of people you'd like to thank is the greatest gift I'm glad to have received.

Chapter 1

Whitney's Wild Ride

Every time Whitney closed the passenger side door of her best friend's Jeep Wrangler, she asked the universe the same question. Was it her time to join the great cupcake bake-off in the sky?

Granted, they'd never been in an accident or injured. Still, Jasmine was the worst driver.

Thinking this ride would be different because she had baked goods for a birthday party was an exercise in poor judgment.

Whitney gritted her teeth and endured the consequences of her bad decision. The two dozen cupcakes were not going to make it.

Her fingers burned from the tight grip she used to secure the box on her lap, taunting Whitney. *Maybe you'll remember this next time.*

But she wouldn't. Because Jasmine was her best friend. And her best friend had the gift of talking Whitney into doing anything.

Most times, it was for their mutual benefit. The others—

they laughed about the shenanigans gone wrong after the blush of *what were we thinking* cooled.

"We're only five minutes away." Jasmine's light reassurance would have worked if the entire vehicle hadn't jostled when she turned sharply in an overcorrection.

Whitney sucked in a breath and elevated the pink box to cushion the contents within.

Trees canopied the sides of the two-lane road. Jasmine kept her sapphire blue eyes trained on the dirt road leading to the house tucked away at the outer edges of Cottage Cove. The furrow in her brow declared her command of the situation. "I couldn't hit that squirrel. Its babies were probably waiting for their dinner."

It was a familiar scene—Whitney and her best friend, Jasmine, rushing, this time, to Jasmine's brother's birthday party.

The two women, the unlikeliest of friends, had been inseparable since their freshman year of high school. Jasmine was slender, sassy, and had a larger-than-life personality.

Whitney preferred to let her light shine behind the curtain. In the way only a best friend could get away with, Jasmine often threw Whitney a surprise eliminating her chance to avoid attention.

This time, it came three hours before the ride that had Whitney questioning the sanity of agreeing to be a passenger in Jasmine's jeep. Jasmine had invoked Whitney's gift of thriving under pressure. "Whit, I'm calling in a favor."

Calling in the favor was unnecessary. Whitney would do anything for Jasmine. Still, using the word "favor" meant the request was a big deal.

"Sure, what do you need?"

Jasmine started with flattery. "You know how you have a magic touch in the kitchen?"

It was more like Whitney filled her alone time with baking.

She used the treats as an excuse to invite herself to people's houses.

"And did I mention you're Jamie's favorite?"

Jasmine's brother, Jamie, may have had a different last name than Whitney, but that was the only thing that kept them from acting like siblings. If one of Whitney's four other brothers wasn't watching out for her, Jamie was. The week prior, he helped her fix a flat tire.

"What does Jamie need?"

"I forgot to mention that he asked for cupcakes for his birthday."

Forgot to mention? Jasmine never forgot anything. She was up to something. Until Whitney could figure it out, she'd play along. "That's easy enough." Whitney mentally adjusted her schedule. She'd skip her mental health walk and drive to the bakery. Her hoodie was pulled over her head, and she was stretching her hands into the sleeves. "I wish I thought of it sooner. I could have bought some this morning when I was at the Sweet Treats Cafe."

When Jasmine cleared her throat, Whitney felt the butter behind her friend's compliments smooth the rough edges of what she was about to ask.

"Jamie likes your cherry-filled, sweeter-than-sin cupcakes."

The impact of the favor slammed into Whitney's chest.

Her heart stopped beating for the minute it took to process.

She had three hours to make cupcakes with homemade frosting and commit to an outfit for Jamie's thirty-fourth birthday party.

Time would be tight, but it could be done. She grabbed the keys off the hook by her door and reached for her purse. "I'm on my way to the store for the whipping cream."

"Don't bother." Whitney heard the car door slam shut. "I'm on my way to get it. Do I need to bring anything else?"

Whitney pored through her cupboard while they discussed the ingredients she needed to fulfill Jamie's special request. Jasmine ended the call saying, "One day, you'll make some lucky guy a happy man. Until then, I'm taking full advantage of your talent."

As Whitney closed the oven door behind two cupcake pans, Jasmine opened the front door of her cottage. Whitney rubbed her hands together to celebrate her accomplishment. She pointed at the oven. "When life closes one door." Then she pointed at the door Jasmine had left open. "It opens another."

Jasmine circled Whitney's dining room table, large enough to seat two people. She held out the carton of heavy whipping cream in one hand, and in the other, she shook the salt and vinegar chips. They noshed on chips while Whitney prepared the frosting.

The knot in Whitney's stomach had her second-guessing the wisdom of eating half the bag of chips before riding in the car with Jasmine. She tightened her muscles to contain the contents and forced herself to remember she'd survived Jasmine's driving in the past, so her chances of making it to the house in one piece were likely.

A mile away from the house, the two-lane dirt road smoothed to pavement. Whitney's shoulders dropped with the change in percussion, and she exhaled a breath. The worst part of the day was over.

Or so she thought.

As the car crept along the drive leading to the Jacobson's seven-room log cabin mansion constructed to look like a ski resort, Whitney counted the parked vehicles. After ten, she decided the number of guests surpassed the amount of cupcakes in her box. "You didn't say it was a full-blown event."

"Why does that matter?" Jasmine craned her neck in search of a space to park her car.

"Two dozen cupcakes isn't enough for all these people." Whitney had assumed that because they were at Jasmine and Jamie's parents' house, Jamie's party would be a small gathering with close friends.

Then again, she saw the flaw in her thinking. The Jacobsons hosted community parties in their log cabin-style mansion. The remote location by the lake meant they didn't have neighbors to disturb and had space for entertaining large crowds. That and everyone liked Jamie.

"The caterer will take care of it," Jasmine assured Whitney.

"Then why did we bring these?" Whitney held up the box that seemed heavier under the tension in her hands.

"Because Jamie asked for your cupcakes." Jasmine tipped a shoulder and flashed her megawatt smile.

Whitney blinked her resignation. There was no point in arguing with Jasmine. Her tenacious friend always won.

The warmth from the summer sun magnified the aroma of the honeysuckle bushes along the walkway, filling the air with sweetness. On the way to the house, Whitney heard a bee buzzing. Intent on avoiding the bee, she walked in an arc away from the general area. The front of her right, low-top, pink Converse All-Star caught on the crack between two of the paving stones.

She stumbled forward.

Having learned from prior mistakes, instead of rushing into the fall to build momentum to recover, Whitney slowed until she came to a complete stop.

She exhaled and grinned. "An Olympic gymnast couldn't have landed better."

Jasmine took the box from Whitney. "Let me take those, Mary Lou Retton."

Even though Jasmine was sarcastic, Whitney couldn't help smiling at the reference. "I'll get the door."

Her feet had landed on the welcome mat with the word "Jacobson" framed by flowers when the door opened. Whitney recoiled away from the cold air and the person behind it.

It took a moment for her mind to reconcile that the enormous body filling the space of the doorway was a friend, not a foe. The man was a little under six feet tall. A hint of a tattoo peeked out from the sleeve of his t-shirt. His close-shaved beard had eliminated the forever young look she'd remembered.

For the second time in less than two minutes, Whitney recovered and stood straight. The boy of her childhood fantasies of happily ever after was standing in front of her as a man looking better than she'd imagined. Her mouth went dry, and her tongue seemed to have grown to a size that made speaking impossible. If she could have talked, she would have said something like "Long time. No see." or "How are you doing, Conrad Hayes?"

Instead, she stood there with her lips pressed together to keep her mouth from gaping. Conrad was easy on the eyes when they were in high school. Time had fine-tuned his muscles, making him look like a human sculpture.

In the comfort of her living room, along with millions of other fans, Whitney had admired him when he was in pre and post-game press conferences.

The cameras hadn't done him any justice.

In person, Conrad Hayes had an almost blinding glow.

Jasmine pushed between Conrad and Whitney and said, "Fancy seeing you here." She passed the box of cupcakes to Whitney, closed the gap, and stepped into Conrad's arms for a hug.

His arms wrapped around her, and he squeezed her tight before picking her up. Jasmine groaned. "I missed this."

"I did too." The warmth in Conrad's voice matched the tight hug. He set Jasmine down on the ground and stepped away.

"You look good." He wrapped his arm around her shoulders and led her into the house.

Whitney watched the scene with amused envy. Years ago, when she was essential to Conrad Hayes's success, the warmest greeting he ever gave her was an occasional wave in the hall between classes. She was a gangly, brace-faced teenager. He was the pride of Cottage Cove, the star football player who went on to be a professional—who forgot about her as quickly as he could brush off the small-town dust from his clothes.

Whitney sighed and glanced around to see if anyone else was near the door. Nobody was there. It was just her and the oversized planter with azaleas. She closed the door behind her and hurried to catch up to Jasmine.

It was only a matter of time before the cupcakes melted.

Chapter 2

Earth to Lumberjack

Torn between staying home or risking unwanted recognition, Conrad waffled on whether or not to attend Jamie's birthday party.

In the end, celebrating his friend won.

Although, the look on Jasmine's friend's face had Conrad questioning the wisdom of his decision. Her honey-brown eyes and long lashes fluttered. They almost worked their female magic, pulling him in to introduce himself and tricking him into saying I'd like to know more about you.

Thanks to a couple of encounters with women who tried using his fame to launch theirs, Conrad had learned to temper his reaction when he met an attractive woman, even though this one had a presence that made him feel like he didn't have to put on airs to impress her. It was too good to be true. She had to be a trap.

Pretend like she's not there, and she'll go away.

Relief cooled his nerves when Jasmine's friend seemed to have picked up on his stay-away vibe. She coolly observed the conversation between Jasmine and him, neither reacting nor attempting to insert herself.

Good, I'll be able to enjoy the night with my friends.

Jasmine pointed at the box her friend was holding. "These cupcakes are a special treat for Jamie. We should make sure he sees them." She scanned the kitchen for a safe place to set down the box. Conrad would have set them on the kitchen island beside the platter of cookies and brownies covered with plastic wrap.

When Jasmine overlooked the spot, he was tempted to take the box and set them there himself, but that would have been overstepping. He hadn't been home long enough to fall into his role as a family friend. When he was a kid, Conrad knew where all the good snacks were stored in the Jacobson's kitchen.

Jasmine traced her steps back to the woman Conrad ignored. The woman's cute rocker-girl vibe poked itself into his field of vision. His fingers twitched against the urge to touch the strand of hair that fell out of the knot at the nape of her neck. He tried pivoting to avoid the woman who quietly cast a spell on him. The harder he tried to ignore her, the deeper he felt the draw of her quiet disregard.

Both women's eyes landed on the refrigerator at the same time. The woman said, "We can hide them in there. It'll give the frosting a chance to recover from your wild driving."

"Oh, don't be so sassy. We made it here in one piece." Jasmine's sandals clacked on the sandstone tile as she crossed the room.

"Conrad, do you remember Whitney?" The refrigerator door exhaled when the seal was broken, allowing the cold to escape. "People fight to get their hands on one of her cupcakes."

He wasn't sure if what Jasmine said was innuendo or fact. The pink box had him leaning toward the cupcakes being that good. Then the name registered, and Conrad turned to face the woman he intentionally ignored. "Whit?"

Awe at the change from the scrawny girl he remembered to

the woman with curves in all the right places overpowered the guilt he felt for being rude. "You've changed over the years."

Back when they were in each other's lives, a spring wind could have picked up Whitney and blown her to the next town. Conrad used to joke that she wore oversized sweaters and Doc Martens to tether herself to the ground. If he remembered correctly, she also wore wide-rimmed glasses. Without them shielding her eyes, he found himself lost in soft- irises.

"It happens." A wash of pink flushed over Whitney's cheeks, and she wobbled onto the heels of her shoes.

Conrad imagined the feel of her cheeks under his lips. He pushed the thought aside. Whitney Stansfield was surrounded by brothers who warned her against men like him. She was one of those people who would go to the ends of the earth for someone she cared about. Under the watchful eye of her brothers, she'd taken a few of those steps for Conrad. He'd also been on the receiving end of her father's don't-hurt-my-daughter-glare.

He bucked against the reminder to stay in his place. They were adults, and it wouldn't hurt to appreciate Whitney's presence, especially when she was with Jasmine.

Whitney and Jasmine were night and day. Jasmine had perfectly styled blond hair, shoes with the pedicure, and jewelry that proudly proclaimed that she was high maintenance.

Whitney looked like she was ready to go to an outdoor concert. Her shorts showed muscular legs. When did she start working out? He guided his thoughts to a safer zone—her face.

"Without your glasses, I didn't recognize you." Uncertain about whether he should hug Whitney in a friendly way or shake her hand, Conrad shoved his hands into the back pockets of his cargo shorts. "You look good."

The corner of Whitney's lip curled to show her lack of appreciation for the assessment that came out all wrong.

Conrad groaned inside. He hadn't meant to say that Whitney wasn't attractive back in the day, but that's exactly how it sounded. What was it about her that had him fumbling?

Deciding the only way to handle the awkwardness was to retreat, he backpedaled. "I should probably go find the guys."

He grabbed the three cans of soda he had left on the counter when he saw Jasmine's jeep on the surveillance camera and nudged his chin toward the door to point out where he was going. "Let's catch up later."

"You better talk to us at some point in the night," Jasmine said. "Otherwise, I'll tell Jamie you can't have any of his cupcakes."

"Yeah, right," Conrad turned and headed for the yard where most people were hanging out. He stepped outside, and the cool of the misting system relieved some of the heat in his face. Usually, Conrad made a good first impression on women. It was the Hayes charm, his father called it.

The Hayes charm was the reason why Conrad avoided drawing attention to himself. At first blush, people talked to Conrad because they were interested in him. Once they figured out he was the son of Austin Hayes, they were more concerned about his family history—*he'd learned about a couple of new chapters in the past year*.

Conrad avoided a small group of women absorbed in their conversation, lounging in chairs on the pool deck. He stepped off the cement path into the grass to create an arc. The greater the distance between him and people outside his circle of friends, the likelier the evening would remain pleasant.

His mind traveled down memory lane—to when he, Jamie, and their friends were teenagers. The cement path was the touchdown line in football, the out-of-bounds for frisbee, and the benchmark for third base in the various games they invented. Conrad eventually reconnected with the walkway that divided the Jacobson's lawn into sections and headed to meet his friends at the far end of the yard.

Free to roam, his mind reeled at what had happened in the kitchen.

Whitney Stansfield. The geeky girl who tutored him through his English, Trigonometry, and history classes grew up.

The last time he saw her was at his graduation party.

Back then, she had braces, and her short brown hair was in a pixie cut that she kept away from her face with a headband. Her hair was long enough to be tied into a knot at the nape of her neck and to have strands framing her ears and neckline. It was a beautiful neckline, too.

Conrad's skin prickled with guilt. He might not have graduated from high school if Whitney hadn't helped him— and he didn't have the decency to say hello. He wouldn't have blamed her if she had written him off as a jerk.

"Hey, Earth to Lumberjack." His nickname blew away the remnants of his reverie. With the awareness of his surroundings slowly returning, Conrad shifted his eyes from the hedges in the distance to his friends, who were watching him with different degrees of amusement. He wasn't sure which one had called him out, so he regarded the three of them with a questioning gaze.

"It's your turn, but I wonder if we should trust you with these darts." Conrad was broad-chested and what he considered a normal height, whereas Jamie was tall and lean. Jamie's mind was quicker, too. Jamie flipped the small arrow that had a protective rubber coating where the point would have been and caught it in his hand.

Conrad held out his hand to accept the lawn dart. "You're worried you'll have to pay up for the dinner I'm about to win."

Jamie passed the small blue projectiles off and stepped to

the side, clearing the way for Conrad to aim for the hooped targets.

Conrad bounced the arrow in his hand to get a feel for the weight. Deciding the weight was similar to a tennis ball, he bent his arm back to throw the dart.

"What took you so long?" Conrad watched his friend Dustin relax his arms on his abdomen from the corner of his eye. Dustin was one of those wide receivers who was bulky, and it was all muscle. If he wasn't a football player, he could have entered the World's Strongest Man competition.

"Jasmine got here with her friend, Whitney."

"Whitney is why he's late," Dustin taunted.

Conrad was used to Dustin's teasing. They had been friends on and off the football field for years. He released the arrow and watched the arc as it flew across the divide. It dropped at the perfect point and landed just inside the target.

"Nice try." He nudged his head toward the ring off in the distance. "But you didn't distract me."

Conrad and Dustin were the original enemies turned friends. They played on opposing teams in college. Conrad played for Arizona State University, and Dustin played for the University of Arizona. It wasn't until they were teammates for the Arizona Cardinals that they learned they were one and the same. They finished each other's sentences.

Although, playing for rival college teams made watching the annual ASU vs. U of A day after Thanksgiving game that much more fun. That wasn't the only difference. In situations where Conrad chose to be cautious, Dustin entered with reckless abandon.

"Did you check out Whitney enough to know if I'd like her?" Adrian, the fourth member of their band of friends, craned his neck to inventory the people wandering around the yard. Adrian looked like Conrad, broad-chested, light brown hair that he liked to wear spiked, close-shaved beard. His brows were bushier than Conrad's.

The question seemed to pull a trigger in Conrad. He needed to protect Whitney. If she was anything like the sweet girl he remembered, she was too kind for his friend. Not that Adrian didn't deserve to be with someone kind. Whitney was the type of person men like Adrian walked over. "Nah, she's the bookish type."

"You got that from a five-minute conversation?" Adrian's question challenged Conrad's intent to protect Whitney.

"I knew her from high school." Conrad made sure to leave out the part where Whitney, two years younger than him, tutored him. By that time, Adrian had graduated from Cottage Cove High School. They ran in different circles, so he probably never knew she existed. Conrad hadn't until he needed her help.

"So, an old girlfriend?" Adrian had, once again, used his gift of goading Conrad. The devious glint in his eyes and Dustin's quiet chuckle were a warning. Redirect the conversation.

"Are we playing a game or talking about somebody who you hope will distract me into losing?" He poised to throw the next dart.

Adrian shook his can, and the last remains of the soda in it sloshed. "I think I need a refill."

If Whitney were anything like Conrad remembered, Adrian wouldn't have a chance with her. He released the dart and watched it glide toward his target. At the last second, a breeze kicked up. The dart landed just left of the hoop on the ground. Conrad uttered a groan of disappointment. He missed.

Chapter 3

Never Have I Ever

The people gathered in small groups around the yard. The carefree atmosphere, the greenery adding color, and vivid aromas captured everything Whitney loved about summer. She savored the scent of meat cooking on the grill and the coolness coming from the mist system connected to the edge of the patio.

Several times throughout the evening, Whitney found her focus wandering toward the direction of Conrad's voice. It called to her, demanding her attention. One time, their eyes met. His gaze bore an intensity that sent flushes of awareness through her. She thought she had outgrown that stupid schoolgirl crush on him. Apparently, she'd only buried it. Just looking at him made her heart do funny things.

She grinned shyly and looked away. *Don't read too much into this.* Conrad had always been intense. She'd ascribe it to his success. The man had drive. He also had made it clear things hadn't changed since they were younger. He was the hot, recently retired athlete who still garnered attention from crowds. She was someone who belonged in the background.

Unspoken wishes from her high school years rose to the

surface. A younger, foolish Whitney would have gone to the ends of the earth if it meant Conrad would recognize her—not as Erick Stansfield's daughter, or Thom's younger sister, or even Jasmine's best friend.

She'd given up on those wishes when her father pulled her to the side after a game. His tough love saved her from embarrassing herself. Conrad's greeting at the door proved her father's words true. Guys like Conrad didn't have time for people like Whitney.

At least he was polite, and she liked that he referred to her by her childhood nickname, Whit. Her cheeks tightened against the grin that deepened with each memory of the fonder moments of their high school years.

People sat in clusters around card tables decorated with linen cloths. Jamie and Jasmine bounced from group to group, thanking them for joining the celebration.

When Jamie and Jasmine were in the same room, it was easy to tell they were siblings. Their dynamic personalities lit the room with positive energy. People under the spell of Jamie and Jasmine's aura smiled brighter and laughed deeper.

Shortly afterward, tables were cleared, and people returned to mingling in different areas of the house and backyard. Whitney joined a group of people playing a game at the cherrywood table, large enough to feed a family of eight people. At first, she just watched and laughed along with them at the outcome of the game. They pushed the game to the side and pulled out another box.

Corrine Henry read the cover to the group. "Never Have I Ever?" She flipped the box to read the description on the side. "This is like the game they have us play at team-building events."

Corrine, a petite blond with bright blue eyes and a dazzling smile, had been friends with Jasmine and Jamie for as long as

Whitney could remember. She didn't talk to Whitney until they were out of college and working in the same building.

Corrine worked at the insurance company at the furthest edge of the outdoor mall. Whitney was in the middle, in the chiropractic office. They had seen each other in passing and waved. When they were at parties, Corrine talked to Whitney for a couple of minutes and was usually whisked away by another friend.

"With a twist." Jasmine tapped her fingertips against each other like a villain. Her coral lipstick made the part she was trying to play that much more realistic. "Think of it as truth or dare for adults. The rules are simple. All of us begin with a hand in the air. I will ask a question. If you have done whatever is asked, you lower one finger. Then you share the story of when you did the deed."

Whitney tightened her cheeks to hold in her reaction to Jasmine's "did the deed comment."

Jasmine noticed and wagged her finger at Whitney as if to say, "I know what you're thinking." She continued with the rules. "We'll do this for roughly five questions. The person with the hand raised at the end wins the round."

After living with four brothers and a sister, not much intimidated Whitney. She sat straight and said, "This should be interesting."

"First," Jasmine raised a finger to impress the point she was about to make. "If there is a question you don't want to answer, say pass. No questions asked. Our goal isn't to cause problems in our friends' lives."

Whitney chuckled inside. That was such a Jasmine move. In one breath, she pretended to be trying out for the role of a Disney supervillain. In the next, she assured her friends that she didn't want to cause them discomfort. Whitney said, "You could always remove the awkward questions."

"Good point." Jasmine read through the questions and separated them into two piles. With each clack of the card on the table, she either said, "I like," or "I don't want to know that."

A friend picked up an "I don't want to know that card and read it." She covered her mouth with her hand and giggled before sliding it back into the pile. "Thank you for not asking that one."

While Jasmine sorted through the cards, people refreshed their drinks and returned to the table with small plates of snacks.

Hoots and cheers from the foosball game on the patio bled into the room. Whitney laughed at the contradiction of how her afternoon started. For a while, she worried about not making it to the party. Sitting amid people who had been friends since high school, she was at ease.

Jasmine cleared her throat and waved the card in her hand. She said, "Never have I ever." Everyone around the table raised their hands.

The pause was longer than Whitney expected, and she found herself leaning forward as though the gesture would pull the words out of her friend's mouth. Jasmine's lips stretched slightly, and she furrowed her brows. "Went skinny dipping."

Several thumbs lowered, and heads turned to see who else had or had not swum naked.

One girl's face glowed red when the person sitting beside her balked. "I wouldn't have pegged you for doing something that risqué. When did you go skinny dipping?" The question started a chain of confessions and giggles.

By the fourth round of the game, Whitney's cheeks burned from laughing so hard. Her heart swelled with the delight of being included. Everyone says you're not the only one, but it was in generalizations. Even though the confessions' content had no bearing on the world at large, it meant a lot to Whitney, who often felt like she was the odd woman out.

After six rounds, she won the game. She had two fingers raised, and the woman across the table was one finger away from being eliminated.

One of the women pressed her hand on the table, cast her gaze toward the guys on the other side of the room, and quickly returned to the conversation. "I have to say, Jasmine, well done on getting a fine display of men to the party."

Another woman raised her glass. "I married the one she introduced me to."

Whitney laughed but held her tongue. She didn't feel comfortable commenting on Jasmine's brother or any of the men who had been friends with her brothers at one point in time. Besides, she knew it was a waste of her time.

"Whitney?"

Whitney's heart skipped a beat when she heard the sly tone in her friend's voice. Whenever Jasmine lowered her tone, it meant she was up to something.

"No." Whitney shook her head. She would not be tricked, cajoled, or nagged into doing something out of her comfort zone.

Jasmine declared, "Whitney is the winner."

Whitney clapped. The women clapped. They joked about the clapping. When the giggles softened, Jasmine picked up from where she had left off. "You have won a dare."

"Oh!" Whitney's smile melted. "I thought we were playing to get to know each other."

Her stomach wobbled. Had she known the prize, she'd have considered confessing to the time she accidentally ate someone else's lunch at work. They figured it out a couple of hours later, and Whitney let them eat hers. Every once in a while, they traded lunches. Because it didn't have an embarrassing outcome,

Whitney didn't tell the story. *That's what I get for being kind. Bad stories and dares.*

She braced herself. Jasmine wasn't mean, but she loved pushing Whitney out of her comfort zone.

"I dare you to tell Conrad about your crush on him?"

"Who doesn't have a crush on Conrad Hayes?" Whitney pushed aside the dare. Maybe if she played it off, Jasmine would think it wasn't risqué enough and escalate to bungee jumping.

"She's right about that," several women around the table chimed in.

Whitney exhaled too soon. Jasmine wore the grin. The same grin Whitney saw just before she was pushed out of a plane when they went skydiving. It was the same grin that she used to pull Whitney into the boat when they went whitewater rafting. The only thing more dangerous than Jasmine's villainous smile was what came afterward.

"One of us is telling him." She crossed her hands in front of her chest. Jasmine meant business.

"Did I mention that I married the guy she set me up with?" The woman's voice was bright with encouragement.

"Can you give me the dare?" Corrine asked.

That struck a nerve. Men tripped over themselves to sit beside Corrine. Something in Whitney bellowed. *Not today, Corrine.*

Whitney knew she didn't have a chance with Conrad. But just maybe, she could tell him the truth in a way that they could laugh about her foolish confession together. And this night would make up for all the nights she was the prop at a party.

For just a couple of minutes, she'd have his attention.

For a couple of minutes, she'd know what it was like to be a part of the it-crowd.

For a couple of minutes, she'd step out of her mold and do something crazy–take a chance.

She'd known what life was like on the outskirts of Conrad's life. At best, life would return to the status quo.

The worst outcome is they'd hit it off. And that wasn't all that bad.

The spark had been ignited. It was time to do something with it. Whitney steadied herself. "What's the timeline?"

Chapter 4

I Dare You

Jasmine tapped the table with both of her hands. "It's time to take things to the next level."

Whitney gulped. She didn't have time to come up with a plan. Her eyes glossed over all the other faces in the room. Where was Conrad? Maybe she'd be lucky, and he went home early.

Her heart pounded against her rib cage like it was tallying each person she skipped over. It stopped with a loud thud when she found Conrad. He glanced away from his conversation, and their eyes connected.

Whitney released a contented sigh. A flare pulsed in Conrad's eyes, and he averted his gaze, returning to the conversation.

A cold chill swept over Whitney's body, bringing memories she had long forgotten. Memories of Conrad walking around with a cheerleader on his arm, passing by Whitney without a second glance.

She threw a withering look at Jasmine. Surely, she wouldn't make Whitney follow through with the dare.

Jasmine grinned. "It's time for Jamie's birthday cake."

The air returned to Whitney's lungs. She had assumed and never been so happy to be wrong. "I'll get the matches."

Jasmine carried the sheet cake to the table, with Whitney following behind with the napkins, plates, and forks.

She connected the flame from her lighter to the first of the rows of candles. "It's time to gather round and sing Happy Birthday to Jamie."

Jamie stood in his place in front of the cake, laughing when the flames flickered their protest. His friends gathered behind him.

One of the friends caught Whitney's eye. His dark hair was longer on the top and cut close around his ears. The ring of gold around his irises seemed to pop. He bobbed his chin and raised his brow to say hello.

The corner of Whitney's lips stretched into an easy smile. Conrad may not have known she was alive, but other men noticed her. The last time Whitney surrendered her crush to being unfulfilled, allowing herself to see that there were other men, she'd found love.

Her entire body warmed with the memory of Geoff. It had taken a while, but she could think about him without the ache of loss. The laughter, brought on by Jamie, who waved a paper plate to blow out the candles on his cake, brought her back to the present.

Life had a way of working out. It could hurt like stubbing a baby toe on the bedpost in the middle of the night, but it always got better.

Somewhere in the middle of passing along slices of cake and the jokes about Jamie's age, Whitney's energy levels depleted to almost empty. She was used to talking to people on a one-on-one basis. While the large group was entertaining, it demanded more than she had to give. She leaned in to whisper to Jasmine, "I'm going outside for fresh air."

When she stopped outside the sliding glass door onto the patio, the night air brushed against Whitney's cheek. The touches of heat mixed in with the softer scents Whitney always attributed to the stars. She wandered to the pool's edge and sat on the deck by the below-ground hot tub. She slipped off her shoes and stored her socks in them. Her entire body relaxed when she immersed her feet in the warm water.

"It's getting to be too much for you too?" Whitney heard the voice before associating it with the person who owned it.

Gradually it registered in her mind that it was Conrad. She tightened her chest muscles and clamped her hand on her chest. There was no reason for her to be afraid. He was a friend nod an adversary. "I imagine you can relate to the feeling."

"What's that supposed to mean?" Conrad removed his flip-flops and sat beside Whitney. He set them on his other side.

"People are fighting for your attention all the time." What Whitney tried to deliver as unconcerned sounded breathy and light. She shifted her focus to the water, hoping it would help her gain her bearings.

"Is that why you've been avoiding me all night?" Conrad asked.

"Avoiding you. Did you know I existed?" Whitney taunted to hide her nervousness. She spent the evening telling herself that Conrad didn't matter, but her heart didn't seem to be paying attention. The foolish thing kept wandering back, trying to attach itself to him.

Conrad tilted away and gazed into Whitney's eyes. The playfulness pierced through all the reasons she listed for why it would be easy for him to overlook her. "You believed I'd forget the person who sacrificed her evenings for an entire year to help me pass high school." He tapped the center of his chest. "That hurts. Right here."

Whitney chuckled. "You'd always been melodramatic."

"It worked." Conrad nudged her. "You showed me mercy and helped me with my schoolwork."

"Mercy? I just tricked you into thinking the work wasn't complicated."

"Aha." Conrad pointed at Whitney. "I was right. Trigonometry was a beast."

"And you tamed it," Whitney nodded her head the way a coach would after his team completed a play.

It was like old times–except they were by the pool instead of the library.

When it was just the two of them, Conrad would let down his guard. Whitney felt comfortable with Conrad because he didn't bristle at her awkwardness. He'd catch the loose book before it fell out of her hand or grab hold of her elbow before she stumbled into a complete fall.

Conrad and Whitney's world was perfect—until other people were there for Conrad to compare against Whitney. Then she'd drift into the background and let him shine like the star he was.

The dare Jasmine issued returned to haunt Whitney. "I dare you to admit to Conrad that you had a crush on him in high school."

Whitney tried to get out of it when they searched for the matches and silverware in the kitchen. "I don't want to sound like a stalker chick."

Jasmine squinted. "How about this? If he brings up the past, you tell him. You can laugh it off as one of those silly teenager things."

"Like that will happen." Whitney rolled her eyes.

Well, there he was, sitting by the pool with her beneath the stars with nobody else around, talking about the past.

Whitney's lip twisted the way it did when she tried to piece together something that should have made sense but didn't. She glared at Conrad, who responded with a questioning expression. "Did Jasmine say anything to you?"

"About?" Back in the day, Whitney had seen a variety of Conrad's facial expressions. There was the "do my homework for me because I'm cute" Conrad. Then there was the "frustrated because this is too hard" Conrad. Her favorite was Conrad after something difficult sank in. The one he was giving her said he had no clue about what she was talking about.

"She dared me to tell you something." The aggravation of being put on the spot somehow affected Whitney's courage.

"A dare?" His face darkened.

"Nothing like that." The need to assure him smoothed over the awkwardness of the confession. "She dared me to tell you that I had a crush on you in high school." As soon as the words left her mouth, Whitney's face burned. "Now, you probably think I'm a groupie." Whitney jumped up, splashing water on the pool deck. Her eyes widened in embarrassment. As she backed away, she said, "Let's forget I said anything."

"Where are you going?" Conrad asked.

"I have to go hurt Jasmine." Whitney turned around to walk away and ran into a patio chair that screeched its protest at being moved with such force. Her hand caught the arm of the chair, helping her regain her balance.

Conrad called out, "Whit! You forgot something."

She had nothing with her when she wandered out to the yard. Whitney thought for sure it was a trick.

"Losing my sanity doesn't count."

Chapter 5

It'll Take A While For My Ego to Recover

Whitney saw the signs. The mouth dropped open in what could only be horror—the eyes widened in a deer-in-the-headlights expression. The arms held out to keep her at bay.

Her father was right! All those years ago, he told her. "Stay in your lane, Whit."

He had gone so far as pulling Whitney out of a crowd of people waiting for Conrad outside the locker room. She was with the cheerleaders, holding their poster board signs, speculating where they'd go for the after-party. Erick Stansfield's presence parted the crowd like a knife through butter until Whitney was the only one left for him to approach. "We need to talk."

Whitney heard the collective gasps. A voice in the crowd said, "Nothing good comes after we need to talk."

Another kid said, "Whitney was such a nice girl. I'll miss seeing her around campus."

Whitney followed behind her father, wishing one of those sinkholes they'd seen on the news would magically appear and pull her to her young and untimely demise.

It didn't. And she survived.

The talk. "Whit, this isn't a good look."

Everybody else thought Erick Stansfield was a hard-nosed driver who pushed people beyond their limits. To Whitney, he was her dad. The papa bear. The man who used to pretend that she was stronger than him when she wrestled with him.

Papa Bear's hand was on her shoulder. "He's a football player that will eventually go pro. You are my princess. Guys like Conrad won't see you that way."

They both averted their gazes toward the crowd. Conrad, with damp hair and his duffel bag full of football gear hurled over his back, was surrounded by girls who went on to be the Homecoming, Winter Wonderland, Valentine's Adventure, and prom queens.

Like a thin needle carefully inserted in a balloon, the truth pierced Whitney's heart. But it didn't break it. Thankful that her dad had pulled her aside to save her from looking like a fool, she released the want of Conrad's attention. Until one day, it didn't matter that he hadn't noticed her.

Why had she listened to Jasmine? Whitney knew she wasn't like Jasmine. That she was part of the in-crowd because of her friendship with Jasmine. For anyone else, the dare would have made sense.

She backed away from Conrad with as much speed as she could muster. "I promise. I'm not a stalker. It was just a dare. And now I will go inside and kill my best friend."

Something cold touched the back of Whitney's leg, and she reached for anything that would save her from the inevitable fall. She felt gravity pull at her, and the chair that tripped her screeched against the cement.

The air left Whitney's lungs, and she saw stars. Some were in the sky. Most of them were from the sparkles in front of her.

Conrad was at her side. "Are you okay?"

And it hit. The look on his face. It was a warning of her

impending doom. Not disgust. Her body warmed as his eyes, assessing for injury, roamed over it.

She leaned on an elbow and tightened to pull herself into a sitting position. "My body's fine. My ego. It'll take a little longer for that to recover."

He rose and held his hand out for her. "Let's get back to the party."

Whitney accepted his help and rubbed the grass off her backside. "I think I'll stay out here."

The grass felt good beneath her feet. It was cool and soft, and – that was what she forgot. Whitney scanned the area around the hot tub for her shoes.

"They're on the chair." Conrad trotted to the chair where he had set them and brought them to Whitney.

A breeze kicked up, delivering notes of his cologne to her nose. Whitney lingered in the fragrance. She could live in that scent forever.

Stay in your lane, Whit. Then she blinked to force herself to return to reality.

"Thank you." Whitney stiffened her body and accepted her shoes. "Just so you know. I'm not some sort of a groupie or one of those stalker chicks."

"I'd say." Conrad smiled, and warmth spread through Whitney's body as it grew into a full grin. "None of them have ever fallen over furniture for me."

He offered her his arm to lean on as she slipped her sock on her foot. "So, other than giving comedic welcome home greetings, what else have you been up to?"

Whitney felt the heat flush through her face. It was cooled with laughter. Conrad had developed a sense of humor since the last time she had talked with him. The embarrassment drifted, and she saw the situation through his eyes. She was his childhood friend's goofy younger sister. Nothing more. Nothing less.

The smile on his face said he was glad about it too. When she laid her head on her pillow that night, Whitney would have to say thanks for the small mercies.

"I'm an occupational therapist."

"Go figure." The surprise in Conrad's voice held sincerity. "I thought you'd end up as an English teacher or something along those lines."

"Liking literature and teaching it are two different animals." Whitney bent down to tie her shoe.

Conrad lowered himself into the chair that was beside Whitney. "It didn't seem like it to me. You did a great job teaching me. I don't know if I'd be here without your help."

The night air stilled. Whitney secured the lace on her other shoe and glanced up at Conrad. "I find that hard to believe. You are the type of person that will do whatever it takes to succeed. I just happened to be lucky enough to be there when you needed the help."

Whitney froze. Lucky enough? Ugh, she sounded like a groupie.

"I mean. I'm glad it was you and not one of my brothers."

Three of Whitney's brothers played football with Conrad. That is how he met her. Conrad was studying with Whitney's brother, Thom. Conrad and Thom were fighting through a passage by Chaucer. Frustrated with their bumbling, she popped in and explained it like it was as easy as boiling water.

The next day, Conrad found Whitney in the library and asked for her help. First with literature, then history, then government, then trigonometry. For an hour a day, until he graduated, Whitney and Conrad studied.

"I'm glad it was me too." Conrad shoved his hands in his pockets.

They were on the patio looking in at their friends. The party had dwindled to the core group, who had gathered in the living room. Chairs had been pulled from other areas of the house, and they sat in a crooked circle.

Conrad's eyes connected with Whitney's. "I missed this."

Whitney's stomach tightened from longing. He meant the crowd, but it sure would have been nice if what he said was about her.

Chapter 6

Can We Pretend?

"Can we pretend like this conversation never happened?" The flush of color, the squeak in Whitney's voice, the memories of all the times they'd been together merged. Conrad felt like he'd been slammed over the head with what he'd missed all those years ago, and the feeling brought a pleasant awakening.

Whitney was adorable—and naive to think he'd let the moment slip. Conrad tucked the conversation away for another time while assigning the moment as another one of their secrets. The first was from all those years ago when she helped him succeed.

He knew firsthand that Whitney was one of those women men worked harder for. Not that they needed to. There was something about the way she expressed appreciation that made a guy want to do a good job again and again. He'd never told her his truth.

Conrad kept a watchful eye on Whitney and followed her into the house. With his luck, she'd fall over a crack in the sidewalk. As a teenager, Whitney lacked the Stansfields' coordination. Her brothers used to joke about it with Conrad when he was at their house.

During one of their study sessions Thom, the closest in age to her, nudged Conrad with an elbow. "She got the brains, and we got the brawn."

It was almost as if it was on cue. Whitney tripped over an area rug, sending a bowl of popcorn skidding across the table.

Thom caught it just before it flew off the other side.

At that point in time, Whitney also lacked the Stansfields' charisma.

A lot had changed since then. Conrad stole a glance at the thick ponytail that stopped in the middle of her back. Somewhere throughout the evening, the knot had fallen loose. The highlights added a soft touch. He couldn't help admiring how cute she looked.

She stopped at the door and pointed to the horizon line. "I could never get tired of that view."

The blue was speckled with white—the Milky Way.

Conrad was in awe of the beauty above and the beauty in front of him. He shoved his hands in his pockets to fight the urge to pull Whitney to him, to wrap his arms around her, so they could enjoy the view together.

Other than how she looked, Whitney hadn't changed. She was the kind of woman a man married.

Not a man like him. Conrad had baggage he was sure would be too heavy for a kindhearted person like Whitney to bear. There was the paparazzi, the women who made opportunities to be in his presence, then the family secrets.

But it was nice to dream.

He slid the glass door behind them. The party had dwindled to the old guard. The group that had been friends for longer than any of them could remember.

They lingered around the living room, sitting haphazardly in chairs with their legs stretched out and inclined toward each other.

Adrian tapped Dustin on the arm and pointed with his chin toward Conrad and Whitney. The look on his face said I told you so.

Conrad rolled his eyes. If Adrian wasn't a football player, he could have been a host on one of those what's happening in famous people's lives shows. He took fragments of information and weaved tales.

If Conrad didn't do something, quick, Whitney would be a victim of Adrian's active imagination.

He frowned and shook his head. It was the universal "knock it off" signal.

The expected sheepish grin never appeared. Adrian winced in pain.

There was a fumble. But where eluded Conrad.

Dustin moved to make room on the couch, and Adrian's eyes darkened like a wolf that had found its prey. He pointed at Whitney and bent his fingers to signal her to sit beside him.

He upped the charm with one of his fake sweet grins to negate her hesitation. "I don't bite. I promise."

"Really, he can be nice," Dustin said.

Whitney's chest shook with the silent chuckle, and the next thing Conrad knew, Whitney—his Whitney—was sitting between his best friends.

His heart bellowed. She had a crush on me. His head chimed in the internal monologue. He had no claim on her.

Jasmine dragged a chair from one of the back rooms to the ragged circle of friends and parked it beside a low-back leather chair. She tapped the chair, "You can sit by me."

Gratitude whittled at the edge of Conrad's nerves. Jasmine

would fix it. He didn't have to take care of things all the time. Jasmine would wheedle and draw Whitney away from Adrian and Dustin.

His eternally kind and sweet Whitney had no idea of the danger she was entertaining.

Her soft laugh at something one of them said confirmed it.

"Did you hear," started the litany of updates about mutual friends. They laughed at the stories from their childhood with the wisdom of hindsight, discussed the causes behind their friends' divorce stories, and mourned the passing of a couple of friends.

Shortly after ten, the group led by Jamie made their way to the kitchen for snacks.

Jamie opened the fridge and cheered, "Score! This is what I've been waiting for." He backed away from the door with the pink box Whitney and Jasmine had tucked away in there earlier.

"It's a good thing I didn't know you had a secret stash in there." Adrian pushed to the front of the group. He ducked his head to see inside the box but didn't get a chance because Jamie pulled it away.

When Whitney's breath hitched, Conrad tried to decipher the meaning. Was she interested in Jamie or the cupcakes?

Jamie winked at her. "Don't you worry. Anything that these hands touch is safe."

"Like the time you—"

Jamie cut her off. "That was the exception, and I more than made up for it."

Whitney pursed her lips, but the gleam in her eye spoke volumes. She and Jamie had a shared history.

Jealousy jabbed at Conrad's shoulders, pushing him to move forward. To claim his position in Whitney's life. Sure, Jamie had been around while Conrad was off playing football. Well, he was back, trying to find his place in the community.

Conrad and Whitney had a shared past they could build upon. If it weren't for Whitney, Conrad's senior year would have been close to impossible to complete. Thanks to Whitney's help, he worried about his schoolwork in the library and had the freedom to focus on football when he was on the field.

Conrad and Whitney's families were the only people who knew about their tutoring sessions in his senior year. Whitney, nor her family, ever called on Conrad for a favor. Not even preferential seats at the district, divisional, or state games.

He owed her a lot but hadn't done a thing to thank her. No wonder she didn't smile at him like she had for Jamie.

Conrad made a promise. When he moved back to Cottage Cove, he would make amends for his oversight.

He stepped closer to get a better look at the cupcakes. The whipped frosting swirled into a dainty peak. Chocolate graham cookie crumbs clung to the crevices formed by the swirls.

Conrad rested his hand on Whitney's shoulder. She stiffened, and the air around her chilled.

He hadn't meant to cause her discomfort. He eased his hand away and smiled to apologize for the offense.

His mind reeled.

Whitney was so friendly when it was just the two of them. Something had changed, but for the life of him, he couldn't figure out what it was.

"What does a guy have to do to get one of those?"

"You've already done it." Jamie extended the box to offer one of the cupcakes to Conrad. "Welcome Home."

The cake practically melted in Conrad's mouth. "This is so good."

"It's why Jamie asks for them every chance he gets," Jasmine plucked a cupcake out of the box.

"She's beautiful, and she bakes." Adrian licked some of the frosting off of his fingers.

Everyone was stealing Conrad's window to give an original compliment. One that would stick. He had to plan a grand opening for his sports training center. The cupcakes would be a hit. He asked, "Do you cater?"

He heard the apology in Whitney's reply. "No, I only bake for friends."

The rejection didn't bother Conrad. He had contributed to the conversation by expressing he valued Whitney's gift. A switch flipped in his mind, and he shook his head. Why was he competing with his friends for Whitney's attention?

The answer came quickly. Because over time, Whitney grew into a woman that commanded men's attention, and she was oblivious to how she affected them.

For the remainder of the night, Conrad stuck by Whitney. He chucked it off as being a result of his earlier inclination to protect her from Adrian and Dustin. That and he felt safe whenever he was by her side. He could let down his guard because she knew him on and off the field. There were no pretenses, just an attraction that she didn't know was mutual.

Before they knew it, the clock struck midnight, and Jamie was walking Jasmine and Whitney to the door. Jasmine hugged her brother. "Happy birthday, bro. Old age looks good on you."

"I wish I could say the same about you." Jamie dodged Jasmine's swipe before it landed on his arm. Brother and sister chuckled and hugged.

Conrad pushed to the front of the conversation and opened the door. "I'll walk the girls to the car."

"Such the gentleman," Jasmine joked.

"So I've been told." Conrad closed the jeep door behind Whitney and stepped away after shutting it. He waved goodbye and watched the car until he could only see the taillights in the distance.

His friends were right. It was a good time for Conrad to return to Cottage Cove.

Chapter 7

Mining on Social Media

Jamie's party reminded Conrad of all the things that made their childhood special. Friends he hadn't seen in years acted like he'd been away for a summer– not joined a pro football team, and traveled around the country for the past ten years of his life.

Tired but not ready to sleep, Conrad pressed his pillows against the headboard and leaned against them. He had a book and the latest Sports Illustrated on the nightstand. But his mind was too busy. Wisps of conversations buzzed through his thoughts. Each one reinforced the smile lingering on his lips. It had been a good night.

Getting to reconnect with Whitney. That was one of life's redo moments. As an eighteen-year-old, he appreciated her. His parents made sure of it. On the nights he was home for dinner, his father would ask about his grades. In between bites, Conrad listed them off. "I have a B in trig, a B in English, a B- in econ."

The letter behind the classes didn't matter to his father. His sole concern was Conrad having the GPA required to graduate.

"How's the head feeling?" That was what his father worried about. Would Conrad's thinking interfere with his playing?

"My head's in the game." Conrad gave him the answer he wanted.

"Whitney's tutoring is working," His mother wiped her fingers on her napkin. "You're remembering to thank her?"

"What kind of guy would I be if I didn't?" Conrad said. During their study sessions, he'd marvel when the concepts clicked. "You're good, Whit. Really good at this. Have you thought about going into teaching?"

She'd turn a lovely shade of pink and joke that he was trying to distract her from the subject.

At the end of their study sessions, he thanked her. Then he'd flirt a little. Just enough to show her that she was special. But he'd never crossed the line because her father would have killed him.

He'd never outright told Whitney that she had saved him. Regret darkened the memory. Conrad was a great athlete at eighteen. His character skills, however. He'd picked up more from his father than he wanted to admit to himself.

Those minutes by the pool were his penance. His chance to give the thank you that was a long time coming. Whitney rewarded him by giving him a glimpse of her great sense of humor. She'd always been funny. Again, he was too stupid to appreciate it when he was eighteen.

Whitney hadn't held his hubris against him. He should have known that she would use it to bridge the past to where they were now. She offered him redemption.

And Conrad had been walking on clouds ever since. The only thing that threatened to ruin his high was when Adrian and Dustin messed with Whitney.

And she was all Conrad could think about. He wished he could pull her out and resume the conversation to learn more about her life.

. . .

He knew she worked with Seth, baked cakes, and had maintained her childhood friendships.

Conrad's phone vibrated with a notification. He eyed it warily. The last thing an active mind needed was more stimulation. Against his better judgment, he reached for the phone and read the message.

"JamieJac just shared a post," lit up his screen.

Obviously, Conrad wasn't the only one having problems sleeping. He shook his head. There were better things to do in the wee hours of the morning.

Then he thought, *maybe Whitney updated her account too.*

Conrad liked Jamie's post-- a picture of him and Jasmine. Jamie captioned the picture with heartfelt words about his sister's support throughout the years and thanked people for making his thirty-eighth birthday special. He had tagged Jasmine.

From there, Conrad mined through Jasmine's friend list to find Whitney. Her avatar, a picture of the view of the lake from Jamie's deck, threw him off at first. The title worked with the image. Whit's End.

Conrad's chest rose with a quiet chuckle. Her younger brother, Ivan, probably helped her make the account. Ivan always said the four brothers drove Whitney to her wit's end.

He scanned the pictures with the most recent in front of him. It had been taken earlier in the day. In an Arizona Cardinals hoodie, Whitney was beside Jasmine, holding a bag of chips and whipping cream. Whitney exaggerated her frown, and Jasmine looked like a game show host. They were adorable. He felt the smile and held onto the warmth.

He imagined they'd still be the goofy best friends all the way to the nursing home. It would be Whitney and Jasmine and Adrian and him. Of course, Conrad would be the one in good shape because he couldn't see himself any other way.

Then he blinked. That was weird.

Jasmine and Whitney had a future ahead of them. Why would he assume that he and Adrian would be a part of it?

Then, he accidentally liked a picture. He hissed and pressed the heart icon again. The last thing he needed was for Whitney to know he was stalking her on social media. He returned to scrolling, keeping his thumb far away from the like button.

The next batch of pictures was taken at a family football game. It was a wide-angle image, probably taken by Jasmine. Whitney was bent, poised with hands in ready-to-run mode. Ivan was beside her calling out the play.

Then something caught Conrad's eye. It couldn't be. Could it? He pinched the picture to zoom in. Whitney was wearing a Cardinals jersey with his number.

A pleased reaction coursed through Conrad's body, having the effect of a glass of orange juice in the morning. It was—he checked the time at the top of the screen. It was three a.m., and his mind and body were ready to start the new day.

Tomorrow would be a bear. Logic told Conrad to put the phone away and get some sleep. Curiosity used the proximity to the information he wanted to continue his quest for knowledge on everything Whitney. What else could he learn?

Pictures at a 5k run told him that she was active. There were images of birthday parties past. She'd posted pictures of cakes she'd baked, concerts she'd attended, and hikes she'd gone on with Jasmine, Jamie, and their crew. The way people clustered together made it hard for Conrad to determine if there was someone special in her life.

Not that it was any of his concern. Conrad was just catching up with a past he'd missed. He had no intention of pursuing a romance with Whitney.

He stopped on a picture of Whitney at a football viewing party. It was dated seven years ago. Her face was fresh, and her hair was in two long braids that ended just below her shoulders. She held up a cupcake, and Jasmine was beside her posing to look like she was seconds away from taking a big bite. They both wore Cardinals gear. Conrad swiped to see the next picture. Whitney wore her Cardinals jersey, and her brother Ben wore a Denver Broncos jersey. They both snarled.

There it was again. Whitney was wearing his number.

At the pool, she said something about not wanting him to think she was a stalker. At the time, it didn't make sense.

Conrad didn't know his smile could get any bigger. But there he was, alone in his bedroom, smiling wider than the characters in children's cartoons.

Whitney said she had a crush on him in high school. If her social media was telling the truth, she had forgotten to mention, that despite his distance, she still had a place in her heart for him.

Chapter 8

Salon Day

The Mystic Muse Salon was rustic on the exterior. Well-placed shrubs and trees groomed with low branches hid the building with glass windows bordered by aged wood. A hair salon, skin center, and massage area filled the interior.

Jasmine had the airs of a queen with her court. It didn't matter to her that the metal foils, some standing on edge, others hanging by the nape of her neck, suited her for a bride of Frankenstein role.

In the chairs beside her, Whitney and her sister, Ericka, hummed under the magic of their cosmetologist's fingers.

"You and Jamie always host great parties." Whitney never doubted the success of a party Jasmine planned. She always had everything organized, and there was always something to keep things moving. The piece-de-resistance was the line of men passing the dishes from one to another, ending with Adrian loading them correctly in the dishwasher.

Jasmine had a set of skills Whitney could only hope to acquire. Thankfully, she used them for the benefit of those around her. That's how their friendship started. Whitney needed help with a group project and didn't know who or how to ask for help. Jasmine shook her head in disappointment, which was funny considering they were fourteen at the time. Her eyes flitted briefly toward Whitney. "You can thank me now."

Thanks to Whitney's intelligence and Jasmine's presentation skills both earned a ninety-eight percent score on the project. Jasmine thanked Whitney for being the work partner who contributed equally, and they'd been best friends ever since.

Ericka shifted in her seat, landing her gaze on Whitney. "What did I miss?"

Whitney said, "I met someone I think you'd like. His name is Dustin." At first, Conrad's friend was a shameless flirt, but as the night progressed, the bravado peeled away, showing a rather large man with a kind heart. Over the course of the night, she connected with the man who had the gift of convincing people that participating in sports as adults could be just as fun as when they were in school. In Dustin's words, "We all are two-year-olds trapped in large bodies. We just need to stretch afterward."

Ericka was always playing in a sports league. It would take some time, but if Whitney had her way, her sister would meet Dustin. From there, she'd let them figure it out.

"Ooh, I agree." Jasmine tapped on her phone screen. "I'll invite him to game night." She scowled at Ericka. "No backing out."

"I'm not making promises." Ericka averted her gaze toward the barn wood shelf stocked with beauty supplies.

"There will be cupcakes," Whitney promised.

Ericka straightened in her chair. "What time and what do I need to bring?"

Jasmine replied, "Dinner rolls."

Whitney pressed a finger against her lips to stop her grin before it started. She and Ericka were as opposite as a pineapple and a green pepper. They worked well together but presented differently. Whitney was girlie, despite or probably as a direct result of having four brothers. Her older sister, Ericka, for the same reason, fit in well with the guys. Growing up, she joined in and led quite a few of their adventures. That left little time for her to learn how to cook. Buying dinner rolls was the safest thing to ask Ericka to bring to a potluck event.

"Are you using them this time?" Ericka's voice was heavy with suspicion.

"She's catching on," Jasmine leaned in her seat and faced Whitney. With the foils in her hair and the hushed tone of voice, she looked like a conspiracy theorist. "We'll have to switch it up next time."

"Let's give her ice cream or a veggie platter." Whitney played along and continued with the whispered talk.

Ericka snapped out, "I can hear you."

"And you love me because we work with your strengths." Whitney smiled to show that it was all in jest and blew her sister a kiss. Ericka was an insightful person, she could convince someone afraid of falling to try and walk across a room, and Whitney had lost count of how many times Ericka had forged peace between the Stansfield siblings. Ericka's weak cooking skills proved that the sister Whitney admired was a real person.

Ericka's pursed lips and scowl said she was not impressed with the joking.

Jasmine said, "Oh, don't be mad. Whitney's turn is coming."

The conspiratorial tone in Jasmine's voice had the effect of a water balloon at a birthday party. Thanks to four little words, Whitney had shifted from giggling at their mutual distrust of Ericka's cooking to cautious awareness of what her friend was up to. Jasmine's superpower was great when she was using it on other people. Whitney shuddered with the reminder that she had gotten a taste of it at the party.

Maybe if she admitted defeat, Jasmine would be satisfied and return to setting up Ericka and Dustin. "Get it over with and say I told you so."

Jasmine shrugged and said, "I don't know what you're talking about."

Whitney rubbed her eyes and relaxed against the tension of expectation. She thought for sure there would be some ribbing or at least a gentle chide. She'd fought hard against Jasmine's challenge. Up until the point where Whitney had the conversation with Conrad, fulfilling the dare, visions of Conrad calling 911 and getting a restraining order lurked at the edge of her mind. "I'm still in shock. He was pretty cool about it."

"He was more than pretty cool," Jasmine said. "You should have seen his face when you started talking to Adrian and Dustin. He looked like a kid who had dropped his ice cream cone."

Whitney brushed off the speculation. She saw Conrad's jaw tighten and the glares he threw when Adrian insinuated the possibility of sharing a spark with Whitney. She assigned it as being a knee-jerk reaction from when they were younger. Conrad was merely acting as a proxy for her brother Thom.

"I bet he'd jump at the chance to work with you on the fun run committee."

Whitney exclaimed, "What?"

The cosmetologist drew back her scissors. "Can you give a warning before you pull a move like that?"

"Sorry." Whitney sank a little in her seat and stewed. The fun run committee was her saving grace and one of the few projects she saw to completion with minimal assistance from Jasmine. Conrad had nothing to gain, which meant he wouldn't help, or worse, he'd see the request for what it was—a setup.

Whitney knew her place, and it wasn't anywhere near Conrad's realm.

That and she'd already invited Dustin to help. He'd been hired for a job with the Parks and Recreation department, making it a mutually beneficial situation.

"Either way, I'm proud of you," Jasmine said. "You stepped out of your comfort zone and took a shot at getting something. She winked. "Or better yet. Someone special."

"I've had my someone special." For a long time, remembering she loved and lost at a young age made Whitney sad. Now, the memory was like a favorite blanket. It protected her from life's cold and occasionally bitter storms. "We are searching for your someone special."

All night, when Jasmine's focus was elsewhere, Adrian regarded her with appreciative glances. Whitney saw the flickers of interest.

Jasmine held up a hand of warning. The cosmetologist stepped away with her scissors and comb poised in a safety position. The chair swiveled, and Jasmine faced Whitney. "I am speaking as your best friend, as the person who hears all your secrets, and the person who will tell your mother about the time—"

She pursed her lips and averted her gaze to Ericka, who had her ear inclined toward the conversation.

"You sound like an eighty-year-old woman. It's time. Promise me. If I'm right about Conrad, you'll give him a chance."

It was an easy promise to make. First, Conrad lived in Arizona. Second, he had hordes of beautiful women throwing themselves at him, which meant he wouldn't have time to give Whitney as much as a second thought. That made three strikes against Whitney. She was out of the game before it started. "Okay. I promise," Whitney said.

"Good." Jasmine leaned back in her chair and swiveled to face the mirror.

Country music chimed through the sound system, and conversations from other chairs filled the silence. Then Whitney got an idea. "Can we invite Adrian to game night?"

Chapter 9

Family Time Whitney

Whitney wiped the sweat off her brow with her forearm. The materials for a project she and her siblings had coordinated were laid out neatly in rows according to size behind the storage shed in her parent's backyard. They'd used flattened-out cardboard to organize the nuts and bolts that would hold the pieces together to make a raised garden. What was set in front of them looked nothing like the picture on the boxes.

"Who's idea was this?" Ivan, the youngest of the siblings, always had the gift of saying what everyone else was thinking and getting away with it. He had a lean runner's body like Whitney but wore athletic gear that matched their older siblings' outfits. In this instance, it was jeans with running shoes and a short-sleeved Under Armour t-shirt.

Whitney was still buzzing. The hum from the excitement of Jamie's party vibrated throughout her body. She didn't care that the project in front of them would take longer than any of them had planned. Every time she tried thinking about something, her mind circled back to the way the night ended. Conrad had walked her and Jasmine to the car.

Ericka, the oldest of the siblings, buckled the tool belt her father bought her for her birthday around her waist. She stretched the ends of her short ponytail, tightening the grip of the band that held her chocolate brown hair out of her face. "Let's make no mistake. This was Mom's idea."

Their mother had dropped several hints. "Wouldn't it be nice if I had a raised garden?"

Or "If I had a raised garden, we could have had fresh herbs in this pasta."

Then there was the guilt approach. "Bending down is getting hard on my knees. One of those raised gardens like my friend, Betty, has in her yard would be nice." She said that one so many times, all six of the Stansfield children mouthed the suggestion behind her back.

While pretending they had no intention of building a raised garden bed, the six siblings had hashed out all the details of their mother's birthday party and the presents three months before the blessed event.

Getting the brothers and sisters to pitch in money for a raised garden bed wasn't the problem. Finding the time to bring all six of them to the same place at the same time to build it was another ordeal.

Finally, they picked a day and decided that whoever could make it would assemble the three wooden boxes that would stand outside the kitchen window one day. The others would paint it and organize the delivery of the gardening materials.

"How's the saying go?" Ivan asked.

"If Mom isn't happy, nobody's happy," Whitney replied.

It was true, too. Whitney didn't know how it was possible, but it seemed like they had bad weather whenever their mother was in a bad mood. One year, when their father forgot their anniversary, a microburst pulled a tree out of the ground.

"You got that right," Thom, the brother that was a year older than Whitney, circled around the pieces of their project. His mocha-brown eyes seemed darker.

Whitney guessed that he was still having troubles with his wife, Grace. Thom and Grace had separated recently. Both said they were fighting for the marriage but needed some space to sort through things before they caused irreparable damage to their relationship.

From what Whitney could read from her brother's somber mood, the space wasn't working.

Thom had seen more heartache in his adulthood than most had in a lifetime.

Whitney wished she could say something to help him with this problem. While Whitney had been in a couple of relationships over the years, she didn't have the wisdom or magic nugget of truth to pass along to him. The longest she'd been in a relationship was six months. It was the same reason, every time. The guy softly let her down. He'd found someone else.

All three times.

Who was she to give advice on how to save a marriage?

"What if we worked in teams? Two of us on one bench, two on the other. One of us can be in charge of reading the directions," Whitney suggested. The quicker they finished, the sooner she'd be able to go home and take a nap.

"That's code for she wants to boss us around," Ivan joked. Being the youngest afforded him leniency. By the time he did something wrong, the older siblings were too caught up in their problems to take issue with whatever Ivan had done. That and he was too cute. Ivan had a grin that he used when he knew he was pushing it and used it the way most people used chocolate syrup on ice cream—with no remorse or hindsight.

Whitney held out the pamphlet with the instructions. She intentionally handed it to Ivan with the German translation facing upward. "Fine, you take over."

"I didn't say I wanted to be in charge." Ivan pushed the instruction manual away like it was rotten food. "I just wanted to point out that you are bossy."

"Duly noted," Whitney took back the pamphlet and silently sniggered. On top of being cute, Ivan was an easy target. When they were little, she made up stories to scare him into bending to her will, like the time she told him that if he ate too many potato chips, he could develop chipitis.

"What's that?" Ivan's eyes were wide like the artist drew in cartoons.

"It's when you eat more chips than your liver can handle. Then one gets stuck." He didn't eat chips for months.

Their dad appeared from around the corner. His eyes were trained on the materials on the ground. "What's going on out here?"

His question didn't fool Whitney. She knew what her father was trying to do. Especially when she caught the wrench hanging out of the back pocket of his jeans. Erick Stansfield had always been a hands-on father. When his kids were younger, he'd pull them into working on a home improvement task with them on the weekends.

And he was the worst with presents.

"Dad, this is supposed to be our gift for Mom's birthday." When Ericka crossed her arms in front of her, she looked like the female interpretation of her father. They both had well-defined jaws and eyes that were so vivid that people often flinched when they had their full attention.

"She has no idea." Erick's eyes roamed around the yard. "She's playing golf. I told her I was staying home to fix the sprinklers." He turned his gaze toward the immaculately trimmed yard that would have made the people from the home gardening shows say, "Ooh."

"Don't mind me. Continue with what you're doing." He

wobbled from his heels to his toes, back to his heels. "I won't bring up the times I signed the report cards when you were afraid to show them to your mother."

The four siblings exchanged glances. There wasn't much of a debate. Their dad was handy with a tool.

"Okay, then. We need to make the base." Whitney pointed to the pieces in the middle. "Two of part A and two of part B." She slid her finger along the illustration. "And it looks like we need four of bolt F."

Her father interrupted her. "What about the nuts? You don't want to strip the wood."

"I wasn't done," Whitney grumbled.

"I was just trying to help," her father said.

Ericka, Ivan, Thomas, and Whitney glanced from their father to each other and sighed. Wanted or not, their father would end up leading their efforts. Whitney, who had always been the bridge between the siblings and the parents, fulfilled her role. "Dad, do you want to take lead?"

Erick pulled the wrench out of his back pocket. "I knew you'd need my help sooner or later." He handed the wrench to Whitney. "I noticed you didn't have one of these, so I brought one along."

"What an interesting coincidence." She spoke to her siblings as if to say, "We should have done this another day."

Once they got started, their father's help proved beneficial. He made the teams even. Ericka and Whitney worked on one of the three containers, and Thom and Ivan worked on the other.

"You know this would have been a great project for Ben to take part in," their father said to Ericka.

"He's at work." Ben, a geology professor at Montana State University, also worked as a consultant for the state.

"I know. Just tell him I'd have liked to have seen him." Erick moved on to the next absent family member. "Thom, how's Grace doing?"

Whitney wanted to apologize to Thom. He didn't want to be there in the first place. Their parents' relationship was a blessing and a thorn in his side. It proved that a cohesive marriage was possible. Thom told Whitney that his inability to get along with Grace might have been a sign that something was wrong with him. "Maybe, I'm cursed," Thom said.

"You are not," Whitney's voice pleaded with him to cast aside the thoughts he used to defeat himself.

"Think about it, Whit. I'm the only one bad things happen to."

"Bad things happen all the time," Whitney argued. "When it happens to somebody else, you'll be strong for them." When she said it, she believed it wholeheartedly. To everyone and everything, there was a season of struggle and a season of ease.

Thom shrugged his resignation.

"She still hasn't come around?" Whitney loved her father. The want of Thom's happiness in his voice added to her esteem of the man who tried to show his kids how to live a good life. Their father could be bossy, intrusive, and sometimes a little rude. His good intentions for his children outshone every one of his flaws.

"I'm beginning to think she never will," Thom bent down and connected the edges of two pieces of wood. The two pieces fell apart when he tried pushing the bolt into the predrilled hole. He exhaled his disappointment. "She's pregnant."

Whitney's eyebrows shot up into her bangs. Everything was about to change in her brother's life. Her silent hopes for reconciliation burned deeper turning into they had to get back together. Thom deserved happiness. Grace deserved to have a husband and a son. They had to figure it out.

"Marriage isn't easy. There's always something threatening

the foundation. It's your job to fight for it. The fight makes the foundation sturdier."

Whitney envied her father's support of Thom and Grace. They'd had it from day one of their relationship. Every guy Whitney liked, her father dismissed for one reason or another. What would he say if he found out the crush she had on Conrad was alive and well and had the chance of growing into something real?

"Dad, she said she doesn't want to fight anymore."

Whitney's heart sank at the defeat she saw in her brother's eyes. Life had given Thom some harsh battles. It hurt that the one that could bring him the most joy might be the one to defeat him.

Ericka and Ivan found the different nuts and bolts used to hold the pieces of wood together interesting. They each bent down and picked up a piece. Ericka pointed at a piece of wood. Ivan nodded and slid it from between Thom and their dad. They worked in silence while Thom and their dad talked.

Whitney pretended to read a manual so she could hear what her father would say to her brother. Erick Stansfield's adeptness at reading people and situations was a gift he didn't dole out freely. So when he spoke, everyone listened.

Erick crossed his arms in front of him. "Son, you know I want the best for you, and I try to let you solve your problems. But I feel like it's time for me to speak. Pregnancy is hard on a woman. You need to believe Grace when she is tired. Maybe, it's time you give her a break."

Ivan secured the bolt on the two slats he connected and stepped away from the finished box. He strode toward Thom and patted him on the shoulder. "Normally, we don't agree with Dad, but he may have a point this time. Look at how many times he got mom pregnant, and they're still married."

Their father's face turned five shades of red, but the soft smile said he agreed with what his son had said.

"Let's get to work on these planters." Ericka spoke in her fake, grumpy voice. "Otherwise, Thom will be a grandfather by the time we finish."

"I'm going to be a grandfather." Their father's face flushed bright red, and his smile widened with wonder.

Whitney had a sweet suspicion Thom would reconcile with his wife. It would take time, and changes were on the horizon. Hopefully, they'd all be ready when it happened.

Chapter 10

You'll Be Like Those Hallmark Guys

Conrad's steps echoed off the walls of the empty building. His vision, a sports center bustling with activity, more robust than the empty building that echoed their footsteps, burned in his chest. In a matter of time, wires that dangled from the ceiling would be connected to computers. Exercise equipment would fill the middle area. Upbeat music pounding through the sound system would blend with the groans of athletes—athletes that sought out his sports center because he had top-level coaches, therapists, and nutritionists. Everything was in position for his return to Cottage Cove.

A vision of Whitney at Jamie's party filled his mind. She was out by herself under the starry sky with the breeze brushing the tendrils of her hair. His next inhalation of air was sweeter and fresher, and invigorating. He wished there was a way to hold onto the feeling.

That day had started with the concerns that pressed on his thoughts. Would people hold his father's sins against him? Would they block his attempts to establish his name in Cottage Cove?

Then he talked to Whitney. Funny, sweet, goofy, Whitney. Despite his indifference from when they were younger, and the years he had been gone, she spoke with ease as though they had been lifelong companions.

If Whitney could give him a chance, it was possible that other people would overlook the skeletons rolling out of his closet like a summer monsoon over parched prairie land. She had done it again. She'd grown his hopes into beliefs. Conrad could be someone other than one of Austin Hayes's sons.

"You did it." Seth Montgomery, the friend who badgered Conrad to return to his roots, patted him on the shoulder. Shortly after graduating from high school, Seth replaced football sprints and hours in the gym with hiking trails and rock climbing. His skin was tight against his face and marked by hours in the sun.

Whitney's brother, Thom, nodded while surveying the space. Thom was older, but he was still the fit guy who could jump to action and catch one of Conrad's throws. "You talked about this when we were in high school. I'll be honest. I didn't see it happening. Good on you."

Many people had different expectations of Conrad. They never said it to his face, but Conrad heard the rumors about how men didn't want their daughters dating him. He also saw the unspoken worry in his mother's eyes and made a promise to himself. Never. Never would he make a woman feel insignificant. In that same vein, he would never tolerate cheating.

After playing with a team for a couple of years, he witnessed the other side of those father's concerns. Several of his teammates, believing the lie fame told them, manipulated women and bartered bad deals. Those guys would be around for a year or two. Then their lifestyle caught up to them, and they'd get traded to another team—to another coach who could manage their attitude.

"I'm not completely where I want to be." Conrad's attention skirted back to his dream that started in the empty building that still had the lingering odors of dust. He shifted his focus to where his office and meeting room would be. The frame for the walls marked off the area.

"You play the game one down at a time," Seth said. "You've contacted the colleges and the sports medicine facilities."

"Yeah, word will get out, and next thing you know, you'll have to open a second location," Thom said. He wandered toward the area where the massage tables and ice baths would eventually be.

Conrad always appreciated Thom. He was slow to approve, but once he supported something, Thom was all in.

Thom's eyes were bright, relaying the vision in his mind. "When people see you at local events, you'll be like those Hallmark Channel guys."

"I don't know about that," Conrad balked. He wasn't planning on falling in love any time soon.

"How do you know about the Hallmark Channel movies?" Seth's face contorted to look like someone who had eaten a sour piece of candy.

"I have a wife," Thom sounded surlier than the situation required. "I know how to stay happily married."

He blinked, and his facial expression changed. He turned to Conrad. "You know– it would be nice to have someone with expertise on the fun run board," Thom raised his hands facing outward. "No pressure."

"The board? I'm more of a hands-on person," Conrad backed away and turned, leading Thom and Seth to the area where the staff kitchen would be. A refrigerator had been plugged in. He passed Thom and Seth a sports drink, and pulled one out for himself, then closed the door. "I could work one of the checkpoints. Or get my team to help with setup and break down."

"Dude!" Thom's brows bent at the middle of his forehead. "What idiot would assign a Division Championship football player to set up and break down a checkpoint? You'd be the face of our public relations team. Do you know how many people will sign up just because you're there? And, did I mention Whitney is the one who started the whole thing?"

Conrad was quickly learning that Thom was also a great negotiator. Thom was the one who suggested the location for the Sports Center. Next, he casually suggested working with the fun run. Mentioning the other person Conrad owed big time —Whitney—tipped the scales heavily toward Conrad's agreement with Thom's request. If Whitney hadn't tutored Conrad, he might not have graduated from high school on time, not to mention the hours he spent with Thom and his older brother Ben on and off the football field.

Although he preferred working behind the scenes, Conrad could see how his presence would support Thom's project. Against his better judgment, he played with the idea of taking on a role with the public relations team. Dustin had mentioned that Whitney had onboarded him. Since then, Dustin had actively promoted the run at all the Parks and Recreation activities.

Conrad focused on the corner where the treadmills would go. For the time being, it was cold cement. One day it would be a running bay with his trainers monitoring their athlete's progress.

If he joined the committee, it could develop into one of those mutually beneficial business deals. They'd use his name to promote the fun run, and his business would garner visibility. He'd make sure to contribute to the runner's experience. "I know a good security team, and I could have some of my trainers in a tent giving tips for post-run stretches. My support staff could help pass out some recovery drinks and nutrition bars."

"It will be like old times." Seth held up his bottle of blue sports drink for a toast. "To the future."

Thom added, "We'll make a difference and be cooler than our parents while we're doing it."

Being cooler didn't hold much sway with Conrad. He'd be happy if he could invalidate the reputation he unfairly inherited from his father. He'd be Conrad, the pro athlete who returned to his roots to give back to the community that supported him for years. Working with Whitney would be his first step toward thanking her for what she had done all those years ago. It would be a good start.

He raised his orange sports drink, and the warmth of the conversation surrounded him. It was like old times. The friends were working together on a project. This time it was one of their makings.

Chapter 11

Avocado Toast

Conrad's nearly-empty house miniaturized his furniture. The white leather couch, large enough to seat him and a friend comfortably, hadn't created a dent in the open area.

The first steps in moving were always the hardest. The lack of a personal touch always drove Conrad to a headspace he preferred avoiding. But that hadn't been important until now. Now, it was time to plan. He had finalized his move to Cottage Cove and needed to find help making it more personal.

A quick inhalation of the aroma from his cup of coffee tickled Conrad's mind toward his plans. He had a busy week ahead. He had to head back to Phoenix, read through a stack of resumes, talk to the project manager, and remember to order groceries for delivery when he returned to Cottage Cove on Friday.

The sound of the front door lock turning sent a surge of adrenaline through Conrad. He hadn't given anyone a copy of his keys.

Conrad set his cup on the glass coffee table and lunged for

the first thing he could grab. He picked up the football he had left on the floor by the couch.

A ray of light widened on the floor, and his brother's tall frame walked through the doorway.

"Don't you know how to knock?" They were grown men, and Kevin still had the annoying habit of just walking in on Conrad at his whim. Conrad dropped the football on the couch.

"What were you going to do?" Kevin gestured toward the football. "Invite me to a game of two-man no touch?"

Conrad's throwing arm had some power. An unexpected hit with a football wouldn't have harmed anyone, but it would have been a strong enough distraction for him to be able to take down an intruder, especially one the size of his brother. Kevin was a good half foot shorter and fifty pounds smaller than Conrad.

"What are you doing here?" The question came out sounding harsher than Conrad intended.

"You're still mad?" The pain that crossed Kevin's face tugged on Conrad's feelings.

"Would I move back if I was mad?" Conrad checked out his clothes. His wrinkled white Arizona Cardinals t-shirt and wrinkled pajama bottoms weren't his best look, but it was better than what he normally wore when he stumbled through his morning. "I thought you were in Switzerland, training."

Kevin, a professional skier, followed the snow so he could either train or coach year-round.

"Mom asked that I stay home for a while." He fixed his steel-blue eyes onto Conrad's. "So we can resolve some issues."

Conrad always wondered why their eyes were different shades of blue. The feeling that he should have known pressed on him, daring him to give in to resentment. Resentment he tried to reject because it would hurt their mother.

Conrad shifted his focus to the empty fireplace. He was the

first to pull away from the stare-down. Kevin had more skin in the game and was willing to fight for it. *They wouldn't have had issues if their parents would have been forthcoming with the truth about Conrad.*

Even so, Kevin handled it better, probably because he was bound by blood to both his mother and father.

As she had several times since the party, Whitney popped into Conrad's mind. A sense of longing accompanied it. His attraction went beyond the pretty face, smoking hot body, or engaging personality. He was at ease when he was with her. It was nothing like the walking on eggshells feeling he had when he was with his family.

"Time will take care of it." Despite the shock of learning they were half-brothers, Kevin clung to the skill of reading Conrad's moods.

He crossed the space and retrieved the loaf of seven-grain bread from the cabinet beside the fridge. "In the meantime, do you want some avocado toast?" Kevin stuck his head in the fridge. "Do you have basil?"

Conrad and Kevin fell into the easy rhythm of making breakfast together. Even though unexpected circumstances had rammed their lives with a sledgehammer of truth that rocked their world, they were brothers.

With a degree of grace that impressed Conrad, Kevin said at the peak of his confusion, "Half is better than none."

Conrad threw his brother a sideways glance. Would they have been as close if Kevin wasn't so vehement about protecting their bond?

Kevin mashed the basil he had cut into slivers with the cream cheese and avocado mixture Conrad had made. "You're stopping by the house to visit Mom?"

Mom had been a loaded word. The tenderness was there, but the scars from anger and the deep stab of betrayal were still sensitive. It took time and resilience for the broken familial bonds to take hold. Conrad relaxed to release the tension building inside him. "Yes, I'm bringing her a jersey." He dropped four slices of bread into his new chrome toaster. He picked off the protective coating and pressed the lever.

Kevin rinsed the bowl he'd used to grind the basil and loaded it in the top rack of Conrad's dishwasher. "How long are you staying?"

"I have to head down to Phoenix for a meeting. But I'll be back next Friday. I plan on staying for the week after that. Will you be here?"

"Hard to say. Dad wants me to stay and help at the lodge this summer." Kevin shrugged, conveying the mutual confusion with the circumstances. It was hard to act like things were normal when everyone was walking around like they might be the next one to drop something that would shatter the already weakened family bonds. His voice changed into his I'm trying to change the subject toward something positive tone. "I heard you were at a party last time you were here. How was it?"

Kevin had mined for anchors to keep Conrad close to home. Love for his brother welled in Conrad's chest. Kevin was the one who fought to remind Conrad that fallouts were opportunities to rise. Through his persistence, he showed Conrad that strength is an accumulation of the little things. He'd said in a variety of ways that most people overlooked the small details. The wise ones used them to grow.

In a flash of a second, Conrad's thoughts made the connection between what his brother was doing and Whitney. Long ago, when it was crucial, she gave him the boost he needed to gain his bearings. Kevin was doing the same thing.

He answered Kevin's question. "It wasn't too exciting. The usuals were there." Conrad twisted the tie in the bread bag and returned it to the fridge. "Whitney's changed."

"Yeah, I saw her when I had to go to Seth's for an adjustment. I almost threw out my back so I could make an appointment for another visit." Kevin munched on a piece of toast.

The muscles in Conrad's back tensed. If Kevin weren't his brother, he'd have punched him.

Conrad froze.

Where had that come from? There was nothing between him and Whitney. Sure, they had a great time hanging out, but it wasn't like he had any reason to get angry because Kevin found her attractive.

Then he thought again. He had every reason to be protective. Whitney had helped him. The least he could do was watch out for her well-being.

He ate the last of his toast and brushed the crumbs from his plate into the trash. "You can hang around, but I've got things to do."

Like?

Conrad said, "Buy some furniture." He thought, *Figure out a way to justify a visit to the chiropractor.*

Chapter 12

An Otherwise Dreary Day

Whitney sighed in contentment. She loved her job at Montgomery Chiropractic Office. It was in her comfort zone—the place where she had enough predictability to relax but knew something would happen to keep her on her toes..

The whitewashed wood flooring and all-white furniture with light gray walls had a cool aesthetic. It almost tricked her into thinking she had outgrown the outsider vibe. But alas, once an awkward geek, always the one who knew too much to fit in but was vital enough to be included occasionally.

Thom casually mentioned, "Conrad should be back from Phoenix next week," and then stuffed his mouth with potato salad. With his not-so-subtle share, Whitney's hopes of hearing from Conrad were batted down like a birdie in the middle of a Stansfield badminton game. Conrad called Thom but hadn't reconnected with Whitney, not even on social media.

Despite Jasmine's encouraging hints, Whitney knew she never had a chance with Conrad. Still, picking up his friendship with Thom said something. The time apart had not damaged their friendship.

Whitney bristled at the imbalance between her and Conrad. He was and continued in his role as a wealthy, hunky athlete, and she remained the middle-class, smart girl that harbored a crush on the man who was way out of her league. There was no reason for him to want to get in contact with her.

Ruby McCleary backed into the glass door leading into the waiting area of the chiropractic office. Whitney rushed to catch the door, making it there in time for Ruby to greet her with a breathy grin.

According to the paperwork in her patient file, Ruby McCleary was in her early sixties. Her short violet haircut and stylish tunics with Birkenstocks gave her the airs of someone in her late thirties.

The scent of cinnamon wafted from the plate covered with embroidered muslin she held out. "I come bearing gifts of thanks." She lifted the edge of the cloth to show Whitney freshly baked cinnamon rolls. "The trick to safely transporting them is using toothpicks."

Ruby set the plate on the counter separating the receptionist from the general seating area. "I made these to celebrate having a normal back."

Weeks ago, when Ruby first entered the office, she baby stepped to the receptionist's desk. Her tightened jaw betrayed the pain she tried to downplay. "I'm sure I'll be fine after an adjustment."

Since then, Ruby had been a regular patient, visiting three times a week. "You shouldn't have," Whitney said, "but since you did, I'll say thank you and have one with coffee later."

"I suspected that would happen," Ruby's eyes twinkled. "Make sure you take two."

Whitney led Ruby down the corridor to the cubby area with the chiropractic table. Not that she was needed. Ruby had been at the office enough times to declare dibs on the room furthest from the reception area. Whenever she was placed in a different room, she'd say, "I prefer the room with sassy quotes."

She positioned her over-the-shoulder purse on the edge of the corner chair. Then she settled into place on the table. "Have you found yourself a nice man yet?" Ruby's dimples appeared whenever she was being playful.

Whitney blushed. At least once a week, Ruby hinted that she had a son or a friend of a friend she "knew would be the perfect companion" for Whitney.

"I don't need a nice man," Whitney replied. "I have good friends and brothers."

"Well, if you ever change your mind, I have a guy that likes to hike." Ruby's eyes glistened like she had relived a fond memory. "My Roy used to love hiking."

Whitney wondered if she'd ever feel that way about a man. The most she had was the exhilaration of finding someone, followed by the uncertainty of the inevitable end. The men she dated were good people, yet she always felt like something was missing. In the end, they said the same thing. "We're better off as friends." Whitney crossed her arms in front of her and leaned against the counter. "I wish I could have met Roy."

She listened to Ruby tell stories until Seth circled the partition. He looked like he could have been one of Ruby's companions in his Hawaiian shirt and khaki cargo pants. He wore a white doctor's coat over his outfit so people would believe he was a doctor. After one appointment, people didn't need the formalities. But he wore it anyway.

"It was nice talking with you, Ruby." Whitney left to give them space for her adjustment.

Ruby called back, "Don't forget about the cinnamon rolls."

Whitney took one and set the plate on her desk for safekeeping.

Later in the day, it proved to be a wise decision. Otherwise, she might not have had the chance to eat one.

Between Seth's chiropractic appointments and Whitney's occupational therapy patients, the office had back-to-back appointments.

In between helping people, Whitney took a call from her brother that began with, "Whit, have I told you how much I appreciate you."

"No. Please no. Thomas." Whitney knew what was coming. They had a fun run meeting scheduled, and her brother wanted her to take notes and make decisions on his behalf.

"Whit. I promised Grace I'd make dinner." She heard the apology in his voice—and the pleading for understanding.

"You're just not coming to the meeting, but you'll still help with the other details?" She'd lost the first battle, but there was still a bigger picture to address.

The long pause tugged at Whitney's heart. Thom was struggling. The 5k fun run was in honor of his friend. But his marriage was on the line.

She sank into her chair. Whitney would have groaned her frustration if she wasn't in an office with thin walls. "You're calling me on my vows." As an official witness to their marriage when they eloped, Whitney promised to support her brother's marriage.

Whitney dated Grace's younger brother Geoff. Until he died on the football field, unaware of a silent heart condition. Having been a victim of love being ripped away without warning, she understood the fragility of relationships. Thom needed her support, and of course, Whitney would give it. The conversation was a formality.

"I'm not bailing on you. I have to step away for a while. Until I get things with Grace back on solid ground."

Grace and Thom's marriage was a testament to Geoff's

influence. So much had been taken from Thom. Thom had friends, but nothing like the relationship he had with Geoff. Grace mourning the loss of her brother, connected with Thom. Love softened their grief, and they married.

Geoff's death birthed Thom and Grace's love. That in itself softened the blow of it being snatched away from Whitney. She lived vicariously through their highs, and, like she would do later in the day, she supported them through their lows.

"Everything will work out. It always does," Whitney muttered, addressing her displeasure with being put on the spot while recognizing that what she said also held true for Thom and Grace. They loved each other enough to work through the rough patches.

"I'll make it up to you," Thom promised. "And you won't be doing this alone. Seth and I found someone in mind to fill in for me. Someone with more experience and connections." Whitney heard a voice in the background. Then Thom said, "We'll talk more later. I love you, Sis."

"I love you, too." Whitney heard the call drop and returned to her day.

Thanks to the active adventure sports season, people who were sedentary for the cooler months dropped in for unscheduled emergency appointments. One thing led to another. Before Whitney could catch hold of her time, it was well past lunchtime, and the untouched cinnamon roll had been moved to the corner of Whitney's desk.

Toward the end of the day, when Seth and Whitney passed each other in the hall, Seth said, "How about I have Michelle call for Gino's pizza and Caesar salad to be delivered." Half of his body was in the next room when he said, "It'll make up for how hard I've made you work today."

Whitney gave him a thumbs-up and turned to greet the next patient on her list. She fingered through the files in the hanging trays until she found the one she was looking for. Their next patient was Bradley Welch. He was a nice man but tended to flirt. Then a thought struck Whitney. *Bradley and Ruby would be cute together.* Whitney added a cleansing breath to the sweet image in her mind and pushed aside the end-of-the-day fatigue. She entered the waiting area to greet Bradley. "Are you ready?"

Bradley spoke to the person beside him, "It's time to get shaken back into line." He pressed down on the arms of the chair and rose. As he reached the full standing position, the gears in Whitney's brain creaked into motion until what was in front of her registered. She shouldn't have been excited, but she was. The person sitting with Bradley. It was Conrad.

Whitney swallowed down the butterflies rising in her stomach, then smiled with her eyes to say hello to Conrad. She nudged her head to say, let's get going to Brad. Conrad tipped his head and reached for a magazine on the table beside him.

Rather than get caught up in why Conrad was sitting in the waiting area of Seth's office, Whitney asked Bradley how he was doing. The gears were moving, and there was no stopping them. Questions swirled in the background of Whitney's mind. She hadn't seen Conrad's name on the appointment register. Was it an emergency appointment? Why hadn't he visited his doctor in Phoenix? Was it wrong for her to be happy to see him under the given circumstances?

When she returned to the waiting room to greet Conrad, he was gone.

She gestured with her thumb toward the empty waiting room and asked Michelle, the receptionist, "What happened to Conrad?"

"He's picking up the pizza for us." Whitney recognized the smitten expression on Michelle's face. It was the same one Whitney had, and she couldn't count how many other lovestruck girls had worn for her first two years of high school.

She wanted to warn Michelle. Look at Conrad, but don't get attached. He doesn't see anything in women like us. Half a beat before she spoke, she stopped and smiled. Having a mutual crush was fun, harmless, and softened the sting of not being good enough. She brightened within the light of their similarities and added a conspiratorial note to her voice. "Do you think he'll drop it off and run, or will he join us for dinner?"

"I wish I didn't have a class in an hour." Michelle's playful groan said Whitney had chosen the right approach. It turned out that casting affection toward someone who was larger than life wasn't as dangerous as she had imagined.

Chapter 13

That's What Happened

Michelle and Whitney wiped down the tables and straightened the rooms' chairs and magazines. Whitney appreciated the help, and Michelle's bubbly personality made the time pass quicker. Her stubby blond ponytail bounced as she whipped from one task to another.

She held up a copy of the *Cottage Cove Tribune.* A picture of Conrad with his friends was on the front quarter panel. The headline read, "From the NFL to Building a Sports Center."

The light of recognition filled Whitney's mind. "That explains Jenny Dalton's Facebook post." Jenny and several of her friends posted memes and gifs about getting married in the near future. The word about Conrad returning home had become general knowledge.

"You should have seen how Conrad was watching you earlier today." Michelle's voice was light. It had a mixture of teasing with you really should take what I'm saying seriously.

"It's probably because I was ignoring him," Whitney said. He hadn't tried to contact her since the party but had rekindled his friendship with her brother. He hadn't made any promises to call her, nor had he given any indication that he was interested beyond the casual conversation they shared throughout the evening.

Still, the part of her that she chose to ignore hoped—hoped that things had changed, and she'd be good enough. It was just as well. Whitney couldn't hold a candle to the women Conrad preferred.

"Well, it worked," Michelle's voice had the air of someone who had just heard a life hack. "After you left, he asked all kinds of questions about you."

Although a shiver of delight coursed through Whitney, she pressed her lips together and forced herself to find a logical reason why Conrad had any interest in her. "Maybe he heard about the 5k and thought it would be good for PR."

"Sure, that's what he was thinking." Michelle flicked the sheet and smoothed it down before tucking it under the edges of the table.

"Have any plans for this weekend?" Whitney had decided there was more to life than Conrad.

He was nice on the eyes, but there wasn't much substance.

She'd probably have more fun watching two turtles race.

It was a lie, but if that's what she needed to keep her heart in check, Whitney was willing to try and believe it.

"I'm going on a moonlit hike with my friends."

Or going on a moonlit hike with her friends would be more fun than spending time with Conrad. Whitney jerked with the awareness that she was controlling her crush on Conrad. Her chest expanded, and years of feeling inadequate fell away. She smiled at Michelle. "You'll have to tell me about it on Monday."

They chatted all the way to the door about all that was entailed in the night hike. Whitney wondered if she could talk her younger brother, Ivan, into going with her. He was always up for a challenge.

She locked the door behind Michelle and mentally prepared for the meeting she'd have with Seth and Dustin. They scheduled the meeting to discuss what they'd done for the past two 5k fun runs and explore ideas for adding to the event. The number of participants doubled from one year to the next, making signing up vendors for booths easier. With Dustin's expertise, it would be that much better. She grabbed her binder with the previous years' information and followed the spicy pizza's aroma to the conference room.

Whitney walked in on the tail end of a conversation. She stopped short to reassess the situation. Dustin and Seth were supposed to be there, but nobody mentioned Conrad, although she should have expected him to be there. He was the one who picked up the pizzas. "We were waiting for you." Seth pointed to the two open boxes of pizza and four plastic containers of salad in the middle of the table.

She slid her binder onto the table and took her seat. "I take it Conrad is filling Thom's slot." Sparks of annoyance surged through Whitney. She had been with Seth all day. He could have said something about the changes. That and it was safer to harbor her displeasure with him. Her brother had his plate full. He had a fractured marriage and a pregnant wife. The last thing he needed was to have Whitney add more complications to his plate.

"Something like that." The way Conrad rubbed his chin set her further on edge. He only did that when he thought about a problem that puzzled him.

There was something the guys weren't telling her. If they were forthright, she could confront the issue. The vague comments and hints set her at a disadvantage.

"Let's eat, and then we can talk strategy for the 5k." Dustin didn't wait for agreement. He grabbed a plate and reached for a slice of the pizza with everything. The other two men waited their turn. "I'll be back in a sec." Whitney ran to the staff fridge to retrieve four water bottles.

Seth met her in the hallway. "I came to help you."

Whitney stretched out the vowels when she replied. "Okay." She handed Seth two of the four bottles.

"I wanted to talk to you, too." He gestured with the bottle toward the wall. "Conrad, Thom, and I talked last weekend. I assumed Thom talked with you about onboarding Conrad." A shadow of concern filled his eyes. "Then I saw your reaction."

The sincerity in Seth's voice tapped on Whitney's instinct to assure him that everything would be fine between them. "We're a team trying to do something good for the community. Many hands make light work. Right?"

Seth's shoulders dropped, and his chest expanded with the intake of air. "I'm glad things are good between us."

Whitney wanted to ask if he was psychic. Her default was to hang the burden of her unhappiness on him. Now that they had reconciled, reality and her expectations differed due to miscommunication. She was stuck dealing with the discomfort of Conrad's presence.

Seth stepped aside, allowing her to enter the meeting room ahead of him. She heard the water sloshing in the bottle as he said, "Leave it to Whitney to remember the drinks."

Whitney handed the bottle in her right hand to Dustin before making a plate of food for herself. She ate with the guys and laughed in all the right places when they made jokes. The prickling sensation that hit her when something was off-target nudged at her.

If Thom had been at the meeting, Seth and Whitney would have glossed over what they discussed in the previous session. Two new members meant rehashing details to pull them up to speed. Seth handed out a bullet point list of items of what they'd discussed or accomplished since the last meeting.

Seth and Whitney had worked together for so long that they had a natural melding of the minds. Dustin was a quick learner, falling into discussions. When they reached a talking point that leaned toward another person's strength, they paused naturally, giving them a chance to pick up the conversation.

Whitney passed Conrad her binder with the spreadsheets she used to organize everything. When Conrad asked questions, and one of them answered, pride in what they had accomplished filled Whitney. The first year they managed the fun run, there were almost more volunteers than runners on the 5k course. Five years later, they had 1000 people registered.

Seth leaned back in his chair and kicked his legs in front of him. "Now that we have filled you in on what we've done so far, we can start our new business with any ideas."

Conrad tapped Whitney's binder with his palm. "First, I want to say what you have done so far has been highly effective. My team navigated your website and found it easy to sign up for the event."

"That's good to hear," Dustin said.

A flash of "that's what happened" took over Whitney's mind. A week prior, the website logged a flurry of registrations. Within a couple of hours, they had fifteen new entrants in the race. Whitney thought it was because a family or a school had signed up.

At the time, she was pleased. She and Michelle celebrated their progress with high fives and an exclamation of, "woot woot." Now that Whitney knew it was Conrad and his "team," she felt foolish. "Your team," she asked. Was he talking about people he played football with? Or an administrative team?

"Yes." Conrad raised his chin, and the gleam in his eye was unmistakable. He was proud of his past accomplishments and intended to show them. "I have a public relations team. We work alongside non-profits. I bring visibility to their organizations. We've been searching for events that align with our vision."

The air left Whitney's lungs, and the muscles at the top of her neck clamped, warring against the tingles promising a dizzy spell. Had she completely misinterpreted Conrad's intention at the party? Her pulse pounded around her ears. Whitney replayed the events with the added details. With each beat of her heart, a different picture formed.

Somebody probably mentioned her affiliation with the fun run. *Babump.*

Interest in the run fueled the change in Conrad from an aloof observer to an active conversant. *Babump.*

Conrad saw that she was alone at the pool and went out there to reestablish their alliance for his success. *Babump*

Whitney would have pressed her palm into her forehead if she could have done so gracefully. He wasn't interested in her. He wanted her help. *It was high school all over again.* She was glad she listened to her gut. In doing so, she had saved herself from a large dose of embarrassment.

"We had a list of suggestions." Conrad walked to a table by the door and retrieved a file. He handed out a two-page document. Each item was bullet-pointed. If she were to hazard a guess, Whitney would have said the bold-faced line items were the more important ones.

"Your website doesn't have a place to contact you if companies want to sponsor your cause. I saw local businesses, but you could get larger donations and swag items from places like the American Heart Association and some larger gear organizations."

It hurt her a little, but she had to admit he was right. The run had grown, perhaps it could have expanded further, but her limited thinking had held it back.

He tapped the paper, "We could have some pre-race

training runs. Either before or after the run, Dustin, Seth, or I could have a healthy heart talk."

Whitney felt herself shrinking beneath the suggestions. Again, he was right. Conrad, Seth, and Dustin had dedicated their life to healthy living. People, especially the younger athletes, would benefit from the extra sessions.

He rattled off a list of other things that Whitney could have done. Instead of suggesting she take the lead, he offered the name of someone who could easily complete the new task.

Conrad concluded his pitch, saying, "With all these in place, you'll have more visibility, more participants, and more money."

He hadn't said it but had made it clear that the benefits came at the expense of Whitney stepping to the side and handing the reins over to Conrad. Her ego wanted to reset its head and fight. To say this project was her baby. Her heart knew it was best if she passed the baton with dignity.

"You've done your work," Seth flipped the paper over and back to the front. "I'm sure if he were here, Thom would be impressed with what you have to offer. But I have to ask, what's in it for you?"

"That's easy," Dustin said. "Conrad is the hometown athlete giving back to the community who believed in him."

"And I'm opening a sports therapy facility. People will be familiar with the name." Whitney noticed Conrad hadn't contradicted anyone. Instead, he agreed and pivoted the conversation where he wanted it to go.

Based on the twists the conversation had taken, it hadn't surprised her when Seth announced, "Conrad will be taking over the empty building in the parking lot across from us."

Whitney's stomach churned with rising nausea, turning the seven seasons pizza into a stone in her gut. Thom said Seth found someone to fill his slot.

They failed to mention that by onboarding Conrad, they acquired a whole team of people to work the fun run. She was no longer necessary. Quicker than it took Conrad Hayes to steal a woman's heart, he had hijacked Whitney's role as event coordinator of Geoff's Healthy Heart Run.

Faster than it took for a popsicle to melt on the sidewalk in summer, the walls of Whitney's heart crystallized, freezing into a fortress. What she had hoped for years had finally happened. Her crush on Conrad Hayes was deader than a corsage smashed between the pages of a thick book.

Chapter 14

Can I Get A Raincheck?

Conrad sat in the back booth of the Morning Grind. The waitress set his cup of black coffee in the only space not occupied by the papers splayed out around him. He glanced up long enough to thank her and returned to reading through the charts and tables in the binder Whitney handed over to him. Her documentation had been thorough. It was almost as if she expected someone to take over the project from her.

Seth slid into the seat opposite him and rested his forearms on the table. Conrad used the Post-it pad Whitney had left in the front pocket to mark his spot. Then, he gathered the papers and closed the binder, setting the information about the 5k run to the right of him.

Seth's smile spoke volumes along the lines of "we did it." When Conrad and Seth were young, they dreamed about their futures. Both talked about doing something that would help athletes.

At the time, they didn't know how it would happen. They just knew that it would. Conrad had the money and business connections for the sports center. Seth brought his medical expertise and professional contacts to help staff the facility. Dreams come true. People often forgot to mention the hard work behind them.

Conrad waited for the waitress to pour the coffee into Seth's cup to speak to him. When she walked away, he checked the time on his watch. "We'll be able to get a round of golf in before I head to Bozeman."

"Ah, you may want to consider a change in plans." Seth tore at the packet of sweetener and watched the white crystals drop into the piping hot, brown liquid. He stirred his coffee and set the spoon on the saucer.

Conrad searched his mind for a disruption that would throw off their timeline. "Is there a problem with the equipment?"

"No, nothing like that." As Seth took a sip of his coffee, Conrad noticed that the ends of his hair were still wet. Seth said, "Whitney meets with people at the park every Saturday morning. A lot of them participate in the fun run."

"She trains people for a fun run?" Conrad flipped open the binder to find the section with the details on training.

"Whitney likes to keep Geoff's parents in the loop. My guess is she'll tell them about the changes in the organizational structure."

"Geoff's parents?" Of course, Whitney would meet with Geoff's parents. Conrad's eyes scanned through the tabs and flipped to the volunteer's pages. He didn't see Mark and Darcy Hill anywhere on the list. Then he flipped to the calendar. The day was blank. "There's nothing in here about meeting with people to train."

"It isn't official. Geoff's dad talks about staying healthy while they walk to the Sweet Treats Cafe to eat cinnamon rolls." Seth caught the server's eye and beckoned her over to give his order. She took their orders and headed to the kitchen.

"There is nothing about meeting with Geoff's parents in the

documentation Whitney gave me." Conrad bristled at the absence of information. They could maximize the publicity by having him, alongside Geoff's parents, talk to kids about heart health.

"Leading up to the fun run, she focused on the scholarships." Seth pointed at the binder. "I'm sure she has the names of the volunteers who run the health tent."

"Why do I get the feeling Whitney withheld some information from me?" Conrad's shoulders pressed into his back to tame the agitation rising in him. He didn't have patience for secrets. One had shattered his world.

"It isn't anything like that," Seth's tone pleaded with Conrad to calm down. "This fundraiser is personal to Whitney. Think about it. Her brother is married to Geoff's sister. Mark and Darcy Hill are her in-laws. The weekend walks started as a way of working through the grief. As more people joined them, they got the idea for the 5k."

"So. She didn't tell me because..." Conrad didn't see where Seth was taking the conversation.

"It isn't an official thing." Seth pushed the sugar dispenser to the edge of the table against the wall and leaned forward like he was divulging a secret. "I don't know if you realized it, but she isn't in charge of any tasks on the list."

"I did that on purpose."

"Oh." Seth sat up straight, pressing back into the brown leather bench. He frowned. "Can I ask why?

Conrad shut the binder. It was obvious that what he was looking for wasn't in there. He slid it away from his place setting. "When we were younger, Whitney helped me out. It's time I returned the favor."

"By taking away what she loved?"

Conrad noticed Whitney had grown silent toward the end of the meeting. At the time, he attributed it to a passing of the baton. She had done her part. Now it was time for him to run with the program.

Conrad's jaw rippled with the rising tension. It wasn't supposed to be complicated. He thought about the end result—the dollars that he could bring in.

The 5k run raised money for scholarships and healthy heart awareness programs. His foundation gained visibility by joining the 5k run, and the scholarship fund got the money.

What he had failed to see was the mixed message. Success took precedence over personal connections. Argh! He wanted to slap the table. He had done it again.

By remaining true to her character, Whitney freely surrendered recognition and maintained connections with those who mattered out of sight. The battle between admiring her and frustration with being excluded warred within Conrad. He was her ally, not some brute who came in to steal her favorite toy.

He shook his head and rubbed his jaw to loosen the tension. He assumed that he had her trust. That was a mistake. Trust is earned, especially after not seeing the person for half a lifetime. "You're right. Can I get a raincheck on the game? It looks like I'll be going for a walk."

He'd eat a light breakfast because it looked like he'd be eating crow shortly.

Chapter 15

Meet The Lilac Lane Walkers

Whitney sat on the stairs of her front porch, throwing a backward glance at the front door of her cottage-style house. It was a tiny house, but it was hers. She bought it, had doubled up on payments, and paid it off. Pride tapped the edges of the numbness Conrad inflicted upon her ego.

It had been three days since he took over Geoff's fun run. Three days of her mind buzzing, trying to figure out where she had failed. Three days of piecing together why Thom, Seth, and Dustin hadn't said anything. Three days of Seth giving her the "are we okay?" sidelong glances.

No, they were not okay. But as long as he was her boss, she had to hold her tongue. So she did. And she needed this morning's walk. The time with friends who didn't care about dollars would do her ailing ego some good. The cinnamon roll at the end of the walk was the literal and proverbial icing. Just thinking about the sticky, gooey bundle of sweetness made her mouth water. Things would get better soon.

She tied the laces of her pink and green camouflage shoes that intentionally matched her pink and gray camouflage shirt and set off for the park to meet the other walkers. The morning air touched the parts of her that were slow to wake, bringing the fresh scent of the moisture on the grass. Life seeped into her joints and muscles, taking the place of the numbness.

For years, Whitney had the event to prove what she hadn't been able to say when she was younger. Geoff's life mattered. More importantly, his death wasn't for naught. Since then, teens had learned about heart conditions that weren't detected by regular sports physicals. They were taught to look for signs to avoid meeting Geoff's end.

Would Conrad stick to that purpose? Or was money and publicity his end goal? If history were any indication, Conrad would choose the latter. He had said as much. With his name and connections, they'd make more money.

Whitney's stomach soured.

Then, a soft breeze touched her cheek, and a sense of peace washed over Whitney. If Geoff could talk to her from the beyond, he'd tell her that contrary to what the heavy feeling in her chest was telling her, it didn't matter who coordinated the fun run. What mattered was that future generations of athletes were aware of heart conditions that affected high school athletes —and their books for their first year of college were paid for.

Whitney popped her earbuds into place, pressed the side of her phone, and became a member of Fall Out Boy. Her body aligned to the rhythm, and the one-sided argument she'd been entertaining for days fell to the wayside, completely disappearing when she spotted the black edge of the asphalt leading into the park.

Ruby's blue BMW and her friend Pauline's yellow Volkswagen Jetta were in the same two parking spots beside each other. The two older women sat on the bench in front of the gazebo. Ruby wore a visor and a pink sweatsuit. Her friend

Pauline had her hair pushed back in a headband. Both women seemed to be gawking at something in the parking lot.

Whitney followed the invisible line between them and whatever caused the reaction. She spotted Conrad and Seth popping out from between two cars and let a soft groan escape. "Why me?"

Conrad and Seth weren't happy with humbling her to insignificance? They had to aggravate her on her Saturday morning walk?

Seth pointed toward the group that had gathered at the entrance of the gazebo, and the men quickened their pace to join them.

She inhaled a breath and reminded herself that Conrad was supposed to be her ally. Or at least that's what he said as he accepted the binder Whitney slid across the table.

There were enough people there, making it possible for her to interact with him superficially. She'd be polite, and that was all he was getting. She pressed forward and stopped in front of Ruby and Pauline.

Ruby leaned around Whitney to gawk at Conrad. "I knew if we came long enough, something good would happen."

Pauline pressed her hand against her chest. "Tell me I've died, and I'm dreaming."

Whitney stiffened to contain the eye roll and pasted on a smile to greet Conrad and Seth. She forced herself to say, "Good to see you."

"This is the perfect day to work on cardio." Conrad's voice sounded like the workout people on videos. He spoke through his smile, "You forgot to mention that you met with people every week."

Whitney talked through her smile. "I handed over the binder with all the details you needed for the fun run."

"Maybe the "walk with people at the park" file accidentally was left on your desk."

The pressure from inquiring eyes fought for Whitney's attention. "Let's introduce ourselves."

She didn't need to call people over because everyone was watching the not-so-subtle argument she was having with Conrad. So much for being polite.

Whitney gestured with her hand, "I'm Whitney, and I've been a member of Lilac Lane Walkers for seven years." She pointed with her hand toward Pauline, who introduced herself. Until everyone in the circle said their name and how long they'd been walking with Whitney. After the last person, Whitney said, "We all meet every Saturday to walk."

An older gentleman raised a finger and interjected, "We also stop at the Sweet Treats Cafe for sustenance."

"Suzie makes the best cinnamon rolls," Pauline gushed.

"On that note, we should head out," Whitney said.

"The first one at Suzie's has to reserve the table," the old man said.

People walked in clusters as they headed for the trail at the end of the park. Conrad and Seth walked on either side of Whitney, making it challenging to buddy up with her regulars.

"I was telling Conrad how Mark and Darcy come and talk with the walkers every once in a while." Seth's long gait gave Whitney an idea. If she waited long enough, she could slow down, and he and Conrad could walk ahead. They liked winning, so it would be natural for them to leave her behind.

"Mark and Darcy are at a family event this weekend," Whitney explained and let it drop. She wasn't sharing that they would be gone for a month. It would serve Conrad well to have to put in some effort. She was done. Done helping him. Done being the stepping stool. Done allowing his charisma to blind her to his selfish opportunism. With that being said, it would be easier if he would stick with the program and do what he did best–leave her behind to run off to join the people that mattered.

A dog that was shin-high trotted down the trail. Seth bent down to intercept the familiar Yorkshire Terrier. "Riley's done it again." If a dog could smile, Riley would have been wearing one.

"Riley is Mrs. Abernathy's dog." Whitney moved toward the outer edge of the path just in case Seth needed help. "He's escaped so often we all know him by sight."

"Why don't you call animal control?" Conrad eyed the dog that walked into the space Seth had made with his body.

The barrage of dog kisses Riley landed on Seth's jaw answered his question. Just in case, Whitney would fill in the blanks. "Mrs. Abernathy is seventy-five, and Riley is like her son. Who wants to send an old woman's child to doggy jail."

"I'll take him back," Seth picked up the dog and cradled it with his arms. The dog licked his chin and snuggled in. Seth's voice softened like he was talking to a child. "Maybe Mrs. Abernathy has baked some chocolate chip cookies."

He reversed his course toward where they started, leaving Whitney and Conrad to watch him walk away and continue their discussion without him as a buffer.

The grumble in Whitney's chest never made it to her vocal cords. But the sentiment was there. If she didn't know any better, she'd have bet money that Seth planned on Riley freeing him from the discussion he brought to Whitney.

Chapter 16

You'll Make Sure of It

The low bushes on the side of the trail passed by in a whirl. Conrad, focused on Whitney, didn't have time to figure out what kind of plants they were.

She alternated from walking so fast that Conrad had to move full stride to slowing and causing him to stumble over his steps. Although a couple of times, he fell behind on purpose to check her out. She looked good in those gray leggings with a long, pink shirt. The outfit outlined her healthy figure, yet was discrete, leaving everything to his imagination.

"You seem kind of cranky. What did Ivan do?" Experience taught him that asking a question where he was obviously wrong was an excellent way to start a conversation.

She froze in place and scowled. "Don't bring my brother into this!" He knew when her tone of voice registered because she flinched. But it wasn't enough to temper her mood. She rolled her eyes and continued walking. "Why do men ask stupid questions when they don't know how to approach a topic?"

"Would now be a good time to point out you answered your own question?"

The straight line in her lips and quick twitch of her eyebrow hinted at thoughts of violence. She'd probably bury his body behind the grove of trees if she could.

Before Seth left, he'd whispered that Conrad may want to retreat.

Conrad wasn't a back-off kind of guy. He confronted problems head-on. The initial clash may be unpleasant. But in the end, just like on the football field, the opponents offered each other a hand and rose to get back in the game. Not that Whitney was an opponent, but she acted like he was.

Whitney rotated her head to the left and then the right. Her eyes fell on the gap between them and the next group of walkers. She hissed, "Why are you here?"

"Isn't it obvious?" Conrad pointed down at his Hoka One trainers and basketball shorts.

"Of all the places to walk. You chose the same park as me?"

Yes, if he had to choose a place to walk, it would be with her. Whitney was his equal, maybe even better than him. But she never threw it in his face. The idea of being anywhere with Whitney exhilarated Conrad. "You were having a meeting for the fun run. Shouldn't I be a part of it?"

"The fun run meeting." Whitney's mouth dropped, and her voice was airy with revelation. Her eyes squinted, and she glared. "And you thought I was sabotaging your leadership."

Conrad's heart rate amped a few notches. The glare was scary. "I thought you may have forgotten to mention it."

"Maybe because these people are my friends. We meet every week because we like each other." She walked backward, "Unlike some people who are only nice because they want something from the other person."

Her lip quirked to the left, and she rested her hands on her waist. "The Lilac Lane Walkers are my friends. Go get your own."

Her dismissal pinched at Conrad's ego but not enough to dissuade him from reconciling her reaction with his expectation.

"Okay, it's just the two of us. Tell me what's going on, Whit."

"You blow into town after fifteen years and take command over Geoff's Healthy Heart Run." The splotches on her face turned a deeper shade of red. "You know what? Forget it. I'm going home." She pivoted and leaned forward to march back to where they had come from.

Conrad stepped in front of her, and she collided with his chest. He caught her by her arms so she wouldn't fall. When he was sure she was steady, he released her. "It's still yours. I'm bringing a team to expand its reach."

She said, "Yeah, yeah. Visibility. Sponsorship. I get it. You can do a better job than me."

A punch in the gut would have done less damage. He was wrong. Whitney didn't get him. "I am trying to make up for all you've done for me." Conrad rubbed the back of his neck. What could he say to get her to understand that they were on the same team?

"What are you talking about?" The steam was gone from her voice, leaving only confusion.

She didn't know. She had no clue that she was the only person who treated him with dignity when he was at his lowest point. Conrad looked up like the trees around them would say, "let me take it from here," or a message would fall out of the clear blue sky. He returned his gaze to her. "Whit. You were my saving grace in high school. I am where I am today because you believed in me."

"But you had crowds around you all the time. You had cheerleaders with your name written on their white t-shirts. Everyone believed in you, Conrad." She had calmed, but her eyes were cold with mistrust. Conrad had seen the look. When her brothers complimented her because they wanted something, Whitney would dismiss them, and they'd plead their case.

Conrad wanted her to understand that he respected her. He owed her. He was trying to reciprocate the kindness she graciously extended him all those years ago. He plead. Plead with her to understand his good intentions. "They were tagging along for the ride. Whit, you got me through my senior year. You saved my dream. It's my turn to help you out with yours."

Her torn expression gutted Conrad. His good intentions had backed her into the corner of remembering the pain of losing her first boyfriend. "He was surrounded by people. I shouldn't have mattered to him. But that's the kind of guy he was."

She paced, stopped, and rested her hands on her waist. "He was always the guy who watched out for the kid who was alone at lunch and gave the cafeteria ladies Christmas cards. And he was taken before he had his chance to make his mark on the world. That's what the run was about. It was a day where Geoff's memory reminded people their health was important."

Conrad had to lean in because her voice softened, relaying how far back in the past she had mentally traveled. She had wrapped her arms in front of her. "Except it's changing into his teammates picking up where he left off because he didn't live long enough to share his message. Pretty soon, people will focus on the messenger and forget about the meaning of the run."

Conrad wanted to pull her into him and comfort her. But that wasn't the apology she wanted or needed. She needed Conrad to treat her like the silent hero everyone except him had known about.

Pieces of Conrad's bravado chipped away, and admiration for Whitney seeped into the empty spaces, opening Conrad to accept that his world would be much better with her in it. She was honest. She was the caliber of person who would tell

Conrad the hard truths. She had just done it. Yes, he'd bring a lot of people. But the limelight would be cast in the wrong direction. He exhaled, to release some of the weight of their confrontation, and to accept the full impact of the humbling.

Geoff was a sophomore when Conrad was a senior, so they played together for two years. But after Conrad moved on from Cottage Cove, Geoff was a fleeting thought that diminished as the years passed. How many other people had moved on after Geoff passed? That wasn't the case for Whitney. She fought to give the guy a legacy.

If Conrad weren't careful, he would fall in love with Whitney Stansfield. He reached out to caress her cheek. His body froze, stopping him from making a big mistake. He closed his hand before easing it back to his side. Her presence had the power to make him forget. Somewhere in the back and forth of his confrontation with Whitney, Conrad had forgotten he was supposed to protect himself from love's prickly touch.

He exhaled and looked up at the sky. He could do this. Maybe by working with Whitney, he'd get whatever drew her to him out of his system, and he'd learn to be a good friend to her. He returned his gaze to Whitney. "The fun run has been about Geoff and will continue to be about him. I know because you'll make sure of it."

Having Whitney by his side throughout the planning was going at the top of the bullet point list he'd made. He and his team needed her to remind them that there was more to a fundraiser than making money.

Chapter 17

We're A Good Team

Whitney's plan half worked. Ruby and Pauline were at the junction of the neighborhood and another trail leading deeper into the park. Conrad tipped his chin toward them. "Let's talk about this over coffee?"

Conrad was sticking by her. She'd used all her sass and all the avoidance moves that worked on her brothers. The man was good.

How many times had she wished that Conrad would press to spend time with her? None of them included it happening when she truly wished he'd fall into a ditch.

Her life had been so disrupted in such a short amount of time that Whitney half expected a microburst to come along and strip the rest of her assuredness, sending her running to Conrad for protection. It would be the universe's way of saying you asked for him. Now that you've got him, what are you going to do?

The nearby row of trees was still. There wasn't enough of a breeze to rustle the leaves.

Her father's advice tugged against her will. *Stay in your lane, Whit.* She'd met guys like Conrad. They worked with the motive of improving their own condition. She'd be safer to remember that his interest was professional.

"I'll buy and throw in the cinnamon roll for good measure." Conrad quirked his lips to the right and smoothed them into a soft grin. His look said I doubt you'll go for this, but I had to try.

Whitney's eyelashes fluttered. She couldn't believe the expression worked, but it had. She couldn't stay upset with him any longer.

"You don't have to buy my breakfast." She had to show some fortitude. He'd already wormed his way into the one project she had. If she budged too far in the agreeable zone, he'd probably try to take her job, too.

"It's my peace offering," Conrad said. "I won't believe you'll work with me unless you accept it."

Whitney's left eye twitched. Had she heard correctly? "Work with you?"

"You're the heart of the fun run." Conrad nudged his head and drifted in the direction he wanted them to go. "Tell me how you got started."

As they meandered down the path with the melody of birds chirping as background noise, Whitney considered her words. "How far back do you want me to go?"

"The beginning."

Conrad was there for the beginning. It was homecoming. Geoff was crowned homecoming king. Whitney was Geoff's date for the dance.

That in itself was a feat. Whitney's father blessed the relationship because Geoff's father was the business teacher at the high school.

The Cottage Cove Hawkeyes were seven points ahead. Geoff caught the ball and was tackled. When the huddle cleared, he was still lying on the ground. He never got up.

She knew telling Conrad that they had made plans to go to

the same college wouldn't matter. Or that Geoff had told her he loved her didn't matter. None of it mattered because Geoff wasn't there anymore. But his life mattered. And Whitney and Geoff's parents decided that if one person could avoid Geoff's fate, his passing wasn't in vain.

"None of us knew a kid could die of a heart attack," Whitney said. For years, she wondered if life took him away from her because she strayed from her father's wisdom. She fell in love with someone who was outside her lane.

"I wrote some research papers on it in college." Conrad sounded neither boastful nor sympathetic. Yet, there was a sound in his voice. "Since then, doctors have been using electrocardiograms to identify athletes with hidden heart problems."

The burst of awareness briefly blinded Whitney. She froze and stared into Conrad's eyes. *Conrad had been touched by Geoff's passing, too.* The ferocity driving her resistance deflated like a balloon with an untied end. Her insides burned with remorse.

His head tilted ever so slightly. His eyes asked the question. "Are things okay between us?"

Silently apologetic for misjudging Conrad's intention, Whitney made a promise to herself. She'd remember that she was only helping Conrad. No falling for him, no giving in to the feelings of wanting to spend more time with him, no more dreaming of what life would be like if they walked out of the stadium holding hands. They were partners working on a mutual project, and that was it. Her lips, curled at the corners, answered his question. The peace between them wasn't there quite yet, but it was only a matter of time.

They blinked and resumed their walk. Conrad and Whitney caught up to the front of the pack of walkers at the point in the path where the walkers turned to leave the trail.

Except, they were walking in the direction opposite the Sweet Treats Cafe.

"It's closed." Nathan, an older gentleman who always wore concert t-shirts, looked almost crestfallen. Whitney could relate.

His friend Jack said, "We're heading back to the cars to drive to the Morning Grind." Jack had a rounder belly than Nathan, yet his calves said he was no stranger to exercise.

"Doesn't that defeat the purpose?" Conrad asked

"I come for the coffee and baked goods." Nathan's voice was bright with pride. He'd set his intention and made peace with it. If Conrad didn't approve, it was on him.

"Yeah," Jack said. "We're only walking to check out the pretty women." He pointed his finger like it was a gun and winked.

Whitney appreciated the comic relief Nathan and Jack brought to whatever situation they were in. They were all talk. Both were happily married and treated their wives like they were queens.

"If we're driving someplace, why don't we all go to my house," Conrad said. "I just bought a new batch of avocados."

Whitney winced at the disconnect from expectation to what Conrad offered.

"You don't like avocados?" Conrad asked.

"Not when I was expecting cinnamon rolls with cream cheese frosting," Whitney replied. Thinking about the frosting melting into gooey sweetness made her mouth water.

"Cream cheese is great with avocado." Conrad's lip tilted upward, giving away that he was intentionally contradicting Whitney.

"Note to self. Conrad is not bringing baked goods to the morning meetings." Whitney's laugh felt light and airy. She liked the feeling.

With that, they turned around and headed back to the

gazebo. The group walked in a small cluster, making it easier to converse. By the time they arrived at the parking lot, Conrad had lured everyone to his house with the promise of a pancake breakfast.

After Conrad gave everyone the directions to his house, people shared what they'd pick up along the way. With plans in place, people hurried to their cars. Whitney waved goodbye as the doors slammed shut behind them. She stretched her face toward the sun to embrace the warmth and headed back to her house.

Jasmine will get a kick out of this story.

Whitney could hear her best friend giving her a hard time for the animosity she had harbored against Conrad.

She was halfway home when Conrad's pickup passed and parked slightly ahead of her. She approached the driver's side. "You want a ride to your house?"

"I'm almost home." She pointed toward the end of the road.

"The sooner you get there, the sooner we can be at my house." His words urged her to run around the back of his vehicle and slide in the passenger side door that Conrad had opened from the inside.

By the time Whitney clicked the safety belt, Conrad's pickup was in her driveway. She pushed the door open and hopped to the ground. Her hand was on the door, ready to slam it shut, when Conrad called out to her, "Whit?"

His use of her childhood nickname mustered all the warm feelings from their sweet memories. "Yes," she replied, half expecting Conrad to ask for help with another project.

"I have a good feeling about this."

"You should. Not too many people can organize a pancake breakfast in twenty minutes."

"I meant us."

Whitney's insides jolted. As much as she wanted to believe

he was talking about their friendship, Whitney suspected his conclusion referred to them working together on the committee. Still, it was fun being with him. It felt like he valued her for more than what she could do for him. He could have approached the whole situation, acting like he was doing her a favor. But he hadn't.

It was the opposite. Conrad had told her that she was essential to the run's success.

Time had changed Conrad.

Whitney liked what she had seen thus far. She started her morning thinking she would need an attitude adjustment—that she needed to remember that her position didn't matter.

Conrad had walked up uninvited and disrupted her plans. He had sought her out and confronted her and her well-intentioned coping strategy. All for the sake of building a bridge and connecting their purposes. Whitney felt less like that gangly girl on the outskirts and more like she belonged. Her smile sent waves of happy energy through her body. She said, "I think we're going to do some great things together."

Chapter 18

Pancakes and Avocados Are Not A Good Combination

Conrad's house was just like him, big, functional, nice to look at, but not any place Whitney would want to visit regularly. She was afraid she'd break something and couldn't afford to replace it.

"I know," he said. "It's a work in progress."

"You don't have a coffee maker?" Whitney leaned a little to the right as though the shift in perspective would add something to the light wood countertop devoid of appliances.

"I have it stored in a safe place." Conrad sauntered across the room like a hunter preparing to show his trophy. He opened a door on the kitchen island and placed his cappuccino maker coffee pot on the counter.

"Why do you have that hidden?" There were so many buttons on the panel that Whitney would have bet her lunch hour that it was self-cleaning.

"It isn't hidden. It is stored in a convenient place." Conrad set it on the countertop beside the sink and plugged it in. "So, I have more counter space for other projects."

"Like?" Whitney liked being in the position of challenging him. Granted, he was right, but it bugged her when he tore through her organization of the 5k. His out-of-sight, out-of-mind kitchen matched his approach to Whitney. Things were there, she just didn't know it until he'd thought it was safe to show her. Whitney put everything out there. She wanted to know what she could touch and what was out of reach.

"When I invite people for breakfast, I have enough cooking space." He filled the carafe with water from the filter.

"Oh, great entertainer, where are your mixing bowls?"

Conrad tipped his head, and Whitney moved in the general direction, finding what she needed to make pancakes.

"This feels like old times," Conrad circled around her, opening the fridge. He balanced several avocados and some herbs with one hand, grabbed a container of cream cheese, and closed the door with his heel. "You and me, working together, to make me look good."

"You don't need my help with that." Whitney had spoken the truth. But it wasn't enough to prevent the compliment from settling on her like a warm blanket. She didn't want to bask in Conrad's appreciation. As quickly as it could be given, it could be taken away.

"You'd be surprised." He pointed at the house that had furniture but no other decorations.

"By the way, what are you doing this afternoon?"

The doorbell rang. The light in his eyes said he'd remember to get the answer to the question later. The butterflies in Whitney's belly slid behind the trap she set and swirled around. Whitney liked working with Conrad, but she'd never, ever, ever admit it.

"Thank you for inviting us over." Pauline handed Conrad two gallons of orange juice. She surveyed the room. "You need a wife."

"You're supposed to say he has a nice house," Ruby walked around them and set the package of solo cups on the counter.

"Jack and Nathan stopped to get their wives. They'll be here in a little while."

She wrinkled her nose at the mashed avocados in the bowl. "Most people have bacon or sausage with their pancakes. You know, maybe top them with maple syrup."

Conrad's ears darkened to a shade of red, and he barked a laugh. "Chips and dip are probably not the best appetizers, but it's what I have."

"Ruby's right. You need a wife."

Whitney focused on the pancakes, like flipping them wrong would result in a national disaster. She would have to agree with Pauline and Ruby. Conrad needed a woman's touch. Yet, she wasn't foolish enough to hope it could be her.

Her heart, however, didn't listen. It bought the fantasy and all the trimmings and lingered in wouldn't-it-be-nice-if-this-were-real land. Especially after Conrad worked alongside her. Their natural rhythm mirrored how she worked with her brothers. She'd stack the pancakes on a plate. Conrad sprayed the pan. She'd pour the batter. He'd add the cooled pancakes to the growing columns in the oven. Instinct guided their movements. While it helped the flow, it upended Whitney's sense of where she was in relation to Conrad. She had never been so in tune with somebody who hadn't shared her last name.

One by one, people filled the once-empty space. The countertop was loaded with cinnamon rolls, deli meat, crackers (that went along with Conrad's avocado dip), and various creamers. Conversations brought the room to life.

In the midst of the lively banter, Whitney saw things from her brother's and Seth's perspective. Conrad was better equipped to handle events.

The large group of people wouldn't have fit in her two-room cottage. If Conrad hadn't joined their weekend walk, they all probably would have gone home.

His easygoing nature set everyone at ease. The men joked, the women playfully flirted, and Conrad went along with it. Every once in a while, he'd slip Whitney a look. He'd raise his eyebrows and smile as though to say, "I see you."

Being seen was another unfamiliar and heady feeling that sent trickles of delight through Whitney. She didn't mind that Conrad was the one creating the feeling. There was something about the way he did it that made her feel safe, cherished, wanted.

A phone vibrated on the countertop. Whitney glanced over to make sure it wasn't hers. She noticed it was Conrad's dad, so Whitney brought the phone to Conrad. The smile faded when his eyes dropped to the screen. "Excuse me. I have to take this."

The phone pressed to his ear. "Hey, what's up?" The light tone from the day was gone. Something about the way his eyes roamed the wall set Whitney on edge. He said, "I'll try, but I don't know if I can make it," and ended the call.

"Is everything okay?" Whitney second and third guessed bringing him the phone. She got the feeling from the tone in Conrad's voice that he wasn't happy to hear from his father.

"Yeah." Conrad shook his head. "No. It's hard. He lied. Never said I'm sorry. Just said it was the best thing for everyone involved. Then expects me to go on with life like it never happened."

Whitney could not relate. Her father erred on the side of being too honest. He said things that bruised egos. Then he apologized for being so forthcoming. "I'm sorry you're going through that."

"Me too. It's why I moved back. The only way to fix a problem is to face it."

"What are you two talking about?"

Whitney bit her tongue against the squeal that rose in her

throat. She had forgotten that they were in a room full of people.

Ruby's eyes danced with laughter. "It must be something juicy to get that reaction."

"I told Whitney that mornings like this are why I'm moving back to Cottage Cove." Conrad turned his face to direct her attention to the people scattered throughout the living room and kitchen area. "I miss this. Just saying to friends, stop by the house and let's have breakfast, and it happens."

Ruby's face softened. "Where we live is kind of special. I forget about that sometimes."

Conrad said, "So, I'm taking your hint to heart."

"Which one? I drop so many it's hard to remember." Ruby's wink expressed her delight in being able to flirt, knowing it didn't mean anything.

Conrad nudged Whitney on the shoulder. "What do you say? How about spending the afternoon with me?"

Whitney stiffened as though it would have the power to sharpen her hearing. Had she heard correctly?

Conrad's lips spread into that crooked grin he gave when he wanted something but wasn't sure he'd get it. "We could look at some home interior decorations, go for some ice cream, and maybe hang out at my mom's. We need time to catch up. That is unless your boyfriend would mind."

Whitney smoothed the front of her shirt, and with the confidence of a kitten, said, "Sure."

Chapter 19

Got Yourself A Good One

Nathan winked and nudged his head toward the counter hiding Whitney. "You got yourself a good one."

Her head popped up, appearing at the counter line. She blew at her bangs.

Conrad saw himself gently gliding them to the side and kissing her on the forehead. His abs constricted from the blow to his gut. She did that to him. Filled his mind with visions of what could be and his heart with fear of what would eventually happen. Whitney was marriage material, and one day, she'd find the guy who deserved her, leaving Conrad with the unholy companions of regret and remorse.

All morning, the older guys had been dropping hints. "Whitney is a great woman." Or, "If I wasn't already married and twenty years younger, I'd go for a woman like her."

He lowered his voice to match the old man's. "We're not dating."

Nathan shook his hand once in a swift wave. "It's a matter of time." His smile dared Conrad to argue.

After a microsecond of silence, ending with Conrad neither

confirming nor denying the prediction, Nathan turned on the heel of his gray Merrells and strolled down Conrad's walkway. He paused at the curb and said loud enough for anyone listening to hear, "You have a nice place. We should meet here more often."

As Conrad waved goodbye, the idea settled. It would be nice to have people over more frequently, especially if Whitney was a part of the group.

He surveyed the room to spot anything that may have been overlooked. Everything in the open space, the couches and chairs facing the fireplace, the tiny dining area, and the kitchen island, were pristine.

It didn't feel as empty anymore. The memories of the people filled the space. It was Whitney's doing. She knew how to pull people together.

Whitney closed the dishwasher door. "I'll let you add the soap."

Conrad was noticing a trend. She had done all the heavy lifting in every project. The 5k run—started by Whitney. The morning's gathering—again, Whitney. If she'd waited, Conrad would have gladly helped.

"You didn't have to do all the dishes."

"I don't mind. Consider it my thanks for hosting us." Whitney dried her hand on a dish towel before folding it.

After Jamie's party, Conrad inquired about Whitney's past. She was an anomaly. Everyone in the community knew her. Nobody knew anything specific. Jamie sheepishly admitted, "Whitney's the kind of person you know has your back. Other than that, I can say she hasn't changed much since high school."

Without her glasses hiding them, her eyes had a glow that invited him to get lost in them. Conrad cleared his throat to chase away the tickle he got whenever his thoughts drifted toward exploring her lips. "It was worth it to spend more time with you."

Whitney stammered and muttered some sounds.

Was the source of her tension caution or resistance to the attraction? Conrad asked the question that had the potential to deliver him a wallop of disappointment. "It's the boyfriend, isn't it?"

Her laughter was a large dose of mirth that remained in the air long after her breathy inhalation.

Conrad wracked his brain to decode the mystery in front of him. "What's so funny?"

"You're funny. Until you took my binder away from me, I was too busy to have a serious relationship." The hitch in her voice said there was more to the story. The quick dash of her gaze toward the door said she'd prefer not sharing it.

Whispers of what she told him that first night came back to Conrad, fueling his confidence. A much younger Whitney had a crush on him. He hadn't seen it then. The similarities between the past and the present prodded him to reassess the attraction. It could be mutual.

Conrad folded his arms in front of his chest, and the wisps of a memory tickled his lips into a smile. Whitney at fifteen with a bright pink binder. She'd walk around with the thing clutched closely like she had confidential documents—not the vocabulary words, geometry theorems, and biology notes for the week. At lunch, she'd sit in the corner of the cafeteria reading through and color-coding them. "You've always had an attachment to binders. It's about time somebody carried yours."

She shrugged away his attempt to pull her into a playful back and forth. "Now, I don't have anything to do."

Conrad got the feeling from the way she said it that Whitney had tied her worth to what she did, not who she was.

"You're scared." He was serious but said it like he was a friend challenging her to a dare.

True to her character, Whitney rose to the occasion. She took a couple of steps, bridging the gap between them, and rested her right hand on her hip. "Of?"

"I'm taking a stab in the dark, here. You think you'll be left out of the conversation."

She jerked away like a cat that had been squirted with a spray bottle.

He reached for her hand, pulling her toward him. "Your voice is too valuable for that to happen. I know firsthand the power behind what you say. You have a gift of taking something complex and breaking it down so the rest of us can absorb the magic in the message."

A sheen of tears glazed Whitney's eyes. She turned away, scanning his barely furnished sitting area. It was enough to accommodate the people they'd invited for breakfast but lacked the welcome-to-my-house warmth. Conrad saw it from her eyes and cringed. He hoped she didn't think his words were as empty as the room. She cleared her throat. "Thank you for saying that."

He gently squeezed her hand for emphasis. "I mean it, Whit. You've always had a voice that breathes life into people. It's time you stopped hiding and bring the world to life with what you have to say."

A lovely shade of pink flushed her cheeks, and she nodded, showing she was processing the truth everyone else knew but she had failed to see. "When did you become so profound?"

Conrad was growing to love the barely-there lines at the corner of her eyes. It was like their curve tattooed her appreciation on his heart. "I think it started my senior year of high school."

He released her hand and looked around his house. He looked at his life. It was time he did something to make it feel like a home. There was one small problem—Conrad was not a shopper. Something told him the solution to his problem was standing beside him. "What are you doing today?"

"If you would have asked me earlier this week, I'd have said finding memes for the fun run's social media accounts. I'm baking a cake for my mother's birthday. Otherwise, I don't have anything that exciting planned." The drop in her voice toward the end warned him that she wasn't completely at peace with the turn of events.

Conrad infused a large dose of charm when he said, "Since I was the one who helped free up your calendar, it's only fair you spend your newfound time with me."

Whitney's jaw dropped, and her mouth formed a cute little circle.

A tingle danced around Conrad's midsection, forcing him to admit to himself that he liked her a little more than was safe for his ego. If Whitney were to ask him then and there, Conrad would have taken his heart out of his chest and handed it to her on a platter, and that was okay—because Whitney Stansfield was the kind of woman who would take whatever Conrad offered her and changed it into something better than he would have dared to think was possible.

Chapter 20

Don't Tell Me You're A Fanboy

What could Whitney say? Sorry, I can't hang out because I have a stupid crush on you. She could have begged off to wash her laundry, but that was the extent of her plans for the day.

That and cooking alongside Conrad felt so comfortable. Like they had picked up where they had left off. They were partners in crime, conspiring for good.

She'd have to remember to thank her brothers for preparing her for the friendship. After years of trying to fit in with Ben, Dan, Thom, and Ivan, doing what guys liked came easily for Whitney. Her brothers always outvoted her, so their movie choices always included guns and fast cars. Or they were playing video games. With her brothers, Whitney avoided fishing excursions. For Conrad, she'd try to touch a worm.

"Okay, what are we doing?" Deep inside, she hoped beyond hope he wouldn't say let's go fishing.

Conrad's response, "I have to go see my mother," was not on Whitney's list of what he'd ask her to do on a sunny Saturday afternoon.

She'd seen Claire around town. Other than the polite smile

and wave, Claire and Whitney hadn't spoken since Conrad's graduation. They'd have close to twenty years of missed mutual events to talk about.

"When would we head over?" Whitney prepared herself for negotiations. Conrad was a man, which meant his timeline would ignore the vital time she needed for showering, followed by the painful process of poring through outfits to decide on the first one chosen, or using the right amount of makeup to look like she wasn't wearing makeup.

"From there, would you want to go shopping for some decorations?"

Whitney frowned. That wasn't on her list either. This was the kind of thing she'd do with Jasmine or her sister Ericka. She didn't want to hurt Conrad's feelings, but his requests were out of the ordinary. She squeaked. "You don't have a girlfriend to help you with those things?"

"Do I look like I have time for a girlfriend? I'm too busy helping you with a fun run." His eyes sparkled with amusement at his joke.

"When you put it that way," Whitney pushed a stray hair behind her ear. "I need time to get ready. And, I don't mean like men do. My soap is different than my shampoo and conditioner."

He chuckled. "For that, I'm glad. Take all the time you need."

All the time in the world wouldn't have been enough because she called Jasmine for help deciding on the outfit. The conversation turned into a back and forth of "I told you so," from Jasmine and "You're making a big deal out of nothing," from Whitney.

Jasmine meant well, but her prodding forced Whitney to think that she should have called Conrad and told him she couldn't go with him in the afternoon. If he asked why she could have said she sprained an ankle when she stepped out of the tub. Except that wouldn't have worked because it was a lie, and Whitney wasn't good with those. She always got caught.

By the time Conrad knocked on the door, Whitney had a pile of clothes on her bed and the weight of uncertainty on her shoulders.

She greeted him, hoping her cargo shorts with her all-stars and a pink Arizona Cardinals t-shirt would impress him. His number was on the back. Even then, she second-guessed. She wanted to show him that he had her support, but what if it was too fangirlish? Whitney nibbled on her lip and pivoted her foot, so she was leaning on the side of it. If there were any signs of concern in Conrad's eyes, she'd change.

His gaze wandered from her head to her feet and back to her face. Whitney looked down at her shirt. "It's too pink." She pivoted on her heel to make a run for her room. "I have something with sunflowers to balance the colors."

He called out to her, "Keep the shirt."

Whitney froze in place. The shirt was what she planned to change. She turned around to see the pleased grin on his face. "I like it."

He wore football shorts with a white moisture-wicking shirt. It was the most relaxed Whitney had seen Conrad since his return to Cottage Cove.

It was the Conrad she remembered from all those years ago. Her worries lifted a little, allowing her to fall into the familiarity of two friends having fun on a Saturday afternoon.

On the way to his parent's house, they talked about little things. Since he'd left Cottage Cove, the neighborhood where Whitney lived growing up was classified as a historic district.

His voice was warm with recollection. "Do your parents still have the hot tub on the patio?"

Whitney rolled her eyes. "That lost its cool quicker than it took the Backstreet Boys to break up and get back together."

Conrad shook his head in disbelief. "They were never really far from each other."

"Don't tell me you're a boy band fan." Whitney turned her face to shield her shocked expression.

"Not exactly. I was a fan of how the girls thought I was hot when I sang their songs at karaoke."

Whitney's head jerked. "I should have seen that one coming." Conrad always had a group of girls waiting for him.

He turned down the street leading to his parent's house. The lawns and hedges were manicured with straight lines that made the bushes look like board game pieces.

The teenage Whitney wished her parents lived in a neighborhood like Conrad's parents. Then she could have coincidentally bumped into him while taking a walk.

As an adult, she realized that never would have happened. People didn't take walks in this neighborhood. The yards separating the houses were too far apart. Cars hidden in garages the size of Whitney's house affirmed the colder side of life in Cottage Cove's more affluent communities.

"We shouldn't be here too long. I need to make sure my mom is okay." Conrad's voice tightened from when they were joking.

"What happened to her?" Whitney, taken aback by the information, wondered if it would have been better if she had stayed home.

"Some things were said, and others remained unspoken." His expression twisted in remorse, and understanding struck Whitney. The voice was deeper because of his size and maturity, but the heart of the guy she remembered was still there. Conrad was the type of person who didn't shy away from a struggle. Instead, he sought out reinforcements.

Whitney reached for Conrad's hand and squeezed it.

Conrad's eyes locked in on Whitney's. In a matter of seconds, a lifetime passed between them. Whitney pursed her lips for effect. Taking on the confidence of the judges on the television singing shows, she said, "You don't have to say a word. We all know NSYNC was the better band."

Conrad jerked and shot her a look that expressed his shock. He had laid his discomfort on the table for her to see, and she hadn't given the expected reaction of sympathy or curiosity.

Whitney knew that wasn't what he wanted or needed. She waited through the silence, allowing the space to fill with the comfort of companionship, and was not disappointed. He had caught the glimmer in her eye. The one that said, you don't have to tell me why. I'll be here for you because we're friends.

A smile crawled across Conrad's lips, and the shadow had left his face. Her joke had broken him free from the tension. He said, "I told you we were a good team."

Chapter 21

We Stopped By

Before Adrian's aunt approached Conrad with the truth about their mutual past, Conrad and Claire were the typical mother and son. Conrad tested boundaries, and Claire asserted them.

She was also his biggest champion. When Conrad struggled in school, his mother was the one who gave the teachers a hard time for suggesting they'd give him easier work. Of course, Conrad accused her of sabotaging his happiness. As calm as a pond on a clear day, Claire said, "Teaching you avoidance of the difficult is not something I'll ever condone."

Twenty years later, he realized that she had prepared him for relationships. They were complicated, confusing, full of conflict. Some situations were brought on by life. Most of the time, problems people picked up along the way and forgot to leave at the door of a fresh perspective muddled what could have been solved with a simple conversation.

Conrad walked around the front of the car and had his hand on the handle when the front door opened.

Claire stood on the front stoop. Her eyes flashed back and forth, assessing the situation. Whitney stepped out of the passenger side of Conrad's car. She kept her hand on the door and waited for the invitation to approach.

Claire's bubble gum pink lips curved to speak her silent approval. She was in her fifties, but people often mistook her for Conrad's older sister.

He had dark wavy hair, and she had straight blond hair. As a kid, he thought it was because she color-treated it. When he found out the real reason for the difference in their appearance, he felt like a fool. But that was supposed to be behind them. Conrad stepped into the arms that comforted him as a child.

Through no fault of their own, things had been rocky between Conrad and Claire. For a long time, he'd put on a good face, but his heart wasn't in it.

Claire was half the size of Conrad, but that didn't weaken her grip. She held him to her with strong arms and breathed in. Conrad, in turn, tightened his squeeze, reassuring her of his love. They'd made it through the other side of their problem.

When Claire stepped out of the hug that made coming home worthwhile, the sweet fragrance from her perfume lingered in the air around Conrad. He waved his hand toward Whitney. "We stopped by to see what you were doing."

She tugged at the bottom of the half apron tied around her waist. "Making art." She looped her arm into Conrad's, "Come inside, and I'll show you."

"Have you met Whitney?"

Conrad's mother squinted. Then her eyes widened in recognition. "It's been forever since I've seen you. How have you been?"

"Like everyone else, I've had my ups and downs." Whitney wore the same shy expression that captured Conrad's attention the first time Jasmine reintroduced her to him. The sweet humility that drew Conrad to Whitney would have the same effect on his mother, which was why Conrad brought Whitney to the house. His mother would see firsthand that Conrad was building connections in Cottage Cove.

He had returned.

Regardless of the past events that yanked at their security, he was willing to fortify his roots with healthy relationships.

His continued friendship with Adrian was the beginning.

His friendship with Whitney would be the first of many to smooth his transition into their hometown community. "We're working together coordinating the Fun Run for the Heart."

"I've signed up to do it with Margie and Ruby."

"Ruby? Very funny. Bakes the best cinnamon rolls. Ruby Lawrence?" Whitney asked.

"Yes!"

Conrad's mother aligned herself with Whitney and led her into the house. "I love how she gets the glaze to stay soft."

"I'm not exaggerating when I say she would win one of those baking shows." Whitney and Claire talked like they were old friends who hadn't seen each other in a couple of days, not people who were loosely acquainted.

Conrad watched as both women left him to close the door behind them. Jealousy and relief battled within him. Claire was his mother.

Then again, the stolen moments with Whitney would reaffirm the mother-son bond.

When Conrad was a teenager, he had friends over after school and on the weekends. His mother made appetizer platters and had the fridge stocked with sports drinks and lemonade. The visits waned to summer and winter breaks when he was in college. A warmth started in Conrad's chest and radiated into his cheeks.

Then came the cold truth. Were it not for his father's indiscretion, his brother, Kevin, would be an only child.

Awkwardness took over.

It was easier to stay away than to endure his father's side glances. But they'd committed to doing the hard things, pushing through until the forgiveness was natural.

Whitney was Conrad's buffer.

Claire easily slipped into the role that made her happy—hostess to Conrad's friends.

Whitney sat at one of the high stools stored under the counter. His mother set three glasses on the counter and filled them with lemon-infused water from a carafe she kept in the middle of the kitchen island. Conrad took a plum out of the pile of fresh fruit stacked in a ceramic bowl his mother had made in a pottery class.

"Are you the reason my son is coming home?" Claire set the glasses on coasters.

"His being here was just as much a surprise to me." Whitney threw Conrad a look that asked him what he had brought her into.

"My mom finds it hard to believe I'd move closer to home because I want to be closer to my family."

"It's too good to be true." Claire's shoulders dropped. "And can you blame a mother for wanting her son to be happy?"

Conrad's eyes darted to Whitney, who found something interesting outside the back window. "Mom, I'm happy."

"I'm glad you finally got some sense." She placed her hand on Whitney's forearm. "We have to catch up. Tonight I'm having a pampering party. Relaxing in the hot tub, playing cards, and getting facials. You should join us."

"We might be out too late." Whitney pursed her lip. It was her way of buying time before she spoke. She probably didn't know she did it. When they were younger, Conrad had watched her do it so many times, he could predict her answer with ninety percent accuracy. She wanted to decline the invitation. Conrad hadn't meant for Whitney to be in the middle. Her presence was meant to soothe his nerves when confronting his family, which he, after the fact, realized was placing Whitney in the center of a fragile situation.

"Oh, I know it's the age difference. Bring a friend. Who can she bring, Conrad?" His mother clung to the tether back into Conrad's life like a puppy that kept its teeth into a toy. It could easily be taken away, but that didn't stop her from trying.

"Can I talk to Whitney for a minute?" Conrad decided the least he could do was make a show of trying to appease his mother.

The Claire from his childhood, the one who loved hosting his friends, emerged. "Sure, I'll get some chips and guacamole while you two work out your schedule." She disappeared into the pantry.

Conrad grimaced to apologize and tipped his head toward the far edge of the kitchen. When they were by the entryway, he lowered his voice. "I'm sorry about my mom. This was supposed to be one of those situations where I tell her we're going home-stuff shopping, and she asks to come along."

Whitney threw a glance over her shoulder. "If we can make it back in time, I'd come. My mom might have some fun."

A soft feeling slid through Conrad. It was like he had taken a full breath and could relax. Whitney had that effect on him. She rolled with whatever life brought her way. He needed to be more like her. He bet if he were, he'd be happier.

Chapter 22

Girl's Night With Claire

Lunch bags decorated with drawings of flowers, filled with a mixture of popcorn, pretzels, and chips, lined the countertop—mini bottles of wine, juices, sodas, and water dotted bowls of ice. Platters of sliced fruit and vegetables were on each corner of the kitchen island. In less time than it took for most people to pick what they were having for dinner, Claire had her house looking like a crafting salon.

Claire invited them to sit in the living room, where she had laid out art supplies for their crafting session.

It turned out that Claire's invitation was the perfect opportunity for Whitney to get the rarely seen, but greatly appreciated, alone time with her mother. When it was just the two of them, Whitney was more at ease with the woman who looked like the template for Whitney.

Mandy Stansfield had long brown hair that she wore pulled into a ponytail. She frequently dressed like her husband and sons in athletic gear but added a feminine touch of jewelry or a tutu. On rare occasions like the one they were in, she wore vibrant maxi dresses with beads.

Whitney's mother picked a colored pencil out of a decorated tin, twirled it in her finger, and set it back in place. "If I had daughters, I would do more things like this."

When she was younger, comments like that hurt Whitney's feelings. At thirty-four, it didn't faze her anymore. They had a family with six children. It was no secret that the four boys were Mandy's favorite, probably because they gave her more chances to dote on them. There were football games, basketball games, then the all-day-long track and field meets. Whitney's sister, Ericka, adapted by proving she could fit in with the boys. The youngest of the group, Whitney, learned to hide in the crowd and let her mother's oversight fall elsewhere.

"I don't have daughters," Claire blinked slowly. Whitney could almost read her mind. She wanted to correct Mandy but didn't know how to do it tactfully. Her face softened when she added, "Which is why I have events like this. It's a way to connect with women who are like sisters, or in the case of Whitney, daughters to me."

She tapped the edge of a coloring page and handed it to Whitney, "After we're done coloring, I will scan the pictures and make an eBook as a memento of the night."

Whitney's mother cleared her throat. "I didn't mean it the way it sounded. The boys demanded so much attention–" Her lips merged into a thin apologetic line, "I didn't have time to do the fun girl things with Whitney."

Whitney's voice had changed from the tightness in her chest. Her mother had spoken correctly. Their lives revolved around her brothers. Ericka learned to run as fast, throw as hard, and play rough and tumble games with the boys.

By the time Whitney came around, the family was deep into Pee Wee football and little league baseball. When her parents weren't on the sidelines, they were camping, and the boys competed with their father to see who could catch the biggest fish.

Whitney learned that if she kept her nose in a book, she wouldn't be at the bottom of a dog-pile, scrape her knees, or worse, learn how to tie a fly to a hook. She was more than happy to play the role of an interested observer. "We had fun, Mom."

She dipped her chin with the pride of a live television show contestant. "I managed to find my place—as the official cook for our outings."

Mandy rubbed Whitney's arm, like it had just occurred to her that Whitney might have felt out of place all those years. Her smile was tender, and her voice was soft with the fond recollection of the past. "It was for her own good. She'd get lost."

"I know the feeling," Claire wiggled her fingers at someone who entered the room. "I was lost in the crowd at the boys' events. It's how I met a lot of these women. The friendships grew during weeks of sitting on those metal benches for four-quarters of more games than I can remember." She excused herself, bounced across the room, and greeted the other woman with a hug.

"She doesn't like me." Whitney's mom picked up her bag of snacks and dropped a kernel of popcorn in her mouth.

"How'd you get that from hello?"

"She said you were like a daughter to her."

"Mom, don't turn a compliment into an insult. Isn't that what you used to say to me when I was a kid." Whitney resented the pleading in her voice.

Her mother gestured with her water bottle toward the room around them. Women were clustered in groups of two, three, and four. Some sat at the kitchen table, and the more agile sat on pillows around the coffee table. "Don't worry. I won't ruin the fun. Besides, I know you love me. You could have invited anyone to this girls' night, but you didn't. You picked me, and I was your first choice. Right?"

"Of course." Sometimes Whitney thought navigating a

tightrope between two skyscrapers would have been easier than deciphering the relationship with her mother.

Claire brought two women with her. "Mandy, have you met Carol and Joann?"

"I'm Carol." Carol waved like she was wiping down a screen. It was hard for Whitney to tell if her cream-colored coordinating linen top and loose bottoms were a casual outfit or expensive pajamas. Either way, it was clear to all in the room that Carol liked nice things. "Adrian mentioned you were working with Conrad on the fun run. We're glad you can join us."

Whitney fought down the urge to mention it was the other way around. She replied, "I bet you're glad he's coming back to Cottage Cove ."

"Our boys. Who would have thought when they became friends all those years in Pop Warner football, they'd stay friends?" Using Joann's response to connect the dots, Whitney inferred that she was Dustin's mother.

"You're the football moms?" Mandy elbowed Whitney and straightened her posture. "Whit only mentioned Claire. But I should have known."

In a picture flash of the moment, Whitney saw the party from her mother's perspective. Conrad and his lifelong friends were the players that brought the Cottage Cove Hawkeyes to the state championship. Her mother sat in the same bleachers as the women at the party but in a different row. Whitney's brothers were second-string players who saw playing time after the Hawkeyes were so far ahead it didn't matter how many points were lost or gained. Claire, Carol, and Joann were the "football moms." They wore the t-shirts with "football mom" screen printed on the back and picture pins of their sons on their right lapel. The three women alternated hosting the team dinners before the district, divisional, and championship games and spoke beside their sons at the press conferences.

If Whitney were to guess her mother's exact words, it would have been, "How did my daughter gain access to such an elusive group?"

"We'd like to be grandmothers one day," Carol sidestepped to the kitchen island.

"Grandmother, I'd be happy if my son would bring a woman home."

"I know you've had your moments with Conrad," Carol said, "But you have to be proud." She winked at Whitney to say welcome to the football mom's party.

Whitney suspected her mother got whiplash. The stern stare said it all. "You didn't tell me you were dating Conrad Hayes."

Whitney raised her pointer finger. "If I could interject." Her voice cracked. "Conrad and I are just friends. We're working together on the fun run." They were building a friendship. She was learning to trust that he regarded her as an equal, and he was trying to reestablish his roots. Romance wasn't on either of their agendas.

"Humble beginnings. Isn't that how Howard and Jody Pierson started?" Claire tipped her head the way moms did when they didn't believe their children but would go along with what was said to keep the peace.

"I think so." Carol wagged her finger as though to say, aha. "Both volunteered at a youth camp."

"I can appreciate your desire for privacy. It can be hard dating someone who is always in the public eye." The gleam in Claire's eye said there was no point in arguing. Anything Whitney said could be used as material to prove her point.

Minds were plotting. Whitney whimpered her resignation. "Can I use your bathroom?"

Chapter 23

Don't Make It A Big Deal

Kevin leaned over the foosball table like his win would earn him something more than bragging rights over Conrad. Regardless of who won or lost, Claire Hayes would be pleased to hear her sons were back on solid ground. The bill of Kevin's cap was on the back of his head, making his eyebrows take on the fierceness of a tiger on the prowl. He growled just before slamming the miniature ball into Conrad's defensive move.

Conrad's cell phone chimed a notification, but he had to ignore it. The foosball game and dinner were on the line.

His smartwatch vibrated with a second notification.

"Are you going to get that?" Kevin gave the handle a hard twist.

He wasn't falling for Kevin's ploy. "Nah, nothing good comes from a Saturday night call." His move chipped the ball in the right direction but missed the target—the small opening at the other end of the table.

"That's what I'm saying," Kevin deflected Conrad's offense with his goalie, sending the ball careening across the board. "What if someone drank too much and needs a ride home."

"Nice try." When they were younger, Kevin used distraction to trick Conrad into taking a submissive position in their games.

Kevin released the handles. "Take the call."

Conrad hit the foosball, and it slid into the goal. "That point doesn't count." He wanted to win, but not unfairly.

He retrieved his phone from the coffee table. There were four notifications from Whitney. The last one said, "I didn't take you to be the kind of person who would throw a friend under the bus."

He pressed the call button. Whitney picked it up on the first ring.

She sounded too cheery. "Hi there. Give me a sec." The phone fell silent.

Conrad mouthed the words, "It's Whitney," to his brother.

Kevin's eyebrows lifted when his eyes widened. "Whitney?"

Conrad sneered and rolled his eyes. "Whatever, dude."

Whitney picked up the call. "Your mom just told all the football moms we were dating." The urgency in her voice said she wasn't pleased. "What did you say to her?"

"You were there. I didn't say anything that would make her think."

"What am I supposed to do, Conrad?" She pipped.

"What did you do?"

"I tried telling her we weren't dating. She said that she could appreciate us wanting privacy." Whitney's voice was almost a squeak. "All the moms are telling her how happy they are that you two have such a close relationship. And now my mom is looking at me like I won a blue ribbon at the county fair."

"She is?" He swallowed hard to keep the smile out of his voice.

"Conrad focus." He heard the snap in the background. "You have to come save me."

Conrad knew one thing. If he showed up at a house full of women to talk to Whitney, they would lose. Their mothers' and their friends' opinions would outweigh the denials. Conrad and Whitney's protests would tighten the collective's grip on wanting to be right. "Save you? I was the one who tried to talk you out of going."

"You can't blame me for wanting some time to paint nails, eat some chocolate, and talk with other women about how men drive us crazy, but we love them anyway." In any other situation, Whitney would have received what she expected.

Then the last thing she said registered. Conrad's abs tightened. "Is that so?" The more they talked, the more he wanted to impress her. The beauty of Whitney was she made him feel like he succeeded–every time. His voice lowered into the tone he used when he aimed to draw a woman's attention. "Tell me what it is you love about me, Whit."

She snapped out, "Right now, nothing."

He felt his lips slide into an easy grin. *Touche.* "Then let me help you. You love my avocado dip."

She took the bait. "That would fall under the drives me crazy category. Who eats things like that with pancakes?"

Conrad's chuckle rumbled in his chest. The back and forth with Whitney was fun.

"If I just drop in to save you, they'll plan our honeymoon behind our backs." The silence was long enough for Conrad to look into his phone to make sure the call was still connected. "Whit, you there?"

"Yes, I have to go. Your mother is smiling at me. We are talking later, Conrad Hayes."

"Yes, in the meantime, have fun. I'll make it up to you, Whit. I promise."

"Yeah, yeah," she disconnected the call.

A curious gaze greeted Conrad. "How does Whitney know about your avocado dip?"

"We had breakfast." As soon as the words slipped out, Conrad wanted to kick himself. "Don't jump to conclusions. We're good friends."

"The kind that convinces you to change your plans. You were supposed to be on a plane this evening."

A flush of energy surged through Conrad faster than he had time to react. He returned to his side of the foosball table and nudged his brother to join him. "Don't make it a big deal." Kevin was ruthless enough to use Whitney to his advantage.

"There is so much to unpack." Kevin tapped the foosball, and it slid to his attack position. "But let me start with this. I support you. And it's about time you had someone in your life that will show you to look beyond what's in front of you."

"What's that supposed to mean?" Conrad deflected the ball and took control of it. He tapped it lightly before slamming his player to bounce it into the goal.

"You have someone who should feel sorry for herself. Instead, she took the kick in the pants life gave her and used it to push other people forward. I hope you realize she will teach you to forgive our father."

The truth jolted Conrad. He straightened into a standing position and heard the clicking of the foosball landing in the goal on his side.

His father had lied to him for the entirety of his life. It would take more than possibly dating kind, sweet, never did anything wrong Whitney Stansfield for him to find any justification for his father's deception.

"Why are you angling so hard for him?" Conrad's jaw flexed.

"This isn't about him." Kevin plucked the ball from the goal and set it in the middle of the table. "I want my family back. Whitney is all about family. The funny thing is you are too. You'll see soon enough."

He pointed at the ball in the middle of the table. "Whoever gets this goal has to buy the steaks we're grilling tonight."

"I already have the steaks in the fridge." Conrad leaned in to play. "I have a better idea. If I get the goal, you consider coming to work with me."

Kevin stood straight. "Did you just prove my point?"

Conrad twisted the arm of the game, and the ball rolled into the opposing goal. He wasn't anti-family. He was pro-reuniting with the brother he almost lost.

Chapter 24

Happy Birthday Mom

Whitney entered her parent's yard through the gate in the back of the house, knowing her mother expected her to walk in the front door. She was aiming to use the element of surprise, hoping it would sweeten the delivery of the cake she had baked for her mother's birthday. In comparison to the raised flower bed, the gift was insignificant. But Whitney knew her mother would love the cake.

Delight with her accomplishment filled her as she slid the latch securing the gate closed. When she turned around, she almost ran into her mother.

Mandy's curious expression briefly disappeared when her eyes flitted toward the back door. "Oh, hello, dear. Why'd you come around this way."

"I was trying to surprise you, Mom," the playful sass in Whitney's voice begged the question, why did I think I'd be able to pull it off? Mandy Stansfield always seemed to have a sixth sense about her children.

Her mom pressed her fingers over her lips as though it were of the utmost importance they'd be quiet. "I'll pretend. It'll be our secret." The tiara and rhinestone jewelry she wore made her look more like a fairy godmother than the mother of six adult children. The jewelry was her mother's trademark. Whenever anyone commented, Mandy explained the need for the baubles and accessories. "When you're a person who can keep up with your boys, people forget there is a feminine side that needs some attention too." And she held true to the explanation. Mandy was the woman who wore tutus over her running shorts at the 5k runs and made sure she wore lipstick even when they were doing yard work.

She pursed her perfectly colored lips. "Have I mentioned that you're my favorite of all the children?"

"Uh-oh," Whitney replied. The cake box was getting heavy in her arms. "Why do I feel like I should run in the other direction?"

"Don't be like that." Her mother tapped her forearm. "You and I have a special bond."

Whitney knew it had to be a big ask. When they were growing up, her mother said she loved all her children equally. She said it when she spent more time with one of the siblings than the others.

The pleading expression in her mother's eyes said it was crucial. Whitney exhaled. Giving in to her mother's request would be easier on everybody involved. Or in this instance, Whitney.

Mandy backpedaled and glanced over her shoulder. Whitney's gaze followed. It was the same backyard, Adirondack chairs around a fire pit, yard edged with marigolds, irises, and the raised planters decorated with gigantic bows near the side of the house.

Then her mother tiptoed and leaned as though she were making sure there wasn't anyone hiding around the corner. She rushed to close the gap. "Can you hide the cake?" The sense of urgency in her voice sent off a wave of alarms within Whitney. "Don't tell me dad is on another diet."

The last time their dad went on a diet, he had everyone in the family eating variations of boiled eggs, bland roasted chicken, and grapefruit. It was so bad the kids drew straws to decide who was visiting.

"No, it isn't anything that traumatic." With a straight face, she said, "You have to get rid of the cake."

Whitney blinked. Surely she misheard what her mother said. There was no way her mother would ask Whitney to toss her birthday cake.

Her mother wrapped her arm around Whitney's shoulder and applied enough pressure to guide her back toward the car. "I'll come to your house tomorrow, and we'll have cake and coffee."

An even worse thought than their dad dieting struck Whitney. "Did someone say something about my baking?"

"You see," her mother said, "I was watching a cooking show."

This was nothing new to Whitney. She and her mother often took notes on cooking shows and compared recipes. They talked like they were experts, not two women from two different generations from a small town. To most of the women in their friend group, melting cheese on top of a tater tot casserole was considered taking a major culinary risk.

She threw a glance toward the house and shifted uncomfortably. "I made the mistake of complimenting one of the men on the show. Your father didn't like it when I said his wife must be happy to go home to him."

Whitney's jaw tightened in a pained expression. She could only imagine how her father would have interpreted what her mother said.

"Exactly. So, your father got it in his head that he wanted to bake my birthday cake." Before Whitney could suggest they have two cakes, her mother said, "So, we have to get rid of what you've baked, or we will hurt his feelings."

"Why send me all the way home and back? Can we store it in the fridge?"

They were at the car door. Her mother shook her head. "We look forward to your cake. If people have a choice between what you've baked and your father's cake, I'll be stuck eating a frosted chocolate sponge. And by sponge, I mean the square we use to wash the dishes."

"So you want us to suffer with you," Whitney joked.

"Yes," her mother opened the car door. "And make sure to get back quickly. Your brother is slicing the smoked brisket."

The traffic on the drive back to Whitney's little house was still mild, giving her the freedom to ponder. Her mother had surrendered her birthday cake to salvage her father's ego. If that wasn't a display of love, she didn't know what would be. Her father would never know how often her mother did things to protect him.

Whitney had been in one relationship where she would do anything for the other person. Long after Geoff had passed, she still would do anything for him. The most recent of her subtle gestures was to take a back seat in the fun run to Conrad. He had more resources, visibility, and connections. By letting go of her control of the fun run, she made it possible for Geoff's memory to inspire people she'd never have been able to reach.

But what if it was more than that?

What if her motivations were conflicted? What if her feelings for Conrad ran deeper than she wanted to admit, even to herself?

She shuddered as though shaking off the thought would make it leave.

It was a crush.

A one-sided crush.

A crush that would go nowhere because Conrad Hayes was larger than life, and she was simply the youngest sister in a large family–a family that talked her into taking a perfectly good cake home because her mother loved her father.

———

Whitney closed the refrigerator door and exclaimed, "Oh, the things we do for our family!" Hard as she tried, she couldn't be mad. Her father and mother drove her crazy, but it was always in the name of love. Who else would send away a marshmallow-frosted double chocolate cake with strawberry filling?

Her mother— because she wanted her husband to feel like his efforts were appreciated.

Whitney lingered in the feelings her parents sparked. If she ever fell in love, she'd want the relationship she'd have with her Mr. Wonderful to be like what she saw in her parents. They'd do things that seemed silly to everyone else but meant the world to the person that mattered.

A seed of a thought tickled the edges of Whitney's mind. Conrad's birthday was in three months. She could do something special for him. Nothing that would draw attention, but something that would show him he was appreciated. She had a gift idea on Pinterest but couldn't pull it off on either of her parents. As far as they were concerned, she was an open book complete with a table of contents and index. All they ever had to do was read her mood, and use the clues to find the information, and faster than a cat found a mouse in the middle of a room, they figured out what she was up to.

Conrad. He'd never figured out that she would give him the best birthday surprise until he walked into it.

Flutters of excitement rippled through her. He'd love it.

She tucked the idea away for the time being. She'd need help from their mutual friends.

She jumped in the car, making a mental list of people who could help her. The plan was fuzzy, but she was committed to it by the time she pulled into the driveway.

Whitney walked the same path she had started fifteen minutes prior. Wiser, she checked to see if anyone was coming around the corner. Her father approached with his finger pressed into his lip.

What is going on? Whitney was beginning to wonder if they were doing something in the house and didn't want her to know.

"I wanted to talk to you about the fun run." Her father spoke with a subdued tone.

Whitney's father recruited his students to work the water stations along the route, so his statement was reasonable. The timing–not so much. "Out here?"

"Can't a man have a conversation with his daughter without her questioning his motive?"

Whitney, caught up in her planning, hadn't heard her tone of voice. Maybe she sounded too incredulous. She smiled softly and shifted into her "you have my full attention" mode. "I'm sorry, Dad. What did you want to talk about?"

"Your mother is going to try and have you hide your cake. Don't do it. I tried baking her a birthday cake. It is horrible." He looked her up and down and bent to see behind her. "Where's your mother's cake?"

"Was I supposed to bring the cake?" Whitney could never lie to her father. It was like he could sense the disconnect between reality and what she was trying to trick him into believing.

"Yes," her father threw out his hands. "Ben brings the vegetables, your sister brings the chips and dips, Thom cooks the meat, we're happy if Ivan shows, and you bring the cake."

He walked toward the fence, craning his neck as though the change in perspective would reveal something different than the empty front seat of her car. "Tell me you left your mother's birthday cake in the car."

"The cake isn't in the car." Whitney was glad to be able to tell the truth.

"We cannot eat that frosted chocolate brick I made for your mother's birthday."

Guilt prodded at Whitney, but she couldn't betray her mother's trust. "What if we made it into ice cream sandwiches?"

"Did someone say ice cream sandwiches?"

Whitney's focus darted to find the owner of the voice. It belonged to Conrad, but why would he be at her mother's birthday party? She turned around to find him holding a white bag with pink dots that swung by the handle on his fingers. "Your mom said I could bring whatever I wanted. So I bought these from Scoopy's Cones."

Scoopy's Cones was Whitney's favorite ice cream stand. They drove by the shop on the way to the furniture store. A line had formed and blocked the front window. Whitney mentioned in passing how much she liked the ice cream. She may have gushed a little.

When she got home from the party and could talk freely, Conrad said he'd make up for his mother and her friend's cajoling when Whitney was at the party. The call ended, and she felt like they were closer—almost in cahoots. Good friends often staged circumstances that had the other questioning the wisdom of following through with the decision. Then the other made up for it. There was Shaggy and Velma, Lilo and Stitch, and she hoped it would be Conrad and Whitney.

Whitney whimpered a little. She didn't know what to expect, but she had hoped for something different than ice cream for her mother's birthday. Something like him showing up at her house with her favorite flavor of ice cream.

She silently laughed at the juxtaposition between her dreams and reality. Of course, Conrad would try to impress her mother. How many times when they were younger had her mother bought his favorite treat knowing he was stopping by the house?

Yep. Her crush on Conrad was definitely one-sided.

The slight pinch of humility didn't hurt as badly as Whitney thought it would. Conrad didn't know, so no real harm had been done. For that, she was grateful. When she had time, she'd rewrite the script to her fantasy of happily ever after.

His grin, crooked, and slightly wicked, dared Whitney to challenge his attempt to regain his position in the Stansfield clan.

Whitney dug deep to muster the energy but found herself empty.

There was nothing.

Her mother's invitation negated anything Whitney or her father could say. She decided to look at the bright side of the situation. In a way, Conrad had come through for her. He had solved the problem of the hidden cake.

Her father's shrug signaled that it was time to move on and enjoy the party. Whitney eyed the Scoopy's ice cream bag warily. "Tell me it's not avocado ice cream.

"Of course not. Your mother likes chocolate swirl." Conrad walked toward the house like they were back in high school, and he was there to hang out with Thom, leaving Whitney and her father standing there with dumbfounded expressions.

After a beat of silence, her father said, "This confirms my suspicions. Your mother hid the cake."

Whitney hustled into the house before he figured out he was right.

Chapter 25

Like The One In Front Of Him

It was a warm, sunny day. The stony glare on Erick's face dropped the temperature by at least ten degrees. The color drained so quickly from Whitney's face that Conrad thought she would faint. Her father's stern expression deterred Conrad from rushing to her side.

"What are you doing here?" Her question sounded more like a squeak. She cleared her throat and spoke again. "I mean. I thought you were going to your mother's house this afternoon."

This wasn't the time to tell her that Conrad had encountered the same results as Whitney. His mother insisted she saw the spark, so there was no point in denying it.

She had gone so far as to tell him that it was cute. She tapped Conrad's cheek and said, "You were like this in high school when you had a crush on a girl."

Then she straightened his collar. "But I can tell when something or, better yet, someone is important to you."

She wriggled her nose in her it's-cute manner. "You get this gleam in your eyes, and your face glows with a sense of wonder."

"Men don't glow, Mom." From there, the conversation shifted to how men have tells they would never admit to.

Whitney's mother calling, mid-denial, with an invite to dinner deepened his mother's pleased grin.

There was only one thing Conrad could do. Move forward. People's well-intended approval didn't make the outcome any different. He had a non-profit to run, a business to build, and he lived in two homes. As much as he would have liked for there to be a thread of truth behind the speculation, he barely had time to nurture his friendship with Whitney, let alone entertain the notion of committing to something serious.

He and Whitney were friends. She was someone he trusted, and at that moment was confused as to why he was at her mother's birthday party. She wouldn't have thought about Conrad dropping in if they were in the same position twenty years ago. Conrad spent more time at the Stansfield house than his own.

The Stansfields' house was the hangout house. People stopped by after the games. Erick always had a ROTC kid in need of a good influence hanging out with the family. Conrad was there because he didn't have to take on the role of the star football player. He was just one of the guys. He hoped that over time, things would turn into an adult version of the routine—passing the time with people he valued and felt the same about him.

He gestured toward the back door. His stomach grumbled as the smoke from the grill touched his nostrils. "It's your mother's birthday. I'm here for her party."

Whitney cast a glance toward her father. A sinking feeling rushed to Conrad's stomach. The cold reception from her father and Whitney's hesitant greeting said there was more than met the eye. What was he missing?

Erick's eyes darted between Conrad and Whitney. Through the furrowed brow and stern glare, he measured what neither Whitney nor Conrad would confess. Especially Conrad. Under different circumstances, he would do everything in his power to prove his mother right.

Conrad was a grown man. Under the critical gaze of Erick Stansfield, he somehow had traveled through time and got caught in his fifteen-year-old mind. He swallowed down the rock in his throat and said, "Hi, Mr. Stansfield. It's nice seeing you."

"Yeah, it's good seeing you too." Whitney's dad threw a glare that yelled, you're not good enough for my daughter. His voice was steady, polite, authoritative. Then, both brows raised ever so slightly. "Mandy tells me that you've been talking to Whit. I didn't know you had come back to town."

And Conrad understood the glare. He had not visited the Stansfields before the invitation to Mandy's birthday party. She probably hinted at the "budding relationship" that had taken place without Erick's approval.

Erick was a traditional man. Whitney was his youngest daughter. From Conrad's admittedly biased perspective, she was the most beautiful woman, inside and out, he had been attracted to in a long time. Before the encounter that had Conrad squirming like an earthworm caught in a gardener's hand, he wondered why she was still single. The fit older man standing behind her, with the posture that said he'd throw Conrad in a chokehold at the slightest provocation, answered the question.

Conrad ran his finger along the collar of his shirt. "Yes, Whitney has helped me get reacquainted with the town." He smiled. "Oh, and we're working together on the fun run."

"Hmm," was all Erick said.

Claire told Conrad about things Whitney's mom mentioned at the party. She had a couple of boyfriends who treated her poorly. "The woman is oblivious that she turns men's heads when she walks into a room, and she's smart." His mother wagged her finger at Conrad, "Don't blow this."

In the standoff with Whitney's overprotective father, second thoughts assaulted Conrad. Did he have what it took to date Whitney?

Mandy appeared from around the corner. "Here's where you are." She lit up like a candle when she noticed Conrad. "I'm so glad you could make it." She walked around Erick and hugged Conrad.

Sweet relief filled Conrad. He breathed in full breaths of air. Glad to have an ally, Conrad said, "I come bearing special gifts." He waved one of the two bags. "Happy Birthday!"

Mandy's tiara caught a ray of the sun and glowed. She gushed, "You are my hero." She wobbled onto her toes in her delight. It was almost like a scene out of the video games Conrad used to play with Thom when they were in high school.

Erick changed from an overprotective dad to an annoyed spouse. He rolled his eyes. "She can be so melodramatic."

"That's what you love about me." Mandy blew her husband a kiss.

Whitney shook her head. "That's how she gets him. Every time."

The dynamics between Whitney's family and Conrad's were different. At first, he checked it off as Erick and Mandy having so many kids. Whitney was the youngest of six. Then something niggled at the back of his mind. They also had different pasts. He stood beside Whitney and whispered, "I'll explain later."

"This better be good," she admonished.

It would. After seeing Mandy and Erick, Conrad decided he wanted a life like Whitney's. One where the dad was doting, almost to a fault, and the mom had him wrapped around her finger. When they were growing up, Conrad had seen Mandy use her powers for good, always elevating Erick. In public, he was chill. In his house, it was a different game. He flirted shamelessly with his wife. Back then, Thom would grumble his embarrassment.

It was a picture of a future Conrad wanted. And what better place to learn how to build it than from the person who lived it every day?

From the outside, the scent of grilled food hinted at the whereabouts of a cookout. When Conrad passed through the doorway, it surrounded him. Hunger hit him hard. The recognition of the missed years hit him even harder. Growing up, this was his hangout. *Why had he stayed away so long?*

The house was orderly. Although, Conrad wouldn't have expected anything otherwise. Whitney's father retired from the military, but he was still an "everything has its place" person. When they were in school, Conrad overheard Erick's students correct each other's organization or lack thereof with the mantra.

Whitney joked at lunch about the possibility of being adopted. At first, the humor hit wrong. Claire wasn't Conrad's biological mother. She had adopted him, and it was the source of his struggles. That was on him—not Whitney, who was oblivious to the changes in his family's story.

Seeing Whitney with her family at her parent's house, Conrad connected the statement with her feelings. Whitney's brothers and sister had the airs of highly disciplined people. They all had great posture, smoothed hairstyles, and neat clothing that wouldn't catch anyone's attention. The five other siblings wore different variations of dark athletic pants and coordinating t-shirts.

Whitney wore a pink eyelet blouse and skinny jeans. She was all about being feminine and didn't seem to mind that she stuck out like a dandelion in a field of pristine grass. She was the flower small children picked up and blew on before making a wish.

Conrad made a wish. Would she wait for him until he had the time and mental resources to pursue her?

He shuddered with the awareness of want. Then he stiffened his shoulders. It had to be the residual of his mother's approval of Whitney. "She isn't like the women you've dated in the past." Claire's eyes gleamed, and she held her hand to her chest. It was something she did when she was excited. "If my memory serves me well, that button of a woman believed in you when you wanted to give up. I'm so glad you came to your senses."

"I'll set this on the table." Whitney took the gift bag he was holding and placed it on a corner coffee table with a stack of greeting cards.

A lot of the furniture was the same, yet everything was different. A neutral beige sectional lined the back wall of the house. In the middle of the three sections sat a glass coffee table. Even though the house was full of people, there were no fingerprints or smudges on the table, and all the cups were on coasters.

Thom waved a tong in the air. "Glad you could make it. You've been all Mom has been talking about."

Time away from Cottage Cove had opened Conrad's eyes to what he had taken for granted. The Stansfields hadn't changed. They remained the same lively bunch of siblings who found meaning in the small town that Conrad had fled.

Mandy batted away Thom's comment. "I was just saying it's nice that Whitney has a special friend."

"Mom," Whitney warned. "I'm not ten years old."

"You'll be spoon-feeding me at the nursing home, and I'll still call you my little girl." Erick's face beamed with love for Whitney.

He threw a scowl at Conrad and as quickly returned to the pleasant-looking man who adored his daughter.

Whitney shook her head and blushed, and her father chuckled softly. Conrad imagined Whitney's bond with her father was similar to his relationship with Claire. They may have rough patches, but they would do anything for each other.

When they were younger, everyone referred to the brothers as a collective. One wasn't too far from the other. Even into adulthood, the trait held. The four of them were in the kitchen organizing the food for the meal. "I'm sure you remember everyone," Mandy said.

Conrad had information about Whitney's family thanks to a mining trip on her social media pages. The twins, Ben and Dan, were the family nomads. They traveled with their jobs but returned to Cottage Cove often. Their chilled gazes meant they either disapproved of Conrad or had forgotten him. He hoped it was the latter.

Thom was married to the only blond in the room. "Good to see you, Grace." She waved the platter that she had taken from the kitchen island. "Welcome to the festivities." The last time Conrad had seen her, she was at Geoff's—her brother's—funeral.

His inner voice warned him. *Tread lightly.* Whitney's acceptance of Conrad chilled when he joined the committee. He had the support of Thom, Grace, and Mandy. But what about the others? And could he win Erick's favor?

Everyone grabbed a plate and followed behind Grace until the table was set. People ducked under arms, reaching for a kitchen tool or plate, and circled around each other in a level of synchronicity that mirrored a well-executed play on the field. An uneasiness hit Conrad. He wanted to contribute but didn't know where he fit in, and nobody volunteered directions.

"Come sit by me." Mandy tapped the chair beside her.

"I wouldn't want to take Erick's place." It was all Conrad had to offer in the way of an excuse. Whitney's father hadn't warmed since the cool greeting in the yard.

"It's okay," Erick said. "I sit by her all the time. You can have a turn." A smile cracked his stoic expression.

Conrad slid the chair from the table to take his place between Mandy and Grace. Thom sat on the other side of Grace, leaving Whitney a spot in the furthest seat possible from Conrad. It was almost as if the family formed a shield around her. Instead of repelling Conrad, the urge to be near Whitney intensified.

Thanks to his mother's urging, Conrad was primed to catch what he missed at the same kitchen table over fifteen years ago. Back then, Conrad and Thom were studying for a vocabulary test. Conrad, recovering from a concussion, struggled to retain the information he had learned. Whitney joined in and made it a game. By the end of the night, Conrad had memorized all the words. She volunteered to tutor him in exchange for tickets to the home games. He wanted to hit his palm against his forehead. *Stupid. Stupid. Stupid.* How could he have missed it? Tutors charged ten to fifteen bucks an hour. The only thing Whitney wanted was a seat to watch him play.

He snapped out of his reverie and mostly listened to the flurry of banter. Whitney's brother, Ivan, threw in the occasional joke about Mandy's real age. She took it in stride, laughing in all the right places and volleying the conversation with idle threats. Ben and Dan challenged the threats with lighthearted reminders that she loved them and would never hurt them. It set off another flurry of laughter along with another round of stories.

The Stansfields had grown, and the love remained. This is what his brother was pushing for. Kevin and Conrad wanted the same thing. Guilt dimmed the charm of the moment.

Conrad should have been with his family. He wasn't good enough for Whitney. But he still wanted to sit closer to her, to make her laugh, to see if she was as into him as he was into her.

Conrad preferred the stories the siblings told about shenanigans from when they were younger. Some involved intense plans to pull one over on Mom and Dad, while others admitted to successful plans to hide something one had done that required rescue from getting in trouble.

Erick sat like a king, watching over his kingdom. He talked to Mandy in low tones, so his voice could be heard, but what he was saying couldn't be fully understood. His calm demeanor and the occasional laughter that resulted in the area over his brow turning red led Conrad's mind toward happier family moments. They hadn't had too many of those in the Hayes house recently. Polite conversation and games passed the time until it was safe to go to friends' houses.

The family rose to clear the table. Again, moving in a pattern that had been established by a lifetime of family gatherings took place. The Stansfield siblings moved synchronously. Rinse the dish, comment on what they liked about the meal, or agree with what someone else had said.

I want a life like this.

The thought came to Conrad so quickly he didn't have the chance to shut it down.

Pinpricks on his arms told him to read the room. He found Ben and Daniel standing side by side with arms crossed, alternating their focus between Conrad and Whitney. If he could read their expression, it would have said, "You're not good enough for our sister."

Conrad was never one to back down. The yearning for a good life with a good woman egged him to make a stance. Either back down, or follow through with his mother's advice, her mother's subtle hints, and the prodding from people he was growing to call friends. A switch flipped. A two-word thought resonated through Conrad: Challenge accepted.

He would prove that he could be as good to Whitney as she had been to him when he was a nobody. Then, when he deserved her, he'd follow through with what he wanted—a life like the one in front of him.

Chapter 26

The Battle Royale

It was a battle royale—brother against brother.

Thom watched through the glass on the side of the door. When he turned around, his demeanor had changed. Gone was the pleasant smile. A thundercloud of emotions clouded his eyes.

He glared at the twins. "You didn't have to be a–" he paused and glanced around the room. "You didn't have to be so inhospitable."

Ben ground out, "He doesn't talk to us for how long, comes in, and...."

Dan finished his sentence, "Goggles Whitney like she is the last hot dog at the cookout."

"He's come to his senses." Thom threw Whitney an apologetic grimace. "Who cares if it's twenty years late."

The living room that had once been a place for them to linger and chat had a great divide. Thom and Ivan were behind the chairs, closer to the door. Ben and Dan leaned forward, their backsides barely touching the couch.

Ivan took Thom's side of the argument. Whitney and Ericka

watched like it was a tennis match. The tension in the room rose like water filling a glass with each volley.

"Where was he when she was ugly? No offense, Whit."

"Where were you when she needed help with the 5k?"

"Trying to make a name other than the grieving Geoff group."

Thom's wife, Grace, gasped. Thom gritted his teeth, and his jaw pulsed with the tension.

Whitney whispered to Ericka, "I think I should go home. It's quieter there." She had to pull the daggers her brothers were throwing out of her back.

Ericka pointed to her backpack purse that was under the dining room table. "Let me get my bag. I'll walk out with you."

They were almost at the door when their father placed himself in the middle. "Look at what you've done."

Whitney and Ericka froze. They exchanged a glance. Ericka whispered, "I'm never bringing the guy I'm seeing to dinner."

Whitney gulped and withered a little on the inside. The attention she didn't want came back to her.

"It's nothing against you, Whitney," Ben said.

True to their secret twin connection, Dan added the end to the explanation. "It just doesn't make sense."

Whitney's cheeks burned in embarrassment. She had basked in Conrad's quiet attentiveness. As her brothers, with the tenderness of a shark in a school of fish, had explained, it was pity. Not attraction.

It must have registered on her face because Ben said, "We didn't mean it like that."

"I know you're just watching out for me." They meant well. She forced a smile and pivoted to inch her way toward the door.

Her mother set the clean glass she unloaded from the dishwasher into the cabinet and said, "Make sure to come back tomorrow with the cake."

Her father and brothers probably got whiplash from how quickly their heads jerked toward Whitney.

"So you baked the cake." It wasn't a question. It was an accusation. Whitney shrank under the disappointment of being betrayed in her father's voice.

Ivan was about to say something, but her mother's stern glare caught him midstream. So he stretched out his "oh," like a note. It started low. He was prepared to take their father's side. The pitch in his voice rose to sound like he found the standoff between their father and Whitney a curiosity.

Whitney winced. They had such a great afternoon, and now, thanks to her, it ended on a low note. She filled her voice with the sincerity of her apology. Her mother was trying. "I'd love to, but I have a meeting tomorrow after work."

They were a little less than three months away from the fun run. The changes Conrad suggested required more meetings, some to make sure nothing was forgotten and others to build team cohesiveness. At least, that was what was in the email Conrad's assistant sent.

"Then Tuesday." Mandy raised a finger to add the unspoken I'm your mother, so you have to agree with me. She softened her stance. "You can help me with my new garden."

"Perhaps others of us could join in this cake and gardening activity," Ivan said. "You know, throw some burgers on the grill."

"It's my long run day, but I can join afterward," Ericka chimed in.

Even though Whitney had looked forward to spending her only free evening on the couch in front of the television, she would be gardening in the raised flower beds she and her siblings had gifted their mother. The best she could hope for was that Ben and Dan wouldn't be there. "I'll see you Tuesday." She pivoted to leave.

"Ahem, did you forget something?" Mandy had her arms wide open and ready to accept a hug.

Whitney walked into her mother's embrace. "I love you, and Happy Birthday."

"Don't listen to your brothers. They're just being overprotective. They've always been like that. Even when you were a gangly teenager." She rubbed Whitney's arms. "Now you're a beautiful woman."

"What we're trying to say is you can do better, Whitney." When Ben didn't say anything, Dan elbowed him. He squirmed to avoid another jab and rubbed at his arm. "If you're lonely, we could set you up with one of our friends who works at the university."

Her mother wrapped her arm around Whitney's shoulders. She led her to the door. "Go while it's still safe." She stopped on the stoop. "And don't listen to your brothers. Follow your heart."

A hum started in Whitney's chest and radiated throughout her body. Her mother's advice removed the sting from her frazzled nerves. "I'll see you Tuesday."

Mandy winked. "And don't forget the cake this time." She scrunched her shoulders and covered her mouth with her hand, stifling her giggle.

Whitney had to smile. Her mother always had a gift of making things better.

Summer had a fragrance all its own. Everything had a warmer smell, and the air was sweet from the abundance of flower blossoms, especially when Whitney passed the rows of lilacs leading to her house.

The drive home softened the rough edges that curled

around Whitney's mood. But the words she'd held on her tongue still danced around her mind.

Who were her brothers to judge Conrad?

It wasn't like they had kept in touch with every person they talked to in high school. Dan and Ben judged with a ruler they couldn't apply to themselves.

Like Conrad, their jobs took them places far from Cottage Cove. They had a small handful of friends they kept in touch with. Yet, they scowled at Conrad behind his back whenever they thought nobody was paying attention to them.

Think about the positive. That's what her mother would say. So Whitney focused on the brothers she sometimes saw too much, Thom and Ivan.

Thom, who was closer in age to Conrad, had treated Conrad like the long-lost friend who returned home. For the better part of the afternoon, they lounged in the red Adirondack chairs in the backyard and relived their glory days. Or that was how Whitney and Grace, who watched them from the kitchen window, interpreted the boisterous laughter.

Or, Thom could have been closer to Conrad because they both had ties to Geoff. The vision of Thom and Conrad dressed in black suits standing in front of Geoff's gravesite pierced through Whitney's aggravation with her older brothers. They weren't there when she and Thom were hurting. Conrad was.

Why hadn't she said something when Ben and Dan were hurling condemnation? Probably because Ivan had. It was hard for Whitney to take up her battles because her brothers always pushed her out of the way and fought on her behalf.

She had barely dropped her car keys on the hook by the door when a visitor knocked.

The hinges groaned their protest at how slowly Whitney slid the door open. It was probably Ben or Dan, and she wasn't in the mood for a forced attempt at reconciliation.

She was about to tell them not to bother. She accepted their apology.

It was Conrad.

Her mouth clamped shut, and the world brightened a little.

Conrad, standing there with his hands in his pockets, with his head tilted at a slight angle, watched her through his eyelashes. That was a look she'd never grow weary of seeing.

Thom's vote of confidence in Conrad inch wormed Whitney's belief. Maybe there was something behind the flutter of excitement that rose in her when she saw Conrad.

Her first inclination was to challenge the flirty greeting. Instead, Ben and Dan's criticism rose to the surface, forcing her to double down on the reminder. They were friends, at best, and worked together on the fun run committee.

His greeting confirmed the correction in Whitney's thinking. "I'm here because we have a situation." A gong reverberated through her body. Pipe down on the attraction and focus on solving a problem.

Whitney straightened her posture, and she was focused.

If there was one thing she appreciated about Conrad, it was his forthright approach. He didn't let time pass. There was no second-guessing his intentions. Whitney held the door wider to make room for him to enter. "Let's talk."

Chapter 27

I Have Baggage

The butterflies in Whitney's belly refused to follow the script. They danced some sort of tango. *Conrad had come to talk.* Their waltz challenged her dinner to stay in her stomach.

She inhaled and regrouped. What would she do if it were Jasmine? They'd have wine and snacks. If forced to hazard a guess, Whitney would say Conrad wasn't a wine drinker. But it was summer, the season of cool sweet beverages. The chairs on the porch would be perfect for a friendly chat. "I have Hibiscus tea in the fridge. Would you like a glass?"

"Sure." His face relaxed. "I don't want secrets between us. I have to tell you some things."

When one person sought out another to divulge a truth, it meant they were friends. All the feelings of uncertainty blew away, allowing Whitney's heart to embrace the strength of their growing bond.

It was official. They were friends.

She felt her heart opening, believing, accepting what she'd denied herself, up until this point. Conrad wanted to be friends with Whitney. Alone. Not Whitney when she was with Jasmine, or Thom, or Seth.

Her heart's whisper filled her body with a glow. *I can be a good friend.*

Rightfully owning the airs of someone who had been in the let's-be-candid talks, she said. "That means we need to have popcorn. The sweet and salty are always good for honest talks."

Conrad followed Whitney to the kitchen that seemed miniature with him in it. He had to back away from Whitney when she opened the fridge, and they had to trade places when she needed to open the cabinet to retrieve the glasses. It was smaller than Conrad's, Claire's, or her parent's kitchens, but Whitney liked it. Everything was within reach when she baked, and it was the perfect size for one person.

She set the drinks on the coffee table in the living room.

"What about the popcorn?" Conrad stood as though he was prepared to return to the kitchen.

Whitney chuckled. If Conrad were anything like her father, he'd talk more if they were doing something. "I pop the corn. You talk."

She set the pot on the stove and hunted through her cabinets for the kernels and the oil. As she expected, he talked.

His voice was far away, like he was digging for words and sharing them as they rose to the surface of his mind. "You see. My family has had some serious issues lately."

Whitney thought back to the end of her mother's birthday dinner. When she said, "What family doesn't?" her voice had the "I've been there many times, myself" tone.

"This was the stuff that, if people were paying attention, would have made it to the TMZ level of conflict."

Whitney paused, assessing what she had taken out of the cabinets and what she still needed for their snack. She set the butter on the end of the row of ingredients and leaned against the cabinet. The anxiety added weight to the air in the room. Whatever it was, Whitney would be there to support Conrad. She crossed her arms in front of her stomach and connected her eyes with his, conveying that he had her undivided attention.

He paused as though he were waiting for her to do something. Whitney moved her hand in a circular motion to signal that she was ready for him to continue the story. Conrad rubbed his chin and paled like the kid who didn't like speaking in front of the class. "It felt more natural when you were doing things."

"I got the feeling this is something that needs me to be present."

Conrad's cheeks flushed, and he rubbed the top of his brows. He was uncomfortable with what he wanted to share. Whitney's attention added pressure. "I knew you were listening. Your ear tilts toward me when you're paying attention."

"It does?" Whitney blushed. What other signals had she accidentally sent out?

"Yes," Conrad squinted. "I'm curious as to what that expression means?"

Whitney's face turned to fire. "This is about you, not me." She twirled around, added the oil to the pot, and twisted the knob at the top of her stove to a level that would be hot enough for the corn to pop.

They fell into a silence brought on by the unspoken agreement. Whitney wouldn't hold Conrad's past against him or use it as leverage in their friendship. It painted her heart with soft strokes of hope. Maybe one day she'd extend the gift of strength that she freely gave to her friends to herself.

The tinkling of popcorn kernels dancing on the metal pan filled the space. Then the awareness of Conrad's observations pricked at the back of Whitney's neck. She shook the pot even though it didn't need it yet. Over the scraping sound, she heard Conrad murmur, "Hmm."

"Continue with your story," she urged.

"I'm trying to figure out where to pick up."

"TMZ." The first kernel popped.

"I'd been a little distant. It was the make excuses for why I couldn't come home for a visit level of avoidance." His body was in the kitchen, but his attention was elsewhere. Or he thought the recipe for apple cider donuts on her fridge was really interesting.

Whitney wanted to give him the space to process, so she continued shaking the pot. "I do that all the time."

"For the holidays?"

Whitney fought the inclination to ask what could keep Conrad away from Claire over the holidays. From where she stood, Conrad was the typical small-town mama's boy. He talked about his mother like she walked on water and acted like anyone who contradicted him had better be prepared for a smackdown. "That bad?"

"Yeah, it turns out Claire isn't my mother."

Whitney dropped the pot on the burner.

"Well, she is my mother. She'll always be my mother."

Somehow, the pain in Conrad's voice gripped Whitney. She moved the popcorn to the back burner, turned off the heat, walked into Conrad's chest, and wrapped her arms around his back. He held onto Whitney. And they stood there in silence. She breathed in the clean scent of his cologne and registered his heartbeat. He held her tight.

Whitney was so different than her brothers and sisters she often wondered if she was adopted. She asked her mother once. Mandy laughed. "I could see why you'd think that, but no, you are all Stansfield." At the time, Whitney was relieved. Conrad's confessions gave her a peek at what it would be like if the answer was otherwise. It was a sharp, crushing sensation. For her it was temporary. She couldn't imagine walking around with the knowledge and the lingering pain.

"How did you figure it out?" Especially with social media and Conrad being on the screen every weekend for months, it would be easy for his parents to reach out to him.

"I was in a car accident. I needed blood. Adrian was a perfect match. I joked that we had always been like brothers. It made sense that he'd be the one to come to my aid."

He stepped out of the hug, shaking his head. "Adrian's aunt said, "You are," like it was common knowledge."

Thinking she was talking about blood brothers, I tapped my stitches and said, "And this will prove it."

He exhaled a long low breath. "Then the room got quiet. Really quiet. Long story short. Dad had an affair with Adrian's mom. I mean our mother. Our mom was best friends with Claire up until the affair. Naturally, the friendship ended. Then my mom died a little after I turned one. Dad took me. Adrian lived with his aunt, and she adopted him. Things got weird after that. But Kevin and I were too young to remember."

Whitney stiffened her jaw to hide her reaction. It was hard with her head swimming in the current of information.

"It was a lot of us looking like that." Conrad pointed at Whitney. "I promised I would never keep a secret from anyone who mattered. I have baggage, and sometimes it's heavy."

"I am honored that you would trust me to help you unpack it." Whitney's whole being settled. Conrad had affirmed her with his actions. By coming over and talking to her, he had shown her that he valued her for more than what she could do for him.

"And, when I brought you to the house, Mom thought I was bringing a girlfriend home, and things were patched between us."

Sensing that Conrad had shared the most difficult shades of

his story, she turned on the heat and placed the pot on the burner. "Can't you bring a woman who happens to be a friend and still be on good terms with your mom?"

The next kernels popped. Whitney slid the pan back and forth over the heat, allowing the kernels the space to expand but not get stuck in place and burn.

Conrad leaned on the counter beside the stove and watched Whitney cook. "This is pretty interesting. I usually buy the stuff in a bag that goes into the microwave."

When the popping ceased, Whitney deposited the popcorn into two smaller bowls. She cut two tablespoons of butter off the end and dropped the square in the pot to melt. "Your way is easier, but I prefer to take something from its basic form and work with its potential."

"Can I ask you a favor, Whit?"

He had used her pet name, which meant it was a big ask. She joked when she replied, "I'm afraid." When she saw the mischievous grin on Conrad's face, she knew she was in trouble.

Chapter 28

Wait For Me

The signs were there. The flushed face, her voice was breathy, and she smelled like one of those expensive perfumes. That first night when they reconnected, Whitney mentioned having a crush on Conrad. It took his mother and her overprotective brothers to point out the obvious. Those feelings were stronger than Conrad had suspected.

Conrad swallowed, testing his throat.

He was with Whitney, looking like a queen of the castle in her kitchen. But tomorrow, he would be on a plane to Phoenix and wouldn't return for a few weeks.

Time was tricky. When he wanted more, it slipped through his fingers. He blinked, and the weekend had passed. Would it work that way when he was in Phoenix?

He wouldn't know if he didn't ask. "What are your plans for the next couple of weeks?"

"Well." Her eyebrows knit together. "I'm having dinner with my family on Tuesday. Then it's the usual. Meetings, meetups, and the typical responsibilities mixed in."

"Meetups?"

"Saturday morning walks."

"I knew what you were talking about." He forgot about the Saturday meetup. "Look, Whit. If I were in a different place in life, I'd take you on some great dates. Buy you flowers. Do things to show you how special you are."

"So this big talk is to tell me that you don't have time for me." Her voice was full and robust, like the jolt from that first-morning coffee. "Why don't you tell me something I don't already know?" She slipped a couple of kernels of popcorn in her mouth and chewed slowly."

Warning sensors blared in Conrad's mind. He should have planned what he was going to say. "My mom. Your mom." He stammered. "I didn't want you to think I was leading you on."

Conrad's body vibrated with energy. Nothing was coming out the way he intended. He flexed his forearms and loosened his fingers. Each action came with an "I told you so." He should have kept his mouth shut. But he hadn't, and now he risked blowing it.

"Oh," she bobbed her head, acknowledging the situation from his perspective. "That makes sense. You're trying to let me down gently. Don't worry about it. I know the spiel. There is nothing between us. We're just friends." She shrank away from him, sliding her small bowl of popcorn on the counter.

Conrad immediately missed the closeness. His words came out in a rush, forcing him to follow through with what he wanted. "I'd like us to be more than friends, but I just don't have the time."

He was grasping at straws. But he'd take what he could get and work with it. That's how he did it on the football fields. Life had to follow some of the rules.

Whitney's eyes pinched to form slits. "What are you getting at?"

"You are an amazing woman. And, we've just reconnected." She'd changed him. He looked forward to hanging out with his family. He liked inviting people who weren't football players to his house. He wanted to reconnect and rebuild relationships with his childhood friends. Highest on the list of his priorities was more time with Whitney. Kevin said it would happen. Whitney had the gift of enticing the better parts of Conrad to the surface. Energy surged through his body. He felt like he could conquer the world. And for her, he would do it.

"I know that when I go back to Phoenix, some guy is going to come along and–" his gaze shifted toward the scenery outside her kitchen window. A ring of flowers surrounded a tall tree. "Say the right things and follow up with his actions, and I won't have a chance."

Her mouth fell open, and her eyelashes fluttered like butterfly wings. She closed her mouth and opened it. It was a breath of silence. Yet, it was long enough for sickening waves to rise in Conrad's stomach.

Then her brows furrowed. "You believe some random guy will wine and dine me when you leave? Wow, you've been gone too long."

The shock in Whitney's voice said more than her objection. She was oblivious, clueless, completely unaware of her charm. He had to browbeat Adrian and Dustin to keep them away from her at the party. During their walk to Sweet Treats, several men gawked at her. One had walked into a bush.

Maybe it wasn't as big an ask as he thought. "Will you wait for me?"

"What am I waiting for?"

Everything within Conrad compelled him to kiss her. His heart railed against his hesitance, adding to the anticipation. His muscles coiled in preparation of approaching her. His conscience reminded him that what he wanted wasn't fair.

This woman inspired Conrad to believe in himself when the odds weren't in his favor. Thanks to her, her first boyfriend,

Geoff, had a legacy. Yet, she never took any of the credit. If given the chance, Conrad would spend his days showing her how much she was appreciated, admired, adored.

"For me. To get settled. To be in a place where I can give you the time you deserve. To treat you right." Conrad meant every word. He'd prove to her brothers and her father and himself that he was good enough for Whitney Stansfield.

"I'm just going to say what I'm hearing. You're too busy to date, so you want to be friends." She picked up her tea and took a sip. All the while watching him from over the top of the glass. Her eyes challenged him to contradict her.

She was correct in her restatement, but she only had half the story. Conrad shook his head. He was at a loss on how to express how deeply she affected him.

Her glass tapping softly on the countertop was his cue. "I'm saying I didn't know until I came home, you're the one I've been looking for." He closed the gap between them in two steps. Before she had time to react, he caressed the soft area beneath her chin. Then he kissed her on the cheek. "Now that I found you, I'm afraid someone with less chaos in their lives will steal you away."

Whitney's fingertips glided along the place where Conrad had kissed her. Confusion clouded her eyes. "Maybe it's because my dad was in the military. That's why taking risks doesn't scare me. My dad always said, "Trust yourself, not the circumstances."

"Is that a challenge?"

"No, it's just a truth." Whitney slid Conrad's bowl over to him. She picked up her bowl and glass of tea and headed toward the front porch.

"That glass of tea isn't going to save you," Conrad charged toward Whitney.

She squealed and ran toward the front door. She pulled it

open, and her father stood there with his hand in the air where the doorknob would have been before Whitney got there. His right brow bent, and his lip curled. He was looking at Conrad when he said, "Why am I not surprised you're here?"

Conrad held his tongue. But if he were to answer Whitney's father, he'd have said, *Because it's obvious to everyone except Whitney that I'm in love with her.*

Chapter 29

I Don't Want To Lose You

Whitney's heart hitched, questioning what her eyes clearly saw. A bouquet of cookies sat in the middle of her desk. Less than twenty-four hours after he had left town, Conrad had a change of heart.

As far as she was concerned, love didn't wait until the circumstances were perfect. She wasn't a guru, but from what she had seen, Cupid's arrow always struck when a person had the chance to prove themselves. She had said as much to him with her words and actions.

In front of her, in the form of a dozen cookies that had to be bigger than her hand with her palm extended, Conrad proved that he had listened. Awe at what she had been afraid to hope for but had been freely given filled Whitney, warming her face, and softening her resolve.

"I knew you'd like them."

The satisfaction in Seth's voice chilled the edges of tenderness within Whitney. "Baked goods are my weakness." Her voice betrayed her vulnerability. She cringed in anticipation of the ribbing or boasting that would come her way.

"Last week was an eye-opener." Seth's voice lacked the cajoling Whitney expected. Instead, it was tender, sincere, kind.

She turned to make sure it was Seth speaking. He wore his Panama Jack button-down shirt and cargo pants, but there was something different about Seth. His grin lacked the playful glint. "I want to make sure Conrad doesn't steal you from me."

Her thoughts froze. Had she heard correctly? She slowly replayed what Seth had said in her mind, connecting the cookies with his admission. "These are from you? It isn't my birthday or anything like that."

He set his hand on the doorframe, pushed off, and leaned back. "I'll admit it is a mildly selfish gift." Then he grinned. "I know you'll share with the rest of us."

Whitney tipped her chin and eyed Seth suspiciously.

His eyes darted back and forth. It was an expression that Whitney was familiar with. Her brothers used it when they wanted something from their mom, and the potential for "no" lurked above the question. "You're an amazing therapist. People trust you. And, I've seen how Conrad works. He'll try to recruit you for his sports center. I don't want you to go."

She bowed her head, her eyes landing on the faux gray hardwood flooring. Whitney had to give Seth credit. He anticipated change, especially when it affected him. Where was the concern about Conrad taking over when they were in the meeting last week?

The dozen cookies on her desk lost their appeal. They were merely bait to lure her into securing clients for his business.

When she was younger, Whitney wished for a kinder father. Hers always handed her truths that were ugly and hard to swallow. As an adult, she saw the method behind the madness. Thanks to his blunt administrations of 'life as he saw it,' Whitney accepted the truth for what it was—a fact meant to help a person reach a decision, not a judgment of her worth. She rolled her eyes to express that she should have seen Seth's logic. "Of course, I'll share."

But she wasn't committing. Seth worked with Conrad and her brother behind her back. Granted, it was to benefit a mutual cause. Still, he could have given her some warning or spoken up on her behalf. Whitney was an asset, an employee, someone who helped Seth achieve a goal. Otherwise, she held no real value to him.

Truth be told, the disappointment with being wrong weighed more than Seth's selfishness. Whitney wanted the cookies to be a gift from Conrad.

She lifted the cookie bouquet from her desk to transfer it to the staff lounge. "I'll set it by the coffee pot."

Seth strolled away from the door and down the hall to his office, calling behind him, "I'll get my cup for a refill and join you."

Michelle rounded the corner with a brown paper bag with twine handles. She held it up so Whitney could see the Louise's Bakery logo on the front. Her hand dropped to her side, and her face scrunched like she was trying to remember something everyone else knew. "Is it your birthday?"

"Seth got these for employee appreciation," Whitney said. "I was heading to the kitchen so everyone could take what they wanted."

"The delivery guy said this was for you." She handed Whitney the bag and took the vase of cookies. When they were situated in the kitchen, Whitney peeked inside the bag, taking out one item at a time. A note written in permanent marker was written on the white napkin. "Challenge accepted."

"What is it?"

"It isn't a cinnamon roll." Whitney showed Michelle a wrapped bagel and a fruit cup.

She sniffed at the bagel overflowing with a green smear

before tightening her cheeks to suppress the laugh bubbling inside her.

"What kind of challenge did you give?" Michelle wrinkled her nose.

"A poorly worded one." Whitney poked at the cream cheese and brought the little dab to her tongue to taste. It wasn't that bad. But she wasn't about to tell Conrad that.

She ripped the bagel in half, passing the part in the paper wrapping to Michelle. "I need to tell a friend that avocado cream cheese is not the way to win a woman's admiration." However, Whitney's words contradicted the happy feeling glowing in her chest.

Michelle mimicked what Whitney had done, first poking at the bagel before trusting the sample. "I wouldn't complain. Nobody has ever had breakfast delivered to me." With that, she took the half bagel, a cookie, and a fresh cup of coffee to her desk.

Morning gave way to afternoon with a steady stream of clients. Whitney was cautious in attributing the quick passing of time to the energy bump from the avocado cream cheese bagel.

Just as she checked her watch to see how soon it would be lunchtime, Michelle walked in with another bag. Whitney's stomach tightened when the scent of cumin and pepper tickled her nose. "Okay, I have to ask. What did you say to get tacos from Manuels delivered?"

"Did someone say tacos?" Seth's head peeked into the office.

"Yeah, someone had lunch delivered for Whitney." Michelle peeked in the bag. "There's a cup of guacamole in here too."

A delighted laugh escaped from deep within Whitney. "He has a thing for avocados."

Seth frowned. "Who's he?"

Michelle's face brightened with recognition. "I told you."

"What did you tell her?" Seth stepped into the room.

Whitney remembered his request from earlier in the day. While she told herself she shouldn't care about what Seth thought, she didn't have the heart to tell him that Conrad had bought her breakfast and lunch and she didn't have to share the gift he'd given her with the office. She tightened her voice into the tone that masked her hints to Michelle not to say a word. "Manuel's delivers."

Michelle jerked and glanced between Seth and Whitney. Her lips puckered to silently say, "oh." Her voice was breathy when she said, "Yes. I told Whitney that she could have tacos whenever she wanted. But she didn't believe me."

Whitney smiled to thank Michelle and quickly regained her composure to address Seth. "Well, now I do."

"And you didn't get any for the rest of us?" Seth shook his head in mock disappointment.

"I'm sorry." Whitney hid the bag behind her back. There were some things women didn't share. Tacos were at the top of her list. "We have cookies in the staff kitchen."

"That's cold, but I get it." Seth backed out of the room. "Michelle, can you call Manuel's and have a taco platter delivered?"

"Sure."

When the coast was clear, Whitney peeked in the bag. She moved the items around to take an inventory of the contents. It had two tacos, the guacamole, a tiny cup of salsa, and a napkin with a note that read, "I heard the way to a woman's heart is tacos with guacamole–C."

Whitney would never tell Conrad that he was wrong. He had her heart all those years ago when they spent hours at the kitchen table studying and joking around. The tacos were the sign that he was after hers.

Chapter 30

I Have A Bad Back

The grass was greener. The sky had a little more shimmer. The sun caressed Whitney's arms. She loved Lilac Lane Park, and it wasn't because Conrad was standing in front of the gazebo with his well-defined biceps pressed against his chest.

Something altogether different rose in her. It was joy. It was a bubble that couldn't burst, and it told her to hold on because she was in for a pleasant surprise. She fought against the urge to walk faster. If Conrad weren't surrounded by a group of people, Whitney would have run and wrapped her arms around him in a hug so tight he would have groaned.

She held her breath to settle her nerves while maintaining her casual pace. It bought her time to appreciate Conrad and take in the full picture of him in his loose Adidas sweats and a plain, short-sleeved t-shirt. His skin glowed to the point that it was obvious that he had spent years focusing on his health. He was laughing at something Adrian said.

Past conversations pinged through Whitney's mind. Adrian was there. Despite all they had been through, Conrad and Adrian were still best friends. Conrad said, "My father's deception tore apart one family and brought another together." It was evident in what they wore. Adrian was in an outfit similar to Conrad's, except his shirt was a light gray.

And there it was for anyone who knew their secret to see. Conrad and Adrian, the brothers, raised in different homes, looked more similar than Conrad and Kevin, who grew up competing for Claire's attention.

Adrian stood with one foot on the bench and leaned against his knee. Nathan and Jack huddled together on the other side of the bench. Nathan glanced over his shoulder. Whitney smiled to say hello, but he returned to the conversation before responding to her greeting. If Whitney didn't know any better, they were planning something.

Off a little way, Ruby and her friends were joking. It looked like a scene from high school, except the people were adults. A gentle appreciation for time's passing filled Whitney. Things had changed. When she was younger, she'd never fit in with the group. Now walking, having breakfast, and talking through problems with them was her normal.

Whitney briefly relished the feeling and joined the group. "What brings you out on this bright and early morning."

"Once I heard this is where all the women were on Saturday morning, I had to come." Adrian's smile almost masked the fatigue in his eyes. It lingered in soft lines on the edges.

According to Jasmine, Adrian was a night owl. He slept until ten, but that was because he was awake until two and three in the morning working.

Jasmine also mentioned that Adrian was the embodiment of a flirt.

Whitney rallied the joke back at Adrian. "I'll have to remember that the next time I need to move furniture."

Adrian rubbed his lower back. "Oh, I have a stitch." He flashed a grin that would have charmed him out of more than helping move furniture. The glint in his eye said he was aware his strategy worked. "Otherwise, You know. I'd help."

"Oh, I see how it is," Whitney said. "It's a good thing I have four brothers." They both laughed at the joke until Conrad's stern glare stunned them both into silence. Adrian cleared his throat, said, "I forgot my water bottle," and backed toward the parking lot.

Nathan flexed and puffed his chest, expanding his olive green, Five Finger Death Punch t-shirt. "If I were twenty years younger, I'd offer to help you move furniture."

Jack winked. "Don't get any ideas. I'm just here to flirt." Then he gestured with his thumb toward Pauline and Ruby.

"Don't worry, guys." Whitney pointed at Conrad. "He's the one who needs help with the furniture." Instead of smiling, as she had hoped, Conrad's face was serious, like he was trying to solve a problem.

Jasmine's red jeep whipped into a parking space. Her voice was louder than the music blaring out the open window. "Don't leave without me."

Glad for a diversion from whatever it was that made Conrad grumpy, Whitney backed away to meet Jasmine. She waited for Jasmine to meet her on the sidewalk separating the parking lot from the grass.

Whitney compared her outfit with her friends. She wore one of her father's ROTC t-shirts, some athletic shorts, and her Saucony trainers.

Dressed in a hybrid tank top, cutoff shorts, and some Teva sandals, Jasmine looked like something out of a Pinterest graphic. Before she knew what she was doing, Whitney checked to see if Conrad noticed. He was deep in a conversation with the two older men on the bench. However, she caught Adrian switching his focus. He could add whiplash to the list of his back injuries. Yet, it warmed Whitney's heart to see that he found Jasmine attractive. *They would make a cute couple.* Whitney tucked the thought away for a time when she could do something to bring the two together.

A couple of other people new to the group had joined as well. So they stood in a circle and introduced each other. Whitney explained the path, and people formed little groups. Whitney added to her introduction of Jasmine to the ladies. "We have been best friends since high school."

"You too," Ruby and Pauline bumped shoulders. "Except for the years when Ruby lived in Lake Havasu, we've been together for our entire lives."

With the introductions in order, people separated into groups and began their trek to the Sweet Treat Cafe for their cinnamon rolls. Conrad took his place alongside Whitney, and Adrian positioned himself between Whitney and Jasmine.

The moisture from the morning dew softened the touch of the summer air, but that wouldn't last long. The weather stations predicted a warm, dry afternoon. Whitney told Conrad, "If you don't have a camelback, I can get one from Mom and Dad's house for you."

"I had one delivered this week. It came the same day as my furniture." His enthusiasm added brightness to his demeanor.

Whitney still had concerns about Conrad dismissing her. He had sent her gifts and meals from local restaurants. They texted back and forth, but he had been too busy to talk. After the newness wore off, he might think she took too much effort.

Seth was the one who explained the lack of phone calls and face-to-face conversations with Conrad. Wearing an expression that begged Whitney to be careful, Seth told her that chairing the 5k had opened opportunities for Conrad. Conrad's assistant had added speaking gigs to his schedule. Seth nudged his chin toward a deli sandwich that was on her desk. "He's had shoe companies offer to make a model for him and nutrition companies asking for endorsements. The way I see it, Conrad owes you more than lunch delivery."

Seth's comments had Whitney once again questioning her expectations. Had she aimed too high by hoping that Conrad liked her for who she was? Was it possible that she had misinterpreted his appreciation?

Conrad was out of her league. He was rich, famous, and handsome. Whitney was a normal woman, who made good money, but what she made in her lifetime wouldn't match one year of Conrad's salary as a football player.

Whitney talked with her mother about dating Conrad while they washed the last of the dishes. Her mother was transferring the clean glasses from the dishwasher to the cabinet when she said, "The way I see it, the worst that could happen is you have some fun, learn more about who you are as a person, and grow into a more beautiful version of yourself. The best that could happen is you find your Erick." Whitney loved how her parents referred to each other as the best possible outcome for a relationship.

"What are you smiling about?" Conrad asked.

"I've always wanted to go to an escape room," Whitney admitted. "So I'm a little excited about today." She pointed at a fork in the road to tell Jasmine and Adrian where they were headed.

"You never said anything to me." Jasmine craned her neck behind Adrian and glared her displeasure.

"It sounds like fun," Adrian said. "What time are you going? I might join you."

"I thought your back hurt," Whitney replied.

"Using my mind won't aggravate my injury," Adrian said. Whitney noticed his gait was strong but didn't have time to point it out.

Jasmine piped in, "I don't have anything planned."

Conrad said, "Whitney and I have a room reserved for six."

Whitney waited for Conrad to add that it was a date. That he wanted some time alone with her. That the idea behind the escape room was having them in a false pressure cooker to see how they handled stress and adapted their approaches. When he said, "Afterward, we're having dinner at my place." She connected the serious expression from earlier with her concerns about merely being a conduit for opportunities.

She felt the loud babump that reverberated through her body, and then the feelings that confused her came to a painful conclusion. She was right.

Even worse, it seemed like Conrad had second thoughts.

Whitney swallowed her disappointment, put on a positive attitude, and dreamed about something nice–like going to the Bahamas, or hiking in Alaska. Anything that would take her away from the grim reality that she had a bad habit of falling for men that were out of her league.

Chapter 31

Whitney's Love Language Is Food

If Conrad didn't know better, he would have sworn his best friend-turned-brother was trying to steal Whitney from him. Maybe stealing was too harsh. Conrad hadn't said anything to Adrian about his intentions toward Whitney. A mile into the trail, Conrad regretted it.

On the surface, Adrian was the guy who acted like he was above any woman that showed him any interest. He said he learned it in college. "Women get overwhelmed by men competing for their attention. I take it easy and let them notice me. Once I spend some time with them, I talk to them like they're normal people and let the attraction build."

It sounded stupid, but it worked.

Adrian was in the middle of Jasmine and Whitney, throwing barbs and laughing when they got a good one in.

Conrad had never competed with Adrian for a woman's attention. They had different tastes. Adrian preferred women he could manipulate with flattery. Women who were attractive but were primarily concerned about how to spend his money.

Whitney was smart, sweet, and whole-hearted. Adrian's attentiveness toward her did not make sense. Then again, they were brothers. Was it possible they had mutual expectations for the type of woman that they'd settle down with? They'd only discussed women they'd found attractive, always avoiding the subject of marriage and family—especially after they'd learned about being raised in separate homes.

To her credit, Whitney tried including Conrad. Every time, Adrian shifted the conversation, leaving Conrad fumbling to contribute. Then he had to figure out how to calm the aggravation rising within him.

At the intersection that would take them to the diner, Conrad decided that he wasn't giving Adrian any room to have time alone with Whitney. With his luck, Adrian would whisk her away, and Conrad would be left standing in front of the hedge with only himself to blame. He tried to play it safe and was looking bad for it.

When Whitney and Jasmine sat at a table to save seats for the group, Conrad found his opening. He and Adrian were in line to order cinnamon rolls. Conrad lowered his voice so the people around them couldn't hear what he said. "Dude, lay off Whitney?"

"Why? Do you have something against me hanging out with her?"

The hair on Conrad's arm rose a little when he heard the defensiveness in Adrian's voice. It was the same feeling Conrad got before a game. Familiar with the reaction, he pushed aside the urge to tackle Adrian and held his cool. "Actually, yeah."

Adrian's face contorted as he passed from one level of understanding to the next until it lit in revelation. "That's why you said I wouldn't like her. You wanted her for yourself." He slapped Conrad on the back, "Why didn't you say something sooner?"

The tension between them drizzled into nothing. They were back to being best friends. Conrad was in a place where he could tell Adrian the truth, knowing it wouldn't be held against him. "Because it's new. We haven't gone out yet."

"When are you going to change that?"

Conrad ground out, "I was—later today."

They were at the front of the line. A woman who looked like the grandma on the cookie packages waited for their order. A light feeling filled Conrad's chest. It was only a cinnamon roll, but the sense of pride in being able to buy Whitney breakfast buoyed his belief that this thing he had with her was moving in the right direction.

Every time he had a meal delivered to Whitney, she sent him the sweetest thank you text. Then they'd text back and forth for a couple of minutes.

Now that he was home, Conrad was ready to pick up where they had left off. His gaze shifted toward the table by the window. Whitney was leaning in toward Jasmine. It looked like they were talking about a picture. Then revelation hit, blocking out the cozy interior with lace curtains and rustic wooden tables with vased flower buds in the center. His focus was on Whitney, who was probably talking about their text messages. Her cheeks, tight with guarded hope, mirrored what Conrad was feeling. The first blushes of their relationship had them questioning and seeking affirmation that it was, in fact, their turn to fall in love.

Conrad and Adrian returned to the table with coffees and pastries for the four of them. Adrian took the seat across from Jasmine, allowing Conrad his place across from Whitney.

He'd have preferred sitting next to Whitney, but it was for the best. With his luck, someone would post a picture of Conrad with Whitney, blowing their relationship out of the water. They needed time to nurture what they had before it fell under public scrutiny.

Conrad leaned forward to speak so only Whitney could

hear what he said. "I've waited two, long weeks to spend time with you."

He couldn't count how many games he'd won without checking the stats, yet if asked, he could tell how many hours and minutes they'd been apart.

Conrad knew he'd remember the surge of adrenaline that coursed through him when he recognized the flush of color rising in Whitney's cheeks and the swell of her chest. It was the first real sign that she was attracted to him. The feeling was mutual.

He'd asked for extra plates so they could share their food. That was a tip from Whitney's father. Erick sat beside Conrad on the stairs of her porch and gave the, "if you love your life, you better not hurt my daughter," talk.

Then came the advice. Pure fatherly pride replaced the glare that had Conrad's stomach clenching. "Whitney's love language is food." He shook his head, "And if you're trying to win her over, share a plate. One time, when they were little, Thom forgot to close the door on Whitney's rabbit cage. Beatrix Potter escaped and never came back." Erick's eyes softened as though he was reliving the memory. "Thom sat beside Whitney, who had been crying like she lost her best friend, and handed her half of his hot dog. The tears stopped, and they've been allies ever since."

The walk to the cafe taught Conrad his next important lesson. Make it clear for all to see, especially Whitney, that he was making room in his life for her. Today, it was as his girlfriend. The deepening want in him said she had an even larger role in his life.

Conrad wavered between certainty and fear of rejection. But he pushed the fear aside. A cinnamon roll had to have more leverage than a hot dog.

When Conrad set the slice of cinnamon roll and half of his

fruit in front of Whitney, her eyes dilated like a camera capturing a moment.

"I know you're disappointed because it doesn't have avocado," Conrad joked. "I'll do better next time."

Adrian's gaze shifted from Conrad to Whitney. He leaned toward Jasmine. "I know as we get older, we miss out on the lingo. Is avocado code for something?"

"Maybe guacamole is a secret aphrodisiac," Jasmine frowned through her confusion.

"Conrad, you will have half the town thinking avocados are some sort of a secret language like the fruit emojis," Whitney complained.

"Then I will have made a positive contribution to society." He loved her disapproving face. It compelled him to stand his ground. Conrad's gut tightened in anticipation when he thought about making up from the small disagreements they were bound to have.

"So is avocado code for let's be really, really close?" Jasmine asked a little more forcefully.

Conrad and Whitney answered at the same time.

He said, "Yes."

She said, "No."

All four of the friends burst into laughter. The feeling pried open areas of Conrad's heart he thought were destroyed by his father's deception. There was a time when he believed he'd lost the gift of laughing and feeling it. He resigned himself to a future of questioning every word spoken, every emotional response, every interaction with those who were close to him. The two people who had the most influence over him, friend-turned-brother and his friend that he hoped would be something a little more were there with him, were showing him how to trust again. The best part—the healing didn't hurt.

Things were much smoother on the way back to the

park. Conrad took his place on Whitney's other side, separating her and Adrian.

Adrian talked with Jasmine, and Whitney gave Conrad her undivided attention. He told her about his talks at the Boys and Girls Club encouraging kids to keep up with their schoolwork while playing sports and how some high school coaches contacted him about speaking at their schools. Whitney listened mostly, occasionally interrupting to ask questions. Before they knew it, they were at the park.

"What time and where are we meeting?" Jasmine had her phone out and her calendar app open.

"What if you and I did something together and let Conrad and Whitney go out alone."

Conrad had to give Adrian credit. He tried.

Jasmine persisted. "It'll be more fun with more people. We can pretend like we're on those race shows."

"You and I can do it another time," Whitney said.

"It's almost like you don't want me to go," Jasmine's challenge was playful.

Adrian averted his gaze toward the trees in the distance. Conrad watched to see how things would play out. Would Whitney tell her friend she was going on a date with him?

"Aw Jaz, I want to go with you, but...."

"I don't like buts, Whitney."

Whitney rushed her words. "It was supposed to be our first date." She nudged her head toward Conrad to explain who the other half of we was.

Jasmine's eyes widened, and her mouth fell open to form a circle. "Congratulations, I had no idea you two were a thing." Then she frowned, "Why didn't I know you two were a thing?"

"Because we're not a thing. Yet." Whitney squirmed, and her face turned a shade of red that was new to Conrad.

He wrapped his arm around her shoulder, drawing her into

his side. It was more to let her know she wasn't alone. His voice was bright but one shade below a full brag. "Let the record show–she said yet."

Jasmine tapped her phone to say I need the details. "I'd still like to go. Can we make it a double date?"

"I don't see why not," Conrad replied.

"Hey, don't I get a say in this?" Adrian said.

"Take it from me," Whitney said, "I've been Jasmine's friend for most of my life. The answer to your question is no. No, you don't have a say. You just come along for the ride and act like you're having fun."

Jasmine preened with pride at Whitney. "If I ever find a man who knows me as well as you do, I'm going to marry him."

Again, the group burst into laughter. Again, Conrad felt the healing effect. He took in the image. This was his future. Adrian would be by his side. Jasmine would be beside Whitney when they started their lives together. His heart settled.

Jasmine's manicured finger pointed at Adrian and curved back to her chest. "In the meantime, you are stuck with me."

If the grin that took over Adrian's face was any indication, he didn't mind.

Chapter 32

Waiting For The Right Moment

Conrad waded through the three inches of water covering the Cottage Cove Sports Center floor. The soles of his shoes sloshed every time they disconnected from the cement flooring. "It's a good thing I came back when I did."

He pushed to get back earlier than planned because he was eager to see Whitney. Otherwise, he'd have been on the golf course in Arizona with a couple of his buddies, and Misty would have been dealing with the mess alone.

She called when he was at the edge of the Lilac Lane Park parking lot. Whitney was still standing in front of her car with Jasmine. He thought Misty was calling to welcome him back to town.

That was short-lived.

The tightness in her voice warned him before he heard the words. "I have some bad news." The pipe leading into the aquatic therapy pool ruptured.

He pulled back into the parking space and told Whitney that he'd probably have to cancel their date. She said the right things, but the disappointment on her face was unmistakable. It had a hint of "I should have known this would happen."

The best Conrad could do was kiss her on the temple, say, "I'll make it up to you. I promise," and go on his way to the sports center.

He assessed the pipe for damage. The valve had busted off, leaving a jagged edge.

"The plumber is on the way," Misty had the foresight to roll up her pants so only her fluorescent Ascics were wet. "He told me how to turn off the main." She looked toward Amy, the clinic's physical therapist, for confirmation of what she was saying. "It took us ten minutes to find it."

"It's a good thing you were here," Conrad had been through more harrowing circumstances. Adding plumbing repairs was a setback, not the end of his project. They had placed some wiggle room in the timeline of the opening. "We didn't have any furniture or carpeting." He sloshed to the wall. The water was well below the socket, so they wouldn't have electrical damage to contend with.

"You won't be so glad when I tell you why I was here," Amy said.

"What's going on?" A little hammer tapped on the side of Conrad's temple, starting what threatened to be a massive tension headache.

She said, "We can talk later."

The pounding deepened, sending waves of discomfort through Conrad's scalp. "That doesn't sound good."

While the plumber repaired the pipe, Amy resigned. She got engaged over the weekend and was moving to Las Vegas with her fiancé. Her departure hurt worse than the headache or the water damage. Amy was his lead sports therapist and would be hard to replace. *It's just a setback,* Conrad told himself.

A setback that had him scrambling to find another therapist for the opening...in a month.

He had the water pumped and fans running to dry the residual moisture. Satisfaction with progress was on the edge of his rattled nerves.

He glanced at his watch and considered inviting Whitney to a late dinner. It wouldn't be as exciting as the escape room, but it would be time for them to talk.

Before he could follow through with the thought, the phone rang with a call from the shipping company. His office furniture was lost somewhere between New Mexico and Colorado.

Conrad's first day back tested his resolve. His mother had spent more time with Whitney than he had. He was forced to spend money on piping. He also had to add finding a therapist and furniture to his growing get-it-done-now list.

For the briefest of moments, Conrad sympathized with his father. How many times had Conrad, as a teen, played the role of judge, jury, and jailer because his father wasn't at a game or couldn't make it to a sports dinner? Life as a business owner was harder than it looked on the surface.

Pity swirled into something hard in his gut. Conrad had almost weakened. He had almost broken his promise to himself. He had almost given himself permission to turn into his father. Conrad curled his hands into his fists. Not today.

He grabbed the phone out of his pocket. Not allowing himself the chance to change his mind, he pressed speed dial. The line didn't ring. Whitney's breathy "Hey, how's it going?" sent waves of relief through his body. The problems were still ahead of him. With Whitney by his side, they didn't feel as heavy.

"What are you doing?"

Her answer followed a metallic clang. "Baking cupcakes."

Conrad's mouth watered with the reminder of the last time

he ate one of her cupcakes. The entire cupcake practically melted on his tongue. "What kind?"

She replied, "Sorry to disappoint. They're not avocado."

Her giggle danced around his chest, tickling its way to his gut. "What about pistachio?" The banter released a little more of the pressure.

She said, "I've seen that on the baking shows. I could try it."

Her response sent waves of pride through Conrad. His voice dropped into the husky tone he used when he was flirting. "Have I influenced the baker's choices?"

"Oh, you have no idea." The soft inflection in her voice made it hard to determine if it was a flirty purr or sound releasing aggravation.

Conrad drew his phone away and gave it a hard stare. Was the certainty a compliment or a warning flare?

His ego told him to go with the positive.

Experience taught him to proceed with vigilance.

Over the years, he saw the signs of his parent's deception and chucked it off to adults being weird. Now he knew better.

He trusted the feeling that he had found his future. That meant proceeding with confidence. He inserted all of it in his voice. "So my plan worked."

"You had a plan?"

"It took some thought, but I figured it out." He leaned back into the folding chair, tilting it on two legs. "People treat others how they want to be treated."

"What about people who are jerks?"

Conrad blinked. Whitney had a habit of seeing both sides of an issue.

Remorse filled him. Statistically, pro ballers married women from their early college years. If he'd paid attention to Whitney when she was in front of him, she'd probably be sitting beside him, talking through possible solutions. She'd rub his shoulders and tell him it would be okay. Regret was a sharp sword.

He'd spend the rest of his life making it up to her.

Conrad answered her question with all the authority he could summon. "They're lashing out in pain. Instead of giving it back to the person who caused it, they're magnifying it by passing it on to someone else."

Conrad knew about being a jerk. He was worse when he found out about his dad's affair. Adrian, who saved Conrad's life, was the recipient of the attitude, salty words, and harsh treatment. He also was the one who called out Conrad's bad behavior. "I get it. You're mad. But I didn't bring this to you. And at least your dad wanted you. Mine left me."

Guilt forced Conrad to change—to look for what people were doing right. He said to Whitney. "You feed people. If you're not doing it with baked goods, you do it by giving them the support they need. I want to be that for you, Whit."

The silence from the other end of the line threatened to take over. Conrad's confidence tripped. Had he said too much too soon? He half hoped the signal had dropped. He settled the chair so the four legs were on the floor and leaned his body forward. "Are you there, Whit?"

Her quiet "Yes," said more than a library of words. She was afraid to believe him.

He rose from the chair and tapped his pocket to double-check that the keys were there. When he felt the lump, he headed for the door. "I'll be there in less than a half hour unless you're making cream cheese frosting. Then I'll speed and be there in fifteen minutes."

It was time to follow through with what he should have done when Whitney admitted her feelings.

He was done waiting for the right moment.

Chapter 33

Cupcake Surprise

Whitney leaned into the kitchen counter and willed her cupcakes to bend to her vision. It didn't work. The piping wilted, sinking into uneven lumps.

Her cupcakes were a hot mess—literally. The timing was off before she started, and she knew it. They needed to chill, but her sense of logic took a back seat to her excitement.

Conrad had said thirty minutes. That was barely enough time to change, let alone mix the frosting and have something presentable when he arrived.

She pasted on a smile and greeted him with enthusiasm she thought for sure would compensate for the fiasco of a dessert.

He settled his hands on her shoulders and tipped his chin, forcing her eyes to connect with his. "What's wrong?"

"My cupcakes are garbage." She grimaced to soften the disappointment. Her baking fails were few and far between. So, when they hit, they hurt. In the past, it didn't matter, but this time. This time, she wanted to impress Conrad.

"It's a good thing I came over for something else." The playfulness in his voice drew Whitney back into the conversation.

His thumb slid on her jawline, and her heart hitched in her

chest. It was too good to be true. She had to be dreaming, but then he pressed his lips against hers. The touch was warm and inviting, and his lips tasted better than any frosting she'd ever tried.

Whitney settled into belief. Conrad kissed her. It wasn't one of those because he was supposed to kisses, either. It gently asked, do you feel this connection between us too?

His voice was husky when he said, "I've been holding off for the perfect moment."

Behind his confident aura, Whitney saw the sweet guy who used to sit across from her at the kitchen table, waiting for approval. "If the tingly feeling in my toes is a sign, I'd say you found it."

"Tingles? In your toes?" Conrad's lips slid into a wicked grin. "So—could it happen again soon?"

"Perhaps." Whitney wobbled on her toes, trying to clear the mixture of anticipation and anxiety that stirred inside her. Conrad had dated cheerleaders, models, and a famous actress. One day, he'd figure out she lacked the cool factor.

How long would it take until he lost interest? If this was like her previous relationships she had two months—then he'd get bored.

She weighed her options. Proceed in fear and live a life of wondering what if, or give it a try. Allow herself to fall into the fantasy with her eyes wide open. It would end, but it was fun while it lasted.

Her cheeks burned with the euphoric feeling she knew she'd have when she told her grandchildren that she kissed a football player in her younger days.

"Do you have chocolate and whipping cream?"

The aura of cool Whitney had worn drizzled, to remind her that she usually came across as awkward.

Conrad had gone from I'm waiting until the time is right to

take you on a date to she didn't dare think of what he had in mind. She replied, "Uh, yea," to buy time to tell him that she wasn't ready to take things to the next level.

"Good, we can make a ganache for the cupcakes."

Her mind rattled at the contradiction between what he said and what she expected.

He chuckled. "Dare I ask what you were thinking?"

"No!" The heat rose in Whitney's cheeks betraying her mental foray. She cleared her throat and turned to lead him into the kitchen. "How do you know how to make a ganache?"

"When I came home from college, I spent time with mom in the kitchen?"

"Really?" Whitney remembered Thom and Conrad hanging out a couple of times before Thom and Grace morphed into a couple. Conrad wasn't as wholesome as the picture he was trying to paint.

"Fine. I took some cooking classes to impress women." A lovely shade of red flushed through his cheeks.

Whitney's ego swirled around in the laughter she contained. His expression said that Conrad hadn't been prepared to handle someone who knew him before he had to work on his skills to entertain women.

Perhaps, they were evenly matched after all. Whitney grinned to set his mind at ease. "Well, let's put those classes to use."

Conrad stood over the stove, stirring the warmed cream and chocolate shavings. "What were you planning on using the cream for?" It wasn't like heavy cream was one of those staple ingredients. "And while we're discussing your refrigerator, I'd like to ask why you don't have avocados?" He pushed his body in front of the pot just before Whitney stuck her finger in for a taste.

She collided into his chest, sending a rush of energy through him. He was right. Taking that cooking class would work to his advantage. "No touching the frosting until it's on the cupcakes."

"Hey, it's the kitchen, not a football field." Her lips curved into a beautiful pout.

Conrad leaned forward and planted a quick kiss on her lips. "I protect what's important."

"Now, there's nothing for me to do."

"Talk to me. Tell me where you'd like me to take you on a date."

"I don't know. A movie? It's summer. We could go for a hike."

They were great ideas, but not impressive. Any guy could take her to the movies or for a hike. Conrad wanted to do something that would blow them out of the water. After going out with him, Whitney would be bored with anyone else. His eyes pierced into Whitney, looking for what would impress her.

It wasn't like he could google how do you impress a woman who dedicated her life to building a legacy for a childhood boyfriend?

He had to give her a memory she would cherish, would hold close to her heart, would make Conrad's intentions clear.

The frosting had glossed into a smooth liquid. He set the pan on a cool burner and dipped a spoon into it. "Now you can taste it."

Whitney reached for the spoon, and he pulled it back. "I won't spill any on you."

Her mouth dropped, but she acquiesced, allowing him to feed her. Her tongue slid across her lips, and her eyes dilated. "Have you thought of infusing it with flavors?"

With one question, she proved her expertise. Conrad had

money, charisma, connections. Whitney was the brains behind the brawn.

An idea for the perfect date clicked into Conrad's mind. "Tomorrow, I'm taking you someplace without Adrian or Jasmine."

Whitney didn't balk or look at him like he was crazy. She asked, "Is this a Converse All-Stars or nice shoe outing?"

It was official. Conrad was in love.

Chapter 34

It Isn't As Romantic As It Looks In The Movies

The rain came in waves. First, it was an overcast sky. Then drizzles dampened the air and were followed by a strong downpour. Blue skies would appear briefly, only to have the cycle resume.

Like the weather outside, Whitney's mood dampened her enthusiasm. She couldn't commit to a hairstyle. The sense that her clothes would meet a soggy demise dimmed her opinion of whatever she chose.

Thinking of looking like the sunshine she wanted, she settled on her yellow Converse All-Stars to go with a white blouse with sunflower patterns and her yellow capri-cut pants. Smiling in the mirror, she celebrated. Her plan worked. She knew that despite the weather's promise of ruining her hairstyle and wilting her outfit, her shoes would be cute.

She heard Conrad pull into the driveway. Rather than wait for him to knock on the door, she grabbed her boho bag and pulled the door shut behind her.

He met her at the passenger side of his pickup with the door open. Whitney sighed softly at his outfit of an untucked button-down shirt with the sleeves rolled to his forearms and some khaki pants. The light color emphasized his tan.

Conrad looked casual yet nice and, most important, dreamy. The clouds above were pouring out rain. It was only fitting that she felt like she was floating on one.

Whitney waited until he was beside her in his pickup for the elation to take effect. She was on a date with Conrad, which meant that soft feeling inside her wasn't a crush anymore.

They were a couple.

Well, almost a couple.

They had kissed, and now they were going on a date. He seemed like he was following through with his promise. If she'd waited, he'd prove that he was worth it.

The dream come true was almost dizzying.

The console filled the space between the driver and passenger seat. Otherwise, Whitney would have scooted to sit beside him. Then she thought better of it. That was something people did when they were younger.

Conrad clicked his seat belt, and delight bubbled inside Whitney. "The Chocolate Palace. I cannot believe I have never been there. I almost couldn't sleep. I'm so excited."

"I'm glad to be the one taking you there." The sincerity in Conrad's eyes sent Whitney's heart into overdrive and her mind even higher into the clouds of what-if. If he didn't stop looking at her that way, she'd start to believe her childhood fantasy of him being her one would come true.

The scent of the rain mingling with the trees added a freshness to the cold, damp, air that stung Whitney's skin. Regret of running out of the house without a jacket prodded her to move closer to the middle of the cab.

Then, Conrad slid his hand in hers, and she didn't mind being cold. It felt like they were at the start of being a couple.

The conversation on the drive was light and easy. Conrad talked about the adaptations to his plans for the Sports Center. Discomfort squeezed Whitney's insides when Conrad told her that before he met Whitney for their date, he had called some friends for suggestions on who to recruit to replace Amy. He'd even reached out to a couple of the candidates.

Although she would have preferred learning the lesson another way, Whitney decided that Ben and her brothers were wrong. That, Conrad liked her for more than what she could do for him.

He should have been working, but he was with her. He could have asked her for names of people that would have helped him. But that wasn't what he wanted. He was content with her companionship.

He was so busy she had to ask herself. Was she wrong to push him to pursue her?

Was her desire for his affection selfish?

Would this outing come back and bite her?

"What's going on in that mind of yours?" Conrad ran his thumb along the soft part of her hand.

Telling him her concerns wasn't an option. She twisted her body to face him. "Is there anything I can do to help you?"

"You've done more than enough, Whit."

His eyes were trained on the road, allowing Whitney the freedom to enjoy his features. The confidence oozed off of him. Sitting in his presence made Whitney feel like she could accomplish anything she set her mind to.

"For as long as we've known each other, you believed in me."

She said, "That was easy."

"And powerful. Hearing that you can do something from

the right person is all it takes to find the power to make it true. You are my person, Whit."

The air around Whitney stilled. Did he mean it the way she wanted to receive it? *You are my person.* It was four little words, but put together in the sequence he delivered gave them so much potential.

"For the record, it was easy to believe in you," Whitney replied. "You've always had a vision, and the heart behind the vision was true."

All the time she had known Conrad, he'd used his position to help others on and off the field. In high school, he volunteered at sports camps to mentor elementary boys. He continued the practice even after he'd been famous by working with teens-sometimes in football camps, but most of the time, he'd surprise kids at the community center and join their football game.

"Can you tell that to a couple of my exes?"

Whitney rolled her eyes. "I'll get on it."

Conrad turned onto a road that had a Main Street America feel. All of the buildings were red brick. Some had signs hanging out from the tops of windows, while others had easel boards promoting the special of the day. Cars were parked perpendicular to the businesses.

Unconcerned that Conrad and Whitney were on a date, the rain fell in steady streams. A puddle splashed despite Conrad's slow ascent into it. He threw Whitney an apologetic smile. "It looks like I'm parking a block away."

Whitney's regret about leaving her jacket at home wagged its finger, giving her a big I-told-you-so. She had her hair pulled back into a ponytail. By the end of this adventure, it would probably look like a frayed rat's tail. Still, visions of rain pouring down her face as she kissed Conrad gave her hope. Not all was lost.

Conrad said, "Were you thinking about kissing in the rain?"

Heat filled Whitney's cheeks, and her jaw opened to deny what was written on her face. She quickly shut it.

He slowed behind the row of cars parked in front of the Chocolate Palace. "Trust me. It isn't as romantic as it looks in the movies."

It was a fantasy that Conrad wouldn't fulfill. Disappointment that it was something Whitney would never experience with him, combined with his confession that he had lived her dream moment with someone else, left a bitter taste in her mouth. She mustered a gust of sass. "For the record, the salty, been-there-done-that persona is not romantic."

His left shoulder dipped slightly, "I don't know what to tell you. I'm a realist."

With the appearance of the dimple on his left cheek, all of Whitney's bluster faded. "I should be grateful. At least I won't get too wet."

She opened the door. Her shoulders tensed in preparation for the onslaught of cold pricks of rain. Then she smiled. "I'll see you inside."

Whitney dodged some puddles by hopping over them. She tiptoed through the ones that were too wide to avoid. She was on the sidewalk, just beneath the awning, when her feet slid faster than her legs could keep up with. One minute she was sliding. The next, she was extending her arms to find her balance, only to fail. She fell, landing on what she would later call the back pockets of her capris.

At the last second, she remembered she was in public and stifled the exclamation of an expletive. She cursed life for betraying her.

The moment was short-lived, but she was wiser for it. Whitney knew better than to hurry and rise. She'd most likely end up in the same position. Besides, it was too late. Her outfit was soaked.

Chapter 35

You Didn't Watch To See If She Made It In The Door?

As soon as Conrad shifted the pickup into park, the rain stopped. It was so sudden he scanned the sky to see if it was a trick. The skies seemed to pass over the town like it was on one of those props riding on a rope and pulley system from a high school drama.

It was just as well.

Whitney would have time to check out the store. Maybe she'd find something she'd like.

Conrad played the mini-movie in his mind.

He'd find her admiring some candy and offer to buy it for her.

She'd decline because that was what Whitney did. She gave freely but had a hard time accepting gifts.

It would be easier to mix oil and water than it would for her to accept kindness.

But Conrad would work on it, and she'd let him buy her the treat.

They'd worked side by side in the kitchen. They worked as a team on the fun run. Today, they'd start the work on the other moments. The little ones that turned into memories.

By the time he reached the front door of the Chocolate Palace, he had a plan. Buy her chocolate. Then some fudge. Then a package to take home.

The soft scent of chocolate filled the air around Conrad when he opened the door. Conrad took in the scenery in front of him. To the right, a woman wearing a pink apron and a pink baseball cap twisted small pieces of taffy in paper. In front of him, people stood in lines around a stand with shelves of chocolate. The walls were loaded with jars of traditional candies. People milled around. None of them wore soft yellow pants.

A frown pressed on Conrad's forehead. He dropped Whitney off in front of the door. She couldn't have gone too deep into the store. Conrad surveyed the area beyond the candy store. A cord separated tables and cozy chairs waiting for someone to take a reprieve from their shopping.

Where was Whitney?

The firm grip on Conrad's shoulder was familiar enough that he didn't react. It was a tight squeeze followed by a tap. Adrian had done it after the games when they lost. Conrad sucked in a breath. What were the odds that Adrian, of all people, would be at the Chocolate Palace?

Disbelief pushed to the front of Conrad's mind. This was supposed to be his day with Whitney. If he didn't know any better, he'd have accused Adrian of trying to sabotage his date. "What are you doing here?"

"My mom loves this place. I bring her here every year for her birthday."

Of course, Adrian would bring his mother to the Chocolate Palace. He was the one who told Conrad about the candy store that attracted people from around the country.

"It's her birthday already?"

"Happens the same time every year," Adrian didn't roll his eyes, but the tone in his voice said he wanted to. He nudged his ear toward the corner of the store. "You have a little problem you might want to fix."

Conrad directed his gaze to an arch leading to another area of the store. Bulb lights were strung along the top, making it look like the doorway to another world.

"Whitney's in the bathroom with mom." Adrian rubbed his chin. For a brief moment, Conrad thought he saw hints of sympathy.

"Thanks." He stuffed his hands in his pockets and surveyed the rows of hard candies. Adrian's presence had him thinking. Maybe he should buy Claire some chocolate.

"If you don't mind me asking." Adrian shifted his weight, indicating he wanted to head toward the bathroom door. "Why'd you just drop her off at the door?"

"It was raining, and I didn't want Whitney to get wet."

Adrian stretched out the first part of his reply. "And you didn't watch to see if she made it in the door."

An uneasy feeling, like a slow-motion sucker punch to the gut, twisted Conrad's insides. He marched to the door. Adrian pulled on his arm before his hand pushed it open.

"You can't just go in there."

"Just tell me what happened already."

The door creaked open. Adrian's mom stopped short, and her mouth dropped slightly. Whitney was right behind her. She was clean-faced, and her hair was tied into a bun at the top of her head. Conrad's chest constricted, and his core tightened. He'd seen a variety of Whitney's looks. This one was breathtaking. It was fresh and pure and had hints of the girl he remembered from all those years ago.

Her eyes connected with his. The disappointment sliced him. She shuffled out of the bathroom and approached him. Conrad wanted to tell her how beautiful she was and ask why she didn't look like this for him more often. Then he'd pull her into his arms, vowing never to let go. The vulnerability pressing down on her shoulders, hunched ever so slightly, said it wasn't the time or the place.

Conrad cupped her cheeks and rested his forehead against hers. She blinked away the residual sadness, but not fully. Her lower lip protruded to form the most adorable pout Conrad had seen. "I'm a hot mess."

The gravel in Conrad's throat almost choked him. The things Whitney Stansfield made him feel. He was willing to spend the rest of his life sorting them out. But it was too soon to tell her. She wouldn't believe him yet. Or worse, he'd scare her. He'd take his time and build memories for them to cherish. He caressed Whitney's jawline with his thumb. "I should have kissed you in the rain."

The pout stretched into a soft grin he couldn't resist.

He knew better but couldn't help it. Right there, in front of the bathrooms, at the candy store, for all to see, Conrad kissed Whitney.

Whitney's point of view

Conrad described Adrian's aunt. "She's one of those people who can tell you the truth, even when it's ugly, and you'll thank her for it."

And she had. The woman, a head shorter than Whitney, walked into the bathroom. Without batting an eye, she said, "Child, you are a hot mess."

On top of her soaked blouse and pants, the beginnings of a frizz threatened to morph the front of Whitney's hair into a cotton ball consistency. Some of her makeup had smeared, as well.

They were too far from home to call for help. So Carol

helped Whitney freshen up. She held Whitney's blouse against the air dryer and told her everything would work out. "I've known Conrad all his life. He won't care if your shirt is a little wrinkled."

Then she distracted Whitney with funny stories from when Conrad and Adrian were growing up. She threw in, "I wish Adrian would find a nice girl like you."

Hesitance pulled on Whitney, but it wasn't like she could hide in the bathroom forever.

She opened the door, and all the fears from her childhood rushed to her heart. "Stay in your lane, Whit."

The makeup she hid behind had muted to near-natural tones—Goodbye, bronze cheeks. The shading to slim her face—gone.

She applied soft pink lipstick she found in her purse to freshen up her look. It was the best she could do with what she had. Whitney braced herself for what was on the other side of the bathroom door.

Conrad swooped in, filling the dark spaces closing in on Whitney. His touch smoothed the rough edges that pricked her heart.

Then from out of the blue, it happened. Right there for all the world to see. Conrad kissed her.

He wrapped his arm around her shoulder and pointed her body toward a store filled with more candy than her sweet tooth could ever want. "How much chocolate is it going to take to fix this?"

The approval in Carol and Adrian's chuckles lit the background, coaxing Whitney along to what was obvious to everyone but her. Bubbles of delight tickled her ribcage. She was in the right lane.

Whitney dared to gaze into the pools of color in Conrad's eyes. They were softened with affection. What she had hoped for was right there in front of her. Conrad authentically cared for and about her.

Everything within her settled.

"I would love one of those turtles. They're the size of my hand. We could share it."

Conrad chuckled. "Yes, we can."

Then she knew the dream was real. She thought with the confidence of someone willing to believe it was her turn to fall in love, *nothing could ruin this day.*

Chapter 36

Someone Took A Picture

Conrad's gaze darted around the room for something. The furrow in his brow said when he found whoever he was looking for, they'd regret it.

Out of reflex, Whitney copied the pattern. She didn't know what she was looking for, so she caught pieces of the restaurant. A half wall made of wood separated the area where they sat from the others. The red brick wall across from them broke the room in half, giving the feel of privacy.

Adrian set his fork on his plate. "What's the angle?"

"I don't know." Conrad's lip tucked into his cheek. He slid the phone across the table. It rotated slightly when it went over a crack.

Adrian picked it up, looked at the screen, tapped, and swiped through several links. "It's some woman named Mountain Chick Climbs. She's wearing a hat that hides her face."

Conrad scanned the room and returned to the conversation. "We'll never find her."

Even though she didn't know what they were talking about, Whitney mimicked their actions. The only thing she saw was people too involved in their own affairs to pay them any mind.

Adrian passed the phone back to Conrad. "That's not that bad."

Conrad's bent brows deepened into a frown. "For now. Once they get the likes, it'll get worse."

The disgust in his voice sent waves of concern down Whitney's spine. "Worse sounds bad?"

He said, "I wasn't ready for this."

Adrian said, "You should always be ready, man."

Whitney asked, "For what?"

"Someone took a picture of us together and posted it to social media." Conrad pivoted in his seat. "If I knew who it was, I'd ask them to take it down. People don't respect privacy."

Whitney stiffened to go against the instinct to pick up her phone and go to Conrad's social media page.

"Too bad," Adrian said. "I could have tried to distract her." He pressed the screen a couple of times and handed Conrad the phone. "There. I removed the tag and blocked her, so she can't tag you. Problem solved."

Carol leaned in and spoke to Whitney. "Yet, he won't help me post pictures of my garden."

Adrian fell into the role of the annoyed child. "You're too old for social media, Mom."

Conrad shook his head as though to say, "I should have expected this from you." His jaw relaxed.

It was like the tension ebbed from him and drifted toward Whitney. The questions chipped away at her good mood. What was in the picture? Her turkey avocado sandwich had lost its appeal, and her chips tasted a little too salty.

"Hey, what's going on?" Conrad took Whitney's hand. "And don't say nothing. I can tell your mind is on a treadmill."

She wanted to accept his comfort. She really did. "Is it a bad picture?"

"I don't think that's possible." Conrad wiggled her fingers.

"It isn't the picture that upsets me. A stranger stole a special moment meant for just you and me. It wasn't hers to capture or share. And she did it for attention. Today, we're a cute couple. The narrative will go along the lines of they were the first to prove it. Next month or next year, someone will use the same picture as a smear campaign. They'll say I'm endorsing a business with a political philosophy."

Worded that way, it made sense. "Note to self. Don't post pictures of what we do together on social media."

"It's safer."

"I told you it was Conrad Hayes." Two women in their late twenties clustered together at the edge of the table. The taller one said, "You probably don't remember me. I'm Sammy." She bent her knee and rested her hand on her waist. "Retired cheerleader."

The woman's long hair, smoothed barrel curls, graceful gestures, and Crest white smile were more than Whitney would ever be able to compete with. Whitney wanted to shrink. Instead, she endured the discomfort, knowing Sammy and her just as pretty friend would go away in a couple of minutes.

"Do you mind taking a picture with me?"

"Sure." Conrad scooted his chair, and the two women took a place on either side of him.

Whitney skirted a glance toward Adrian and his mother to share her disbelief. Conrad had just issued a proclamation against pictures and attention, and the two women had disproven his point.

They didn't know that he was on a date. They'd interrupted their meal, so they'd have something to brag about.

Adrian and his mother wore pasted-on grins.

"Do you mind?" Sammy stretched her arm, handing Whitney the camera.

Wisps of deja vu clouded Whitney's vision. This was one of

those lose-lose dilemmas. Take the picture and risk a list of negative repercussions. Declining would mean risking alienating fans.

She positioned the camera, zooming it so as much of the background would be gone. Then she tapped four times. "Hopefully, one of those will work."

"All of them are great." Sammy smiled.

Her friend said, "Share them with me. Before you forget."

The lines came into focus, and the cloudy feeling hardened into a familiar feeling Whitney had nearly forgotten. It was that time outside the gym. The social rules applied to her. If she waited outside the stands for Conrad, she opened herself to criticism. The cheerleaders and rich, pretty girls worked outside those parameters. She had outgrown her braces and gained weight, and got a job making decent money. Yet she still wasn't good enough.

They were back at the table, with Whitney helping Conrad manage factors outside his control—to maintain his reputation.

The women walked away. When they were out of hearing range, Whitney said, "I set it to the filter that blurs the background."

"Whoa," Adrian marveled under his breath. "She's a good person to have on our side."

Yes, she was. But this time, Whitney had a choice. Was it worth it to be blurred in the picture of Conrad's life?

Chapter 37

I Dare You

Before their lives toppled and they were in rebuilding mode, Conrad's father gave him all kinds of tips and tricks about women. After the extent of his father's experience with women was brought to light, the tip-sharing ceased.

Conrad's life turned into a maze, and around every corner was a challenge. He could have used some help navigating it.

Ever since Whitney had taken the picture, she'd been sweeter than the batch of pistachio fudge tucked away in a pink bag in her shoulder purse. His father would say, "It's a bad sign when a woman has been pleasant for too long. Either she's planning to murder you. Or, you're one bad decision away from sleeping on the couch and getting good morning kisses from the dog."

The rain had subsided, making it a beautiful day to walk through the town and visit the shops. Whitney oohed and ahhed in all the right places, was complementary of anything he suggested, and had gone as far as to thank him for the excursion. "This was a nice break from my weekend routine. If we didn't come here, I probably would have binge-watched a cooking show."

Where was the sass? Or sarcasm? She hadn't thrown him one smart comment to volley back with a joke.

Either Conrad had done so well there was no reason to worry, or he had done so poorly she didn't bother to attach any emotion to any of his suggestions.

Conrad tested the waters. "Maybe we could come here another time with Thom and Grace."

She didn't pause for thought. She surveyed the shops from one end of the block to the other and circled around to take in the shops on the other side of the street. "I bet they'd say yes." She pointed at the ice cream shop on the corner, "Grace would want to stop there."

There was his sign. Whitney loved her brothers. So much that she made it a point to run in the opposite direction when they started talking about an outing. Their interests were too dissimilar.

Something happened, and she was not happy with Conrad.

He tapped on her elbow, guiding her into the little bookstore. It smelled of old paper, and the books were stacked by subjects. Conrad didn't care about the store as much as they'd have a quiet place to talk, and maybe perusing the books would distract Whitney, and she'd come out from behind the wall she'd put between them.

He bought her a hot tea, and they wandered. Her attention zoned in on the baby section but quickly returned to where Conrad was guiding her. The cookbooks would force her into her comfort zone. She picked up *101 Ways to Make a Cupcake* turning her face as the pages flipped. When one caught her interest, she stopped and studied it.

He'd offer to buy it for her. Her overly congenial disposition hinted at her refusal. Conrad stood close to her, leaning in to see the picture. It was a cupcake with fancy paper. The icing had gold flecks and chocolate shavings. Just thinking about tasting it after it came out of her oven made Conrad's mouth water. He swallowed and pressed ahead.

"I dare you to tell me what's bothering you."

Whitney surveyed the area around them. Conrad mirrored the behavior. It was just the two of them in the store. The clerks at the register were in the midst of a heated discussion.

"Do you want me to go first?"

He didn't wait. He held up his hands, raising a finger with each phrase. "I think you're mad at me. I want you to bake that cupcake in the picture. I want to go home. To keep it interesting, one of them isn't true."

"Oh," she set down the magazine. A pleasant smile filled her face. He didn't know how she did it, but the woman shimmered happiness like she was a Disney character. "We can go."

Her lack of sass broke the façade of her disguise. She intentionally chose the wrong answer to avoid a confrontation.

In this situation, Conrad's father would have said something short and expected change. One time Conrad had been privileged to witness a spat between Whitney's parents. Her father, the military officer, the war veteran, the guy who had to corral four strong-willed sons, morphed into a puppy that wanted approval. It worked. Her mother groaned against the frustration of their disagreement and buckled. They'd made up.

That was what Conrad wanted, and this was his first chance at it. He added some purr to his voice. "How do I make it up to you?"

"There's nothing to make up." Her voice said she wasn't affected by him. Her dilated eyes and the quick nostril flare told her truth. She wanted them to make amends, but what bothered her was stronger.

When she hurt, he hurt. He pressed on the soft area below

his collarbone to soften the dull ache in his chest. "The dare was to tell me how you feel." Conrad caressed her arm. Whatever she had to say couldn't be that bad.

The words rushed out of her mouth in one quick flow. "I feel like you're embarrassed to be seen with me, and maybe this is a mistake."

"It was the picture." She'd been caught in the snare of his fame. They couldn't change the past, but they'd set a foundation for their future. Her feelings were more important than someone taking a social media grab. He set both of his hands on her shoulders. "I don't want you doing things that make you feel uncomfortable."

"You made her day. If I were in her shoes, it would be the highlight of my weekend. Who knows, maybe even the year." She took his hand and squeezed it, reassuring Conrad. "It's not uncomfortable. It's new, and it's something I'll have to adapt to."

The woman's character was driven by her head and her heart. She knew the rules of the game but didn't like playing them. This he could work with. "Whitney, as far as the rest of the world is concerned, I haven't had a girlfriend. I won't post pictures of you because it's the first line of defense to protect you from drama." If they weren't in a public place, he would have been more affectionate with her. He'd risked it once at the candy store. Twice was tempting fate. "It's bad enough that I have to deal with this. It isn't fair to have you suffer from people's intrusive curiosity."

"I get it." Her lip quivered and stretched, ending with a dimple piercing her right cheek. "I don't like it."

"Would you like it if I took you to the ice cream shop?" He picked up the cookbook. When it was closer to his birthday, he'd ask her to bake those cupcakes for him. "After I paid for this book you don't want."

His heart hitched at the cheeky grin she used as a reply. On the surface, it was a small victory. Inside, Conrad felt like he'd won one of those once-in-a-lifetime awards. He had proved to himself that he could break away from his father's example. Conrad had a singular focus, and she was standing in front of him, ready to go get some ice cream.

Chapter 38

Frozen Watermelon Ice

Thom and Grace had reconciled. It was as clear as day when Thom gave his wife a sweet peck on the cheek. "Call if you need anything."

Whitney wanted to ask her brother if she was included in the parting words spoken like he'd hurdle walls or run through fire.

Whitney waved goodbye, not that it mattered. Thom backed away with his eyes zoned in on his wife.

Grace's face glowed like a Fourth of July sparkler. Her beauty dazzled Whitney, who hadn't decided if the radiance was from the life growing within Grace or the renewed love between husband and wife. Or had both blessings released an untapped essence?

At the end of the driveway, Thom bumped into a trash can. Grace smirked and shook her head. "Watch where you're going. Little Tomina needs a healthy dad to change her diapers."

Thom flexed. Whitney's stomach tightened. She was going to get diabetes from her brother and his wife's Hallmark Channel PDA. "Eww, save it for when you're at home."

"Just wait." The light in Grace's eyes softened, reflecting a pleased warmth. "One day, it'll be you and Conrad."

"I highly doubt it." Grace and Thom had a shared history that brought them together.

Grace started as the annoying little sister of one of Thom's friends and grew into the one woman her brother couldn't live without. "Geoff brought Thom and me together. I get the sneaking suspicion he's doing the same thing to you and Conrad."

"I don't follow."

"When we were younger, Geoff was the typical brother. We'd fight because he avoided me. I was the younger sister who thought he was my personal hero."

Her eyes glistened with a mixture of pride and sadness of a person who walked daily with someone in their heart because they weren't there in body. "But when I was grounded to my room, and he had the chance to play without me under his feet, he changed. Geoff would sneak into my room and play a quiet game of cards with me. He couldn't stand it when I was alone and sad."

Grace's memory blew on the cinders of loss in Whitney's heart. Geoff struck up a conversation with her on a gray Friday afternoon in the school courtyard. She was alone at one of the picnic tables, reading a book. She had long forgotten the book but remembered the joke he had told her.

Boundaries didn't seem to matter to him, either. His hip lined with hers, and his shoulders filled the once-empty space to her right.

"I came to save you." Then, he handed her a piece of licorice. It was the first gooey candy she had eaten after having her braces removed.

The memory warmed Whitney. The world was a better place because Geoff had been in it. "But I'm not sad."

"Before Conrad came back to Cottage Cove, you were alone." Grace snapped her finger in the air. "And don't go all Kelly Clarkson telling me the difference between alone and lonely."

"Woo, pregnancy has made someone spunky." Whitney wished she had half of Grace's confidence.

Grace pushed open the door to the garden shed. She spoke over her shoulder. "It's called being married to your brother who is exactly like you. So I've had practice with the Stansfield independent bravado."

It was hard to argue when only one of the six adult Stansfield siblings was married.

Grace rubbed her belly. "You know what else? I have a craving."

"Oh, goody." Whitney rubbed her hands together. "I get to have sympathy cravings. What are we eating?"

"A frozen watermelon ice."

"I have the feeling I am going to love this role."

Second thoughts reared their ugly head when Whitney and Grace took their place in the line that extended to the bathrooms.

Grace stood on her tiptoes. "If my counting is right, fifteen people are ahead of us."

The line shuffled forward. "Correction. Fourteen."

"Because that one person makes all the difference." Whitney's eyelids fluttered, but she prevented them from going into a full eye roll.

"What do they say about great minds?" Jasmine and Adrian got in line behind Whitney and Grace.

"They like Frozen Fruit?" Whitney curled her lip into a goofy snarl that said she wanted to complain about the circumstances but didn't have it in her. It was a warm day, and the surge to the Frozen Fruit shop made sense.

The line shuffled, taking them to the middle of the store. "I should go to the restroom," Grace said.

"I'll go with," Jasmine offered.

"I'll hold our place in line," Whitney said.

"And I'll watch out for Whitney," Adrian's tone joked that Whitney was the troublemaker of the group.

As soon as the door closed behind Jasmine, Whitney released the question she'd wanted to ask for weeks. Ever since Jasmine and Adrian had gone to the escape room, Adrian was all Jasmine talked about.

"So I hear things are going well with you and Jas. I'm happy for you."

"We have a good time when we're together. But we're just friends." Adrian threw a furtive glance toward the bathroom. "Women like Jasmine deserve a guy who's better than me."

If Whitney hadn't heard it from Adrian's mouth, she wouldn't have believed he'd said something so self-deprecating about himself. He'd been a loyal friend to Conrad.

While Conrad was the face of the non-profit and the sports center, Adrian was the person who laid the groundwork for the meetings and events. He did a lot of work and took none of the glory. "You're a good man with a good heart, Adrian. Jasmine needs someone exactly like you. I know you'd treat her right."

"Any guy with a good head on his shoulders would treat her like a queen." His eyes darkened in apology, and his lips tightened into a thin line. Adrian shook his head before looking away. When he returned his gaze back to Whitney, his demeanor had returned to normal. I have baggage she doesn't deserve to see."

He was so matter of fact Whitney blinked as though she'd see another side of Adrian between the opening and closing of her eyes. "We all have baggage."

Adrian leaned forward and whispered conspiratorially.

"How many people can say they found out when they were in their thirties that they had a brother."

Whitney's heart ached. Adrian was aware that she knew his truth. Somehow Conrad's father's secret overshadowed Adrian's belief in love. It softened the irritation of Conrad hiding his relationship with her.

She got the feeling that speaking with Adrian candidly would relieve her of a burden of her own. Maybe they could make peace with Conrad's odd approach to relationships. "One day, we will discuss our mutual friend's secrets."

"What secret?" Jasmine and Grace's faces were bright with curiosity.

"He's buying shaved ice for all of us."

Jasmine's frown said she wasn't buying it. Her silent acceptance said there wasn't much she could do about it.

"So, why don't Grace and I find a table?" Whitney crooked her elbow with Grace's. "I want blue raspberry, and she wants–"

Grace picked up the sentence. "Sour watermelon. But just a small one. When I have too much sugar Tomina uses my intestines for a trapeze."

They backed away, leaving Jasmine stunned and Adrian wide-eyed.

"Was that too much information?" Grace asked.

Whitney enjoyed the giggle she got from their reaction. "Yes, and it was worth seeing their faces drop."

They found an umbrella table outside the door, behind a gated area. Whitney sat in the chair closest to the planters that lined the edges of the eating area.

When Adrian and Jasmine returned, they discussed their plans for the weekend. Jasmine suggested they double date, but Whitney begged off. "Conrad's meeting with candidates for the sports therapist position. You can hang out with me and watch the Hallmark Channel."

"No, thank you," Adrian said. "I'd rather get a root canal."

Whitney's brother, Ivan, talked to her over the fence. "Whit, can I talk to you for a minute?"

"Sure." She pushed the chair back and walked to the edge of the eating area so they could talk over the fence.

Ivan's voice was soft with apology. "You know I support this thing you have going with Conrad. But I think you should go into it with your eyes wide open."

She looked over at Adrian, Jasmine, and Grace. They were the picture of summer. Three friends eating shaved ice, laughing, and looking like they didn't have a care in the world.

She returned her attention to her brother. His expression was as chilled as her frozen watermelon ice. Except, it didn't promise satisfaction or sweetness.

Chapter 39

Visit to Main Street

Conrad saved Main Street for last because it would be at the top of the list of reasons Jess Richardson would want to live in a small town. Not just any small town. She'd want to live specifically in Cottage Cove.

After her success with several WNBA players, Jess Richardson was one of the most sought-after therapists. The players she worked with attributed their new successes to her physical, mental, and nutritional changes. Sports therapy franchises around the nation were vying for her attention.

Cottage Cove needed her. She'd draw professional athletes looking for an out-of-the-way place to recover. Several pro teams hosted football camps in nearby Three Creeks, so the area already had a reputation for welcoming athletes.

The strategy was simple. By the time Jess stepped on the plane, she'd be close to deciding that she needed Cottage Cove too. So far, she'd met the sand volleyball players at the sports complex.

She'd partnered with Conrad in a couple of games, challenging him when he'd missed a chance for a volley. They'd won a couple of matches, garnering an invitation to the Sunday afternoon unofficial tournament. Jess begged off, citing family commitments while suggesting a rematch was possible.

After that, they watched a couple of fast-pitch softball games under the summer sky. In an early morning impromptu soccer game at the park, she held her own in a match against the other sports therapists and coaches—that had to be a sign that she was close to agreeing to work with Conrad and his team.

He parked the car, and they walked toward the Sweet Treats Cafe. Jess seemed to have a positive comment about every store they passed. The bookstore would be a fun place to take her daughter. The dress shop would appeal to her sister when she visited, and the bakery would inspire her to keep up with her training.

She pointed at the indoor shaved ice stand. "If the line weren't so long, I'd say let's try some of that." Conrad surveyed the line that extended to the back door. His gaze froze on a familiar ponytail. Whitney?

She looked up at Adrian as though he were the only man in the room. Conrad tightened against the slivers of ice stabbing at his gut, pushing him. He'd been so concerned about turning out like his father it never occurred to him that he could take on Claire's role—the one who had taken a back seat to the best friend. No. He decided. He wasn't like his mother. He would not accept anything less than what he gave. One hundred percent commitment.

That was a matter that could be dealt with later. He had to recruit one of the best therapists to join his team.

Conrad averted his focus to where it belonged—on Jess. "The next time you visit, we'll make sure to stop here first."

"Next time? You're that confident?"

"Yes, I have a secret weapon. Are you ready to see it?" He tapped her bicep and pointed at the Sweet Treats Cafe. From where they stood, he easily saw plenty of tables for them to sit and talk.

It was also out of the zone where he could see Whitney and Adrian. He threw one look back and saw Whitney laugh. Adrian always knew how to impress women.

The feeling of gravel rolling around Conrad's stomach was enough for him to look away. Remorse and relief fought for dominance. Conrad thought Whitney would be different. His mother insisted she was good people. Apparently, she was as bad a judge of character now as she was thirty years ago. Conrad had a consoling thought. At least he learned about Whitney's propensity to stray now and not after they were married and had a toddler.

He returned his gaze to the cafe and forced a chuckle. "It looks harmless. But I know several people who walk miles with this place as their final destination."

"This I have to see." They strolled side by side to the cafe, with Jess noticing the finer details of Main Street. The flowers, the piped music, and the creative use of miniature cottages in the window displays.

A cinnamon-scented breeze wafted by them when they opened the door. "Oh, I think I'm in trouble." Jess sounded like a kid that had walked into a candy shop. "I can smell the cream cheese frosting."

"Let the record show, I warned you." Conrad guided her to the line. "Ask, and you shall have."

Jess shook her head and grimaced, showing the fight with temptation. "I don't think I could eat one by myself." She took a step away from the counter as though the pastry would jump out of the display and force its way into her stomach.

"We could share," Conrad offered. "That way, you'd get a taste without as much guilt."

"Deal." Jess bounced on her toes. "I'd like an unsweetened iced tea, too."

The cashier smiled her recognition of Conrad and quickly straightened her expression when Conrad told her the order. "We'll have one cinnamon roll, two plates, one coffee, and one unsweetened iced tea."

They chose a seat by the front window so Jess had a full view of the quaint cafe and the mountains that jutted from the top of the stores across the street.

Jess sliced into her half of the cinnamon roll. "This looks like one of those towns on the covers of those cozy romance novels. I'm surprised we haven't seen any weddings."

"It's still early in the afternoon," Conrad pointed at his watch. "A couple hours before sunset, there will be some happy couple declaring their eternal love for each other."

"You say that with such sarcasm. I take it you haven't found your one." Jess's arched brow invited him to be honest.

Conrad thought back to seeing Whitney and Adrian at the shaved ice shop. "Not yet."

"Yet." Jess waved her fork. "You're optimistic."

"About you joining our crew, definitely," Conrad winked and pointed at her with an air pistol. He leaned forward, resting his elbow on the table. "Seriously though, what are the odds you'd consider it."

"I'll be honest. I have two more meetings this week. So far, The Cottage Cove Sports Center is my first choice. But I have several things to consider."

"Look at what we have here." Whitney's brother Ivan nudged a gray-faced Whitney in the elbow. Her arm moved against the prodding. "I don't mean to horn in on your conversation, but I had to introduce myself. My name is Ivan."

Jess twisted in her chair and wiped her hand on her napkin

before shaking his hand. "I'm thinking about moving to Cottage Cove."

"What isn't there to love?" Ivan exuded a charm that impressed Conrad.

"I know it's great for me, but what about kids?" Her question challenged Ivan.

"I may be biased because our parents work in the school system." He pointed with his thumb toward Whitney, who had her attention on the one plate between Conrad and Jess. She must have realized she was frozen because she turned her gaze to Ivan.

Conrad studied her expression. Was she avoiding him? She answered his question by turning her attention to Jess.

Ivan talked like he was pitching the community for personal reasons. "We have one of the best school systems in the state. Because the class sizes are smaller, the teachers don't let the kids get away with much." He tapped Whitney on the thigh. "Help me, will ya." Then he eased a chair over from another table and sat beside Jess.

If Whitney could have shot darts at her brother with her eyes, he would have been impaled, if not dead. Her smile apologized for her brother's abrupt approach. "We have a great community art and drama program. The children's choir performs every Christmas. Their show draws people from all over the state."

Ivan nodded at every point Whitney made. "What else are you looking to know?"

Jess tilted her head and alternated her gaze from Conrad, to Whitney, to Ivan, and back to Conrad. "You weren't kidding."

"About?" Conrad didn't like the feeling of uncertainty around him. Whitney and Ivan had an entire conversation without speaking a word in front of him. Then they pulled Jess in.

"You'd save the best for last. So far, you're the only prospective job that could answer my question that quickly. The others gave me, can we get back to you, and replied a few days later with stats."

"We're glad we could help." Whitney waved and backed away. "Nice meeting you."

Her eyes never connected with Conrad's. He tucked the tidbit of information away. Whitney was a puzzle and not an easy one to solve. In one instance, she was helping him recruit Jess to move to Cottage Cove, and the next, she was avoiding him. When he had the time, he'd tear it apart to figure out what it meant.

Ivan remained glued to his seat. "If you have any questions, I'd gladly answer them."

Conrad cleared his throat and tried piercing Ivan with his go-away look. "I don't mean to be that guy, but we were in the middle of something."

"Oh. Right." Ivan got up from his chair and returned it to the table. His voice turned cold. "Didn't mean to intrude."

Conrad shrugged off the drop-dead glare Ivan threw his way before exiting the cafe, rested his arm on the table, and continued his negotiation with Jess. "Do you want to visit the community center to learn more about those kids' programs?"

Chapter 40

Walking to Forget

It took some finagling, but Whitney finally accomplished her mission. She had Adrian and Jasmine together. Thom and Grace were joining them on the hike.

Whitney shared the plan with Thom and Grace. She'd get Jasmine and Adrian talking. Then she'd casually slip into a slower pace and walk with Thom and Grace, leaving Adrian and Jasmine to explore their mutual attraction.

"Why don't you focus on your own love life?" Thom asked, sounding slightly annoyed.

All she had to say was, "Because Conrad is working with Jess." Conrad had a short window to pull Jess up to speed on how the business was working. Ivan had hinted a couple of times that Conrad's interest in Jess may have been more than professional. He'd used the pictures of Conrad and Jess in the newspaper to prove his point. They were sitting together in the bleachers with their heads leaned together.

Whitney remembered the conversation on their date. People take pictures to promote their agenda. She pushed Ivan's speculations into the gray chatter zone in her mind and supported Conrad by giving him the space he needed.

Not being able to act like they were a couple in front of Jess resurrected a host of her girl-on-the-outside-looking-in feelings, but that was Whitney's issue, not Conrad's. So Whitney swallowed her pride and focused her energy on something that would make her happy–Adrian and Jasmine, and Thom and Grace. One represented love's potential, the other love fulfilled.

And there they stood—the five of them in front of the trail map. Thom's finger glided along the jagged line that broke onto a fork. "We'll head east here, so we can circle back."

If they walked comfortably, it would take a little more than an hour to complete the hike. Would three miles be enough time for Adrian and Jasmine to connect?

Whitney planned to find another way to force them together if it wasn't. Maybe lock them in a room and pretend she lost the key.

"That'll be perfect," Grace said. "Afterward, we can stop for lunch at the Bistro. They make the best huckleberry sorbet."

Jasmine's face brightened. "I'll gladly join you in your frozen sweet cravings."

More time together. Whitney loved how she and Grace seamlessly worked together toward common goals.

Whitney recognized the glow on Thom's face. It was the same expression her father wore when their mother approved of something he had done.

"Then let's get going," Thom waited for Grace to take his side, and they walked past the brick restrooms and last chance to fill their water bottles.

Jamie sat, leaning forward, on the cement bench meant for hikers to rest or appreciate the view. It all depended on if they were at the beginning or end of their journey.

Jasmine stole the words out of Whitney's mouth when she asked her brother, "Which of these rocks have you been hiding under?"

His glance slid toward the mountain behind him. "I was taking care of business."

"Is that code for tending to your wounds in the absence of friends and family who care about you?"

Stories had circulated, but nobody had confirmed the details. A woman stayed behind at Jamie's party. She was responsible for the first couple of weeks of radio silence. Images of them, faces glowing, arm in arm, looking like the picture of a couple in love, filled Jamie's social media posts. Then silence.

Jamie replied to Jasmine's texts confirming he was alive.

Jasmine's unhappiness with her brother was authentic.

"Sorry, I needed time to sort through some things."

Jamie sounded more defeated than apologetic, like that time he was supposed to catch the winning play, but the other team intercepted it. He couldn't have done anything to change the outcome. But that didn't ease the heaviness of the disappointment.

Jasmine sidled up to her brother. "We have three miles to make up for the lost time."

And like that, Whitney's plan crumbled. She inwardly groaned. It was never this hard on reality TV.

They walked side by side on the trail softened by fallen pine needles. Jamie talked over his shoulder. "Conrad's birthday is coming up. Do we want to have a party at the house?"

"He needs it," Adrian said. "He's working like he has something to prove. The break will do him some good."

"He could be working to forget," Jamie replied.

"Then he's succeeding."

Whitney saw Adrian's gaze flick toward her. Suspicion made her eyelids feel a little heavier. The hike was her idea. Except for Thom, everyone accepted the invitation, no questions asked. At the time, she thought it was because their schedules were free. Now she wondered. She kept her voice casual to sound like she was trying to keep the conversation flowing. "Jamie, how did you know we were here?"

His reply, "Adrian told me," tapped on her suspicions, rousing them to full alert. They knew something she didn't.

"I knew he'd come if you were here," Adrian said. "You make it hard for people to feel sorry for themselves."

Whitney took Adrian's point to heart. She tried isolating herself after Geoff died. She just wanted to be home alone and linger in his memory. She didn't have it in her to care about her friends or family.

For months, she walked through life like a zombie. Jamie, home on school break, insisted she take a walk with him and Jasmine. They walked in silence. She breathed in the fresh air and listened to Jamie and Jasmine argue over whose idea it was.

Their banter amused her. The next day, she walked alone. It progressed to walks around the park. Sometimes with her siblings, others with friends, and gradually including Geoff's parents.

"Do you care to share what problem we're walking off today?" Jasmine broke away from Jamie and forced herself between Whitney and Adrian. He veered from the trail and had to hurdle a small bush to avoid crashing into it.

Whitney organized the walk to match Jasmine and Adrian. They came because they thought she had a problem. Whitney wanted to be upset but couldn't. Her brother and friends paused their lives without question.

"Let's just say I have this friend," she said.

"Friend," Jasmine's voice rose in her "okay, I'll play along" tone.

"And she gets along well with this guy."

"Kind of like you and Conrad."

Whitney breathed in and exhaled, "Oh, nothing like Conrad and me. She is a perfect match for this guy."

Jasmine froze. "Stop. What's going on with you and Conrad?"

Rather than sugarcoat that the texts between them were reduced to "How was your day?" and the conversations centered on following up on an action item for the fun run, Whitney replied like her answer was par for the course. "Nothing. He's too busy for a relationship. Now on to my friend."

Jamie called back. "Keep up, ladies."

Adrian had caught up with Jamie and walked beside him. "Remember, this was your idea."

Thom and Grace were so far ahead of the group Whitney could only identify that it was them by their matching navy and maroon hiking jackets.

They were so far off of Whitney's plan, she raised her arms in the air and yelled, "aahhh!" She took Jasmine by the hand and ran to catch up to Adrian and Jamie.

The men who had been friends for most of their lives looked at each other as though to say whose turn is it to handle this? While holding Jasmine's hand, Whitney forced her way between Adrian and Jasmine. "Why do you have to make things difficult? Jasmine, you are the friend."

She released her hand to gesture toward Adrian with her palms facing up. "Here is the guy whom you obviously are attracted to." A flush of pride rushed through her. "I used whom correctly."

Adrian and Jasmine spoke simultaneously, "No, you didn't." They looked at each other and chuckled.

Jasmine said, "Isn't she cute?"

Adrian said, "Remember that time when we were on the senior trip and—" His voice trailed off as they progressed down the path.

Absorbed in their conversation, Jasmine and Adrian left Whitney and Jamie behind. The breeze whistled through the pine needles. She said, "You don't have to talk, but if you ever need someone to listen, call and tell me to break out the hiking boots. Or walking shoes. Or wine if you prefer."

A grin slid across Jamie's lips and just as quickly vanished. "Thanks. I'll keep that in mind."

They fell back into silence. Whitney couldn't help admiring the view of the lake off in the distance. From where they were, it seemed as though it would go on forever. Experience and her map reading skills taught her that there was more to navigational skills than met the eye.

Adrian, Jasmine, Thom, and Grace wandered around the meeting place at the fork in the road.

Grace surveyed the scenery. "Next year, at this time, we'll be here with little Erick." Thom rubbed her belly before kissing it. "Did you hear that little guy? We're already planning family outings."

The further they got into their pregnancy–the more Thom acted like their father. As time passed, Whitney couldn't help comparing. Her brother was a contradiction to Conrad, who strived to be nothing like his dad.

"Everyone, move in for a picture." Adrian held out his phone so people could see how they fit into the screen. They scrunched together: Thom's arm wrapped around Grace and Whitney. Jasmine leaned into Adrian. Jamie was behind his sister, holding his fingers up like bunny ears. Adrian snapped the camera several times and promised to share the picture when they were within a cell signal.

Their smiles said they'd been friends through thick and thin. Time nor distance breached their bond. Whitney's smile said, thanks to them, she felt a little better about life.

Chapter 41

It's The Little Things

Whitney pursed her lips. A soft hmm danced within her exhalation.

"That is a love-sick sound." Jamie's voice intruded on Whitney's exhalation from wishing Conrad was there. Sadness flicked across his expression, and he returned to being affable. "I know the feeling, well."

Whitney thought she had kept her thoughts to herself. She smiled her apology. First, for bringing a damper on their great day and for the sadness she saw in the shadows behind Jamie's eyes.

It was almost as bad as the time Jasmine, Jamie, and she ate some pizza that had been left out too long and got food poisoning. They were both heartsick, and somehow sharing the pain stripped away some of the bite.

They started down the trail. The silence between them was a comfortable companion. At the beginning of a switchback, Jamie said. "I never thought I'd miss the sight of a bra hanging from the doorknob—or finding a dirty coffee cup in the sink."

Whitney knew what he was talking about. She acted like it drove her crazy when Conrad brought avocados to add to her fridge, but deep down inside, the quirk delighted her. It was Conrad's way of saying he trusted her with a piece of him, and she was there for it. Today it was avocados—Secretly, she hoped that maybe one day, he'd trust her with his heart. Ever since that day, she saw him at the Sweet Treats Cafe with Jess, it felt like Conrad had faded. Now. She only saw shadows of the man who made her feel like she was important. "People act like it's the grand gestures that matter, but it's the little things that make someone stick to your heart." She said that as much for Jamie as she had for herself.

Jasmine threw her brother a sympathetic glance. Her soft smile thanked Whitney for being the person Jamie was comfortable talking to.

The feeling was mutual. Jamie was there when Whitney had tried on bras with his sister, and learned how to use makeup, and she suspected he was listening when they had the teenage late-night girl talks.

Jamie said. "Go ahead and get it off your chest. You know you'll feel better once you do."

And he was in tune with her silences.

"I can't compete." Whitney kicked a pebble. She thought she was special when she'd shared a cinnamon roll with Conrad. That things between them were above the best friend's smart younger sister string that held them together. Then he'd turned around and shared one with Jess. Jess was athletic and kind and worthy of being in the newspaper beside Conrad. She was a better fit, but that didn't matter. It was too late for Whitney to turn back. She was in love with Conrad.

Jamie said, "You shouldn't have to compete. You bring a lot to your relationships, Whit. Look at all you do for your friends, your family, the community. If Conrad, or any other man for that matter, can't see that you are a light that brightens this world. He doesn't deserve you."

Like the warmth of the sun, Jamie's words seeped into the sore spots in Whitney's heart. She did do a lot for people. Not because she wanted anything. She just liked making the world a better place.

Up ahead of them, Jasmine pushed into Adrian, and he stumbled and as quickly recovered. He wagged his finger playfully at her. They were too far ahead for Whitney or Jamie to hear the conversation, but the body language said they were willing to admit the spark had grown into an ember.

Like Jasmine and Adrian. She had pushed to bring them together. "Thanks, Jamie. I'll keep that in mind."

They were halfway down the mountain when Jamie picked up the conversation. "I feel like I should point out that Conrad notices you. He's just too busy right now. I have a feeling that if you give it time, it will work out."

"Ah, time. It seemed so long when we were younger, and now we don't have enough of it."

Jamie fell into the agreeing tone of voice. "And it is so unpredictable. I wish life came with something like a cookbook. We have timelines for being able to drive, to vote, and to buy a beer. But the important things are so vague."

Maybe Jami was right. Time and space were what Conrad needed. That Whitney could give him. She breathed in to add some enthusiasm to her voice. "Let's focus on something that'll cheer up both of us. I have a great idea for Conrad's birthday."

"Why do I have a bad feeling about this." Jamie moved to the left to avoid a rock in the path.

Whitney moved to the right and ducked to dodge the swipe of a low-hanging branch. The idea had given her an energy boost. She joked, "Because you're worried Conrad won't share his cupcakes?"

"Because Conrad doesn't like attention." Jamie said it the

way someone would explain why the sky was blue. It was just one of those things that was a given.

Jamie was right. That's what made several of the ideas on her Pinterest board perfect. They'd recognize his day without drawing unwanted attention.

Whitney's finger went from her lip to her temple. "You can have a big celebration."

What she planned was so clever Conrad would never see it coming. It would be the ultimate birthday surprise. "Jamie, what did you like best about your birthday party?"

"You won't like my answer." The brief appearance of Jamie's bad boy grin said the hike had brought him deeper down the road to recovery from his broken heart.

Whitney's response conveyed her delight with his half joke-half truth. "Can you give an answer that you can share with the class?"

"I like it when you try to act like you're in charge."

"Act? I am." Whitney sassed. The banter was a good sign. The Jamie everyone knew and loved was back.

Whitney stuck out her tongue, and Jamie laughed. The sound was light, yet it opened enough space to remember who they were. She was Whitney, the youngest daughter in a family of four boys, and he was Jamie, the older brother responsible for tormenting Whitney and his sister. Somewhere between the roles, they had prodded, cajoled, and celebrated their milestones.

They met Jasmine and Adrian at the next turn in the road. "For someone who is pregnant, Grace sure can walk fast." Jasmine directed their attention to Grace and Thom almost at the end of the trail.

"On a serious note," Jamie picked up the conversation he and Whitney were having. "The birthday cards were the best. I waited until the next day to read them. Remember when we were little and looked for money? Now it's all about the sentiment."

It made sense that he said it in front of Jasmine. She had helped Whitney organize the party, having gone as far as including a last-minute cupcake request.

The rhythm of the ground greeting their feet as they worked with gravity for their descent lulled Whitney. They had grown into people who read the cards. "That's it," she exclaimed. "Jamie, you are brilliant."

"You're just now figuring that out?" he joked.

"He is?" Jasmine's grin said she was glad her brother was in brighter spirits.

Whitney's idea was too big to change her focus and add a comeback to Jamie's ribbing. "What if we got people to write what they would in a card to Conrad on a strip of paper? Then we could attach the paper to the bottom of ribbons for helium balloons and fill his office with them."

"That sounds cute," Jasmine said, "but how many people can we get?"

Whitney knew they could pull it off if they all worked together. "Adrian, you could get notes from former teammates. Jamie, you and Thom could get players from high school." The more she talked, the more Whitney realized that the friends would have just as much fun. And it would be a light, pleasant moment to alleviate the stress of having to work so much.

"Jasmine, you could help me with the local friends. I was hoping you could help tie the cards to the helium balloons. Adrian, you can help us break into his office."

The more Whitney plotted, the brighter the vision. Conrad's office would be filled from wall to wall with balloons. A note would anchor the balloons so that he could reach them.

"What about the person who doesn't pay attention to the word surprise?" Jasmine asked. "There's always one."

"We'll tell people it's for a birthday book we're presenting at the birthday party.....that Jamie is hosting."

They had all grounds covered. People would know it was a surprise and be less likely to tell Conrad about their note. Even if they did, they would tell him what he already knew about.

Over lunch, they typed lists into their phones. The excitement between the friends grew with each name added to the list. When they got to one hundred people, Jasmine shook her head with admiration. "The Whitney I remember is back."

Chapter 42

Swag Bag Event

In a little under two weeks, over two thousand runners would descend upon Cottage Cove, and the Fun Run Team was ready for them. Tables, bags, and boxes of materials for the swag bags filled the corners and center area of the training room.

Whitney leaned away to get the full image of Conrad's face. The square jaw, the bright eyes, and the determined expression were a welcome change from when he first moved back to Cottage Cove. He was no longer the man who looked like he questioned whether or not he'd made the right decision. Now, he was a little more than proud of his accomplishments.

Whitney was too.

True to form, their friends, family, and community members showed up to support the efforts. Seth, Dustin, and Ericka led a team of teachers from the high school, stuffing swag bags for the event entrants from A to H.

Whitney's, Conrad's, and Geoff's parents formed a team, taking the third corner of the room. They were in charge of the entrants with the last names of I-L.

Conrad's staff and an additional ten volunteers ushered supplies or stuffed bags for the entrants of M-Z.

Jasmine and Jamie argued over who would be in charge of hospitality and social media posting for the day. Conrad solved the problem. "Both of you do it. And in the downtime, help whatever team needs it with random tasks that pop up."

Brother and sister seemed happy, using their sibling rivalry to feed the competition to see who got the better angle or the funniest wording for their posts.

Whitney and Conrad met at the snack station in his office every half hour to discuss the progress. She discarded her empty sports drink container and gave Conrad the kudos he deserved. "I am truly impressed." Even the music, playing through the sound system, matched the vibe."

He nudged her shoulder with his bicep. "It's easy when someone else laid a sound foundation." The laughter in his eyes brought Whitney back to when she thought he would steal the event. It had been the opposite. He'd posted videos telling Geoff's story, ending it wondering how the world would have been different if he knew he had underlying heart issues.

The committee had worked together for hours, replaying the scenarios in their mind, so the progress aligned with the vision. Gather people to have fun doing something healthy, remind them to monitor their heart safety, and raise money. At the end of the school year, athletes of any sport at Cottage Cove High School would have money for books when they started college.

She wrinkled her nose in a silent reply to the I told you so buried in the light behind his eyes. He'd said they'd make a great team, and all the activity in front of them proved him right.

They separated, with Conrad turning to the left and Whitney to the right. The crinkling of the blue and gold shoe bags drowned out the chatter, making it hard to hear any specific conversation. Still, it didn't interfere with Whitney's understanding of what people were saying. They were verifying that each bag had recovery drink samples, gels, a coupon for a cinnamon roll at the baked goods stand, a pamphlet educating people about heart health, a race number, and a t-shirt.

Boxes of filled bags were stacked at the edges of the tables.

Thom and Grace joked and flirted while stuffing bags. Whitney looked at the clipboard in her hand. A feeling that things were off unsettled her. A table separated her from being alongside Thom and Grace.

They were there alongside her from the beginning. This was their dream child as much as hers.

Thom stuffed a shirt into his swag bag and passed it down the line to Jasmine. "Look at how far we've come, Whit."

Five years ago, young and driven by a vision to make a difference, they spitballed ideas. Whitney surveyed the room. Their little dream had taken on a life of its own.

Jasmine dropped a filled bag in the box behind her. "You have outdone yourself."

Her brother pressed a bag into Jasmine's hands. "At the rate you're working, we'll never get done." Joking was the way Jasmine and Thom had communicated. One would criticize. The other had a smart comment.

Jasmine stuck out her tongue, grinned, and added a t-shirt and a number to the nylon bag. She passed it to her brother, who added a protein bar, some goo, and drink mix powder.

Whitney set the clipboard on the table's edge and crawled under it to position herself beside them.

One of the volunteers gave her a friendly smile and shoved a stack of numbers into Whitney's hands. "I've written the names and shirt sizes on the bottom. Distract Jess so I can get a chance to say hello to my future husband."

Whitney laughed. "Jess, I didn't know you were a taskmaster?"

Jess said, "She says that because of the newspaper article."

Pictures of Jess and Conrad promoting the Sports Center made the front page of the newspaper. The photographer used live shots of them playing volleyball at the Parks and Rec department.

A sinking feeling hit Whitney in her gut. For weeks, people speculated that Jess and Conrad would be the new it-couple." They both denied the rumors. Jess said her love interests were eight and ten years old. Conrad said he didn't date people he worked with.

Whitney trusted his response. The leggy blond batting her eyes and twirling her hair stirred a pot of emotions she thought had been laid to rest.

Sure, privacy had its benefits, but it, too, invited unwanted attention.

Conrad tipped his head back and laughed at something the blond said. Like the anvil in the cartoons, comparisonitis hit Whitney. The only thing missing was the stars circling around her head. In their place, questions loomed around her.

What if the blond was better for Conrad?

What if, like when they were younger, Whitney was only supposed to help Conrad find his legs?

He was established, and if the results of the run were any sign, he was set to accomplish some amazing things.

Was it time to let go?

This isn't the time or place. Whitney tucked her chin and focused on something she had control over, finding the shirt sizes that corresponded with the information on the race tag.

"Whitney, can you slow it down? Not all of us have aspirations to win a swag bag stuffing contest." Whitney told herself that Jamie was joking.

It didn't work. The comment landed atop the image of Conrad and the blond living a better life if she'd move to the side.

Jamie must have sensed the change in her because he gave her bicep a playful tap. "I was joking, Whit."

She forced the strong side of her personality into her voice. "Or, did you just remember that I hid the cupcakes?"

Jamie clutched his hand to his chest. "You hit where it hurts."

They chuckled and returned to filling the bags. Whitney appreciated Jamie and was a little sad for him. She didn't know why the girl he liked left him, but she hoped the woman came to her senses and they reconciled.

She read the room, taking inventory of all the people. Maybe one of them would be a good match for Jamie.

Conrad tapped on Whitney's elbow. His eyes scanned the room. Every time they landed on a corner, they darkened like he was trying to form a play, but it wasn't working. He nudged his head toward the door. "Let's go talk in the conference room."

"Can I talk to my sister for a minute?" Thom hooked his elbow into Whitney's.

Whitney allowed herself to be led away. "I'll meet you in the conference room as soon as we're done."

Adrian cut them off in the middle of the room. The three of them huddled together. Adrian swung his arm around Whitney's shoulder. She imagined from his tone of voice that it was close to what he was like in a huddle. He shifted the direction of his face slightly. "I've talked to Jess and Rene. They'll message me to let me know when Conrad has signed out for the day."

He nodded at Thom. "Jasmine and Grace have sneaked away and are at the desk across the way, cutting the messages. If Conrad asks where they are, you tell him Grace complained about a backache, and Jasmine volunteered to take her home."

"Whitney, you got the hard job. Get him to go home and stay home." They all looked over their shoulders. Conrad sat on the table's edge with his arms across his chest. It was his pretending that he wasn't paying them any mind pose. They all knew about it, but none of them called him out. A couple of times, Adrian and Jamie bragged about dropping hints when he wouldn't listen to their advice directly.

All the bad feelings from earlier vanished, and Whitney was back on solid ground. She loved Conrad and had rehearsed telling him. The surprise would leave no room for doubt and open the door for her to tell him that she did it because she loved him. He'd say that he was blown away by his surprise.

Whitney's fantasy had gone as far as Conrad sharing that he was in love with her too but hadn't said anything because he was waiting for the perfect situation.

Whitney had been looking for ways for her friends to face love. This was the first time she'd done it for herself. An energy she couldn't control swirled around her. She was scared. Mostly, she was proud. She'd fight her fears of not being enough and hold onto her faith in love.

Chapter 43

Never Ever

Conrad had been working on the laptop for so long that the heat from the battery warmed his legs. A stack of papers with more highlights and tabs than ants at a picnic taunted him. He had a lot of reading to get done before his meeting in the morning. He pressed send. His nomination for the "Making A Difference Award" was submitted. In time, he'd know if he'd written a compelling story.

Whitney was the picture of focus as she huddled over her iPad in Conrad's family room. Her legs were curled beneath her, and her back was angled against the corner of the couch. Pieces of her hair floated above her hairline.

"There's a zucchini festival in Three Creeks the weekend after the run. We should go." She glanced up from her screen, her focus roaming the room, stopping on Conrad.

He'd joined her and Seth for lunch at the chiropractic office. They'd talked for a little while after their business meetings and made sure to check in on each other every night. Even though they never had enough time to do anything as a couple, she'd been so patient and supportive and available.

If there were one complaint Conrad would have about what

was growing between them, it would be that Whitney spent more time with Adrian and Jamie than with him. They were always posting pictures on social media about their group activities or joking back and forth in the comment streams.

When he posted anything on social media, she gave his posts a like or the occasional, ha-ha.

"Where are you seeing this?"

"I'm reading about it in the newspaper."

"On your tablet?" He ran his fingers along the documents in front of him. Conrad preferred print. You could touch it, circle it, and, as the colors that danced in front of his eyes proved, highlight important information.

She showed him the screen that was unreadable from across the room. "It's either that or being out of touch with what's happening in the community."

"Let me look at my calendar and see."

She said, "Okay."

Conrad heard the unspoken, "I knew that was going to be the answer, but I had to ask."

"If I can't make it, what will you do?"

The blue light from the screen reflected off her chest. "I'll ask my sister. If she says no, I'll ask Jasmine, Jamie, and Adrian. We'll make it a group activity."

"Or you could come hang out at the Sports Center."

"That's how I want to spend my free time. In a gym, watching athletes train, and women goggle at you."

She had a point.

Conrad glanced at her phone screen. Their friend group, minus him, was the image on the lock screen. Adrian was at the front, Whitney was to his right, and Jasmine was to his left. Jamie and Thom were behind him, with Grace between them. Their smiles were bright with accomplishment, and the proximity reflected years of companionship.

He was doing something and couldn't make it that day.

A notification of a text coming in from Adrian dropped down to the middle of Whitney's phone screen. "Will 8:00 tonight work?"

"What are you doing tonight?" Conrad asked the question out of curiosity. Making time for Whitney would have to be intentional. He could reschedule his morning meeting, giving him an hour to sleep in after what would most likely be a late-night game night with friends. Thinking about the break gave him a jolt of energy that he'd use to get through the paperwork faster.

"Just hanging out." She didn't look up from the screen. She didn't make eye contact. She didn't want to tell him. Something was up.

Whitney thought the accusation was playful until she saw the tightness in Conrad's jaw. "Are you talking to Adrian behind my back?"

His one big issue was lying. She had to tell him the truth without giving away that they had planned a little surprise for his birthday. It was hard coming up with something big enough to show that he had a lot of friends who thought the world of him without bringing attention to him. Conrad didn't like social media.

She took a gulp of air and dived into the conversation. Every word mattered. She had to tell the truth without giving away what his friends had conspired to do on his behalf. "Yes, but it isn't what your face says you think it is."

"Then what are you doing with Adrian behind my back?" His voice challenged her. She needed to come clean.

Her jaw already hurt from holding in the truth. He'd know what they were doing in the morning.

She just had to hold him off until morning.

Jasmine and Adrian said this might happen. Jasmine said, "Conrad can read you like a book. If he finds out, it will be from you."

He was going to be surprised. In the morning, he'd be all smiles, and they'd laugh when he thought about how hard he tried to get it out of her. She grimaced to express that not telling him was harder for her than for him. "I can't tell you."

"Can't or won't?"

His face was cool. Neither angry nor hopeful. She imagined it was what he looked like under the helmet on the football field. He looked at everything from every angle before reaching a conclusion.

That helped. She'd throw a little out there. Enough to say he could trust her, but not give away that their friends had joined together to give him the best birthday surprise. Because of the party planned on Saturday afternoon, he'd never expect them to decorate his office on Thursday.

Whitney stretched out the word "Both." Then, she closed the screen protector on her tablet. The conversation demanded her full attention. She set her feet on the floor, wiggling her toes on the cool hardwood. "Trust me. You'll find out why when the time is right."

"Now, Whitney. The right time is now."

She'd expected the insistence. Why had she left her phone on the countertop? The situation could have been avoided if she'd stored it in her purse. The plan was simple. She'd hang out with Conrad, taking him away from the office so Jess and Rene could get things ready for Adrian and Jasmine to bring the balloons, helium tank, precut curling ribbon, and roughly 200 birthday notes from friends around the world.

He would do some "quick reading" in the comfort of his home. She'd be there for moral support, and they would go out for a quick bite to eat. While she and Conrad were eating California tacos at Manuel's, the makeshift crew would inflate the balloons, attach the messages, and fill his office with birthday greetings. When he walked into the office, his staff would greet him with cupcakes she baked and stored at Jess's and yell, "Surprise."

"I'm sorry. There isn't much to tell." She worked across the parking lot from him. She held in the grin, knowing he'd run over to the chiropractic office, pull her into the break room, and say the same words. He'd say I'm sorry—for being a crank and hug and kiss her.

"Not as sorry as me." The muscle in his jaw ticked, and Whitney's stomach dropped. She imagined it was probably what the player that tried to go up against Conrad on the field experienced just before their bodies clashed.

He rubbed his eyes. "This isn't working. I wanted it to work. If you can't tell me what you're doing with Adrian, I will assume the worst." He shook his head. "I should have seen this coming. It would be best for everyone involved if we go back to the way it was."

The way it was? What did that mean?

Whitney was about to ask him when he said. "It's not like we're so deep into this that we can't take a step back without feelings getting trampled. Let's take a break. It's better if we work as friends."

It was the same line as the others before him. Whitney knew what came next. In three or four weeks, she'd bump into Conrad arm-in-arm with someone else.

They got along so well.

He couldn't mean it.

Especially after he found out they were talking to coordinate his birthday present.

This was where she had to focus on the finish line. The reconciliation. She tightened her hands into a fist and wiggled her fingers upon the release to rid her body of the tension.

This was not in the plan.

Going back to the way things were was not in the plan.

Going back to the way things were stomped on her feelings.

His immediate jump to going back to the way things were proved her initial concerns were right.

That the purpose of their relationship was to help his career. That guys like Conrad overlooked the value of women who were smart, and kind, and more times than not, gave more than they took.

She couldn't go back to the way things were because she was a different person. She was the fool who trusted love instead of her history.

Whitney had never wanted to be wrong more than she had at that moment.

She could step out of her lane. She could believe in love. She'd be safe. She wouldn't get trampled. That's what she wanted. That's what she was fighting for.

"Can we wait a couple of days and decide then? Maybe, after your birthday." She emphasized the word after.

There was the hint explaining why she and Adrian were talking. Without telling him, she'd told Conrad they were planning something for his birthday. She bit her lip and held her voice. Now that it was out there, he'd only need a couple of seconds— to decipher the reason for the text.

That would make it even sweeter. They were up to something but keeping the element of surprise. Then, when he saw it was a discreet surprise that wouldn't garner social media attention, he'd feel bad about his minor overreaction.

Still, the threat hurt. It meant what Samantha said was possible. There were options out there that Conrad had been considering. Whitney buffered the ache with an obvious truth. Samantha was just trying to get under her skin. Conrad wanted to be with Whitney. *Didn't he?*

"To give you time to get your stories to match. No. It's now or never." He stepped away from the counter. It was a sign that he was making room for her to leave. *He didn't.* Whitney's skin felt clammy.

This could not be happening.

How could he dismiss her that easily?

"Can we talk about this tomorrow?"

The steel in his eyes. The steady set of his jaw contradicted everything Whitney thought she knew about Conrad. It said that the man she loved probably never existed. It was all a ruse to gain her trust, and he'd intended to discard her after he got what he wanted.

The truth punched her in the gut.

It was all a game. Offense and defense were strategies meant to bring Conrad the win.

The biggest disappointment—Whitney's foolish heart hinged on hope. Hope that people changed. Hope that people learned from their mistakes.

In this case, her stupid heart had hoped that Conrad would appreciate what he had overlooked all those years ago. In doing so, he'd have proved her father wrong.

Whitney was disappointed in Conrad. She was disgusted with herself.

She'd been warned.

Her keys, hanging by a carabiner on the loop, jangled with the movement of Whitney's purse. It was her sign. She'd leave with dignity. There would be no awkward stumbles or having to return because she left the keys on the table.

Now, all she had to do was fight the growing lump in her throat. She'd waited for what seemed like a lifetime for him, and he couldn't wait one night.

Life sucked.

Whitney swallowed the rocks threatening to close off her vocal cords.

Her focus shifted to the flooring she didn't slip on, to the shoes she slid her feet into without losing her balance. She murmured, "At least this time, I know I tried."

Years of what-ifs had been answered. What if Whitney had a chance? She'd had her chance and learned that Conrad could throw her away like a pair of old socks. The ache was worse than the wondering.

Whitney grabbed her phone, making a large arc to avoid contact with Conrad, toward the doorway she walked through without bumping into the frame, to the crack in the sidewalk she skirted, and every little detail she used to avoid because her eyes always zoned in on Conrad.

She sat in the driver's seat of her car and ground out a promise. "Never again."

She would not let a man that close to her heart. Ever. Especially Conrad Hayes.

Chapter 44

Something Along the Lines of Uh-Oh

Whitney was gone. The silence of her absence deafened Conrad. It poked at his nerves. Each jab drove energy he couldn't contain through his muscles.

Whitney had come to his house so they could have more time together. After he finished some work, they planned to have dinner at Manuel's. The weekend was going to be busy and offered little opportunity for them to be just them. They had a party at his parent's house on Saturday, and Sunday was the practice drills with the managers of the different stations. He'd carved out this time to be with her.

A niggling tickled the back of his mind. His role on the committee freed up time for her. Time to do whatever she wanted with whomever she pleased.

Whitney. Sweet, faithful, giving more than she received, Whitney.

Was that it? He hadn't given enough, and she sought affection elsewhere.

"That was on her." Conrad argued with the empty room.

He'd told her from the beginning that he didn't have time. That he wanted to wait.

She pushed, and when he couldn't meet her needs, she looked elsewhere.

That had to be it.

But why with his brother?

Whitney knew Adrian was Conrad's Achilles tendon. He loved him like a brother—well, he was his brother. Even though he didn't mean it, Adrian was the sign that everything Conrad believed about life could be stripped bare in a matter of seconds.

Why would she entertain betraying him with Adrian?

The acid in Conrad's stomach challenged him. It was time to set some boundaries with Adrian. But he had to wait. Cool down. Both would have to give up Whitney. That was the only way it would work. If he didn't, Conrad would make both of them miserable.

He paced a circle around the kitchen island and sat down. He had work to do. Except, he'd read a page and didn't understand a word.

He had to get out of there to a place where the air was empty of the conflict. Conrad shoved the papers into a file, climbed into his car, and drove to the only safe place–his office. It would remind him of why he moved to Cottage Cove in the first place. He parked in the back and shoved the car keys in his pockets. With his luck, he'd lose them and have to call for help.

He saw the light under the door and ran his hands through his hair. *Can't anyone do anything right?* When the door opened, he saw lights. Lights in front of him and the mini-explosions going off in his head.

Could this day get any worse?

If he hadn't stopped at work, someone could have robbed him. What was wrong with people?

Even worse, the closing staff hadn't turned on the alarm. A

potential robber would have made a clean getaway. Conrad shut the door behind him, locked it, and ran the schedule through his mind. Who was scheduled to close?

Jess and Rene.

They were the most responsible among his staff.

Voices drifted through the open area, leading his attention beyond the gym equipment, behind the front desk computer, to the slightly ajar door of his office.

It wasn't secretive voices he'd expected. They were loud and boisterous. If Conrad didn't know any better, he'd have said it was Adrian and Jasmine. But that wasn't possible because Adrian was meeting Whitney at 8:00.

He glanced down at his watch, which was ten minutes ago. A drizzle of uh-oh sank into his stomach. He sensed the possibility of a call trying to explain that he was out of line would be in his near future.

In case it was foe, not friend, in his office, Conrad picked up a baseball bat from the equipment box in the corner. He edged along the wall, listening for hints of danger.

When he was ten feet away, he had a clear view of his office. Adrian was standing with scissors and ribbon.

Conrad dropped the bat and marched into his office. "What are you doing here?"

Adrian flexed and tightened his muscles like he was ready to pounce. Jasmine squealed. Jess and Rene were in the corner, frozen with paper strips in their hand. Strings hanging from the ceiling drew his gaze to see where they had come from. Every inch of the ceiling was covered with helium balloons.

The conversation with Whitney exploded with clarity. *Can I tell you in a couple of days?"*

His gut clenched with disgust and then melted into despair. She'd pleaded with him. Please *give me time to explain.*

He was responsible for the heartbreak in her voice when she said, "At least I tried."

Anger turned into electricity inside his body. He ran his hands through his hair fighting the urge to rip it out.

Jasmine's voice trembled with awareness. "Conrad, why aren't you with Whitney?"

The weight of Conrad's head was almost too much for his neck when he leaned back. He stretched his arms, and his biceps landed on his head.

If he could, he would have buried his face in his biceps. But they weren't big enough to hide what he had done. "Because I thought she was meeting Adrian."

He was in an office full of balloons with ribbons hanging within his reach. Most were anchored with folded sheets of paper.

A small stack of notes was on the edge of his desk.

"You saw my text and assumed that I was meeting with your girlfriend for a hookup?" Adrian looked like he wanted to strangle Conrad with the handful of ribbons he was holding.

Conrad couldn't blame him.

The text message. His gaze searched the area around him as though he'd see the disconnect. In light of his office being decorated, it made sense.

"Every time she wasn't with me, she was with you." Conrad had seen it. They were looking buddy-buddy at the ice cream shop. Her phone screen was a picture with Adrian in the center. How many times had they been together in "group gatherings"?

"Because she was trying to set us up." Jasmine snatched at the stack of papers on the desk. "Whitney has spent months trying to get us to see what was obvious to everyone else. And, she thought I was blind?" Jasmine shoved the slips of paper into Conrad's hands. "My job here is done."

Conrad had been so busy he forgot that the next day was his birthday. He dropped into a chair. Why had he been such a "my way or the highway" Neanderthal?

He had to get a hold of her.

He could fix this.

They'd talk, and everything would be fine.

Adrian waved the ribbon in the air and searched the area around him. "What do I do with these?"

"I can't answer that question and be a lady," Jasmine was at the door. She glared at Conrad. "The sun doesn't shine there."

Adrian threw the ribbons that landed on Conrad's chest and slid on the floor. "We rode in the same car."

They ran to the front door and pressed into it. The locked door resisted their attempt to exit. Their eye rolls, that almost looked synchronized, said, "We are stupid."

Then they scrambled to the door Conrad had entered. He heard the lock clicking shut.

Well, he was right about some things. The Sports Center staff was good about locking the door, and Adrian would choose a woman over him. He'd been wrong about which woman.

Rene and Jess were side-by-side, wearing variations of the same pained expressions. Jess cleared her throat. "I know it's a day early." She twisted her hand in a soft-hearted display of spirit fingers. "Surprise."

"Weeks of work and poof, it's ruined." Rene scowled and marched out of the office. Jess grimaced and followed behind her, leaving Conrad with a bright reminder of the consequences of his stupidity.

Chapter 45

List of Things I Should Have Known

Whitney walked and walked, and walked some more. She walked into the darkness that hid her. When the pain in her joints ached the loudest, she took a recovery break in the gazebo of Lilac Lane Park and used every logical reason why it wasn't appropriate for her to cry, temporarily damming the inevitable barrage of tears.

Her face was pressed into her hand, and her palms pressed into her eyelids. It was best to be safe than sorry.

"I have been looking for you all over the place." Jasmine's sandals slapped her heels after the three stomps up the gazebo steps. Her presence collided with Whitney as she took her place on the bench beside her.

Jasmine wrapped her arm around Whitney's upper back. "Do you have ways to get payback on your Pinterest board? If not, I have some ideas, but they're not as cute or creative."

"How did you know I was here?" Whitney straightened to face her best friend. She was supposed to be in Conrad's office tying birthday greetings to balloons.

Jasmine shrugged. "Lucky guess."

Jasmine's voice was too cheerful. Something had gone awry.

Whitney hadn't told anyone about the argument. She wanted to wait until she was level-headed and could say what happened in a clear, concise way that didn't cause drama. Jasmine's presence said that despite Whitney's best intentions, drama had taken place.

If she waited long enough, Jasmine would talk. She tucked her lips into her mouth and waited for Jasmine to spill the truth.

"Fine." She tapped her knee like it was a tripwire. The next thing Whitney knew, her best friend was pacing in front of her. "Adrian, Jess, Rene, and I were in the middle of hanging the balloons. We only had maybe ten to go, and guess who comes rushing in with a baseball bat."

Whitney was horrified. She didn't call her friends because she didn't want to disrupt their progress. But maybe she should have. "I should have warned you. Man, I'm just ruining everyone's lives." If this was the price of the pursuit of love, Whitney didn't need it.

"I can tell you have the wrong idea. Conrad thought we were burglars. He walked in on his surprise." Jasmine grew still.

Her calm was unsettling to Whitney. That meant more bad things were coming her way. She braced herself and waited.

"Then he told Adrian that he thought you two were cheating. I am so sorry, Whitney." She settled into the seat next to Whitney. "My joy brought you pain. I don't know what to say."

The pain in her chest pushed out the words. "Just tell me. Tell me how long it will take for me to ignore these feelings I have for him. Please, tell me how long it will take to forget that I just wanted to be with him. How long will it take for my heart to stop jumping when he walks into the room?"

Whitney sucked in a deep breath hoping the chilled air would cool the burning in her throat. "He didn't have to take me on trips or buy me presents or take me out. I was happy with the little bits of time we had together. But he never wanted me."

The tears trickled, and she swiped them away like they were mosquitoes. But like the little pest that nibbled away, leaving discomfort as payment, the tears refused to go away. "He was only being kind because I was helping him."

She pleaded. "Tell me how long I'm going to have to carry this until I stop feeling stupid for believing him."

"I don't know, honey." Jasmine rubbed her back. "I don't know. But can I ask a question?"

"Sure." Whitney sniffled.

"When was the last time you were in love with someone?"

Whitney felt her forehead wrinkle in confusion. Her lungs accepted a full breath. Her throat was jagged but hurt less, like some of the pain had been shaved away. "What does that mean?"

"That means I've known you since before we had to wear training bras. This is the first time since high school you've been in love and believed someone could love you back."

"And I'm not good at it."

"You were great. You glowed. You accepted our compliments." She nudged Whitney's shoulder. "You picked up a little sass. I'm proud of you." Jasmine stretched her arm around Whitney's shoulder and tightened her grip into a side hug. The reassurance lulled Whitney to a place where the sharp corners of her ache lost their power to slice her tender heart. This also was the first time she'd cried over a breakup. In the past, she'd merely accepted that she wasn't worthy of love. With Conrad, it was different. He'd never said he loved her, but he had taught her to love herself. And that was why she gave herself permission to love him.

"You, my friend. This was the bravest thing you had ever done for yourself. I'm sorry things worked out the way they did, but I'm proud of you."

A voice broke through the darkness. "We are too."

Jasmine jumped into a pose with her hands angled outward. A beam of light cut through the entrance to the gazebo. Whitney held her hands in front of her face to shield herself from the blinding effect. Jasmine squinted and tilted her head to slide out of the path of the light.

"What are you going to do? Go all Charlie's Angels on me." The light slid down to Jasmine's feet. "In those strappy sandals, no less."

Whitney had heard enough to know the voice. "Mom, what are you doing here?"

"Conrad stopped by the house looking for you. He said you had a miscommunication. That is man code for I messed up. We called Thom, who guessed you'd be here. And here we are."

They heard a click, and a light starting in the middle of the gazebo filled the space.

"How did you do that?" Jasmine's gaze wandered the area.

Ericka pointed at the electric plate that was just inside the arched entrance. "The light switch."

Whitney sighed. It was just another thing to add to the list of things she should have known.

Whitney fought with the lock to the front door of her house. Her head vibrated with pain. It was nothing that a couple of Tylenol and ten years of sleep couldn't cure.

Her nerves were too wound for sleep. Her grandmother used to say the home shopping network had cathartic properties. Whitney waited for a sign that it was a bad idea. The still night air didn't present any objections. She plopped on her couch and picked up the remote. "It couldn't hurt."

A lady with perfectly styled hair and jewelry she probably found in the network's costume room gushed. "We had this tiramisu cheesecake at a bridal shower. Our only regret was not buying two."

The cool floor sent waves of awareness through Whitney's feet. She flexed them, tipping her toes to lean forward. For five easy payments of fifteen dollars, she could have the cheesecake delivered to her house within a week. That would definitely fix her headache. If not, she'd freeze it and save it for an emergency.

A soft tap on the front door saved her from making the call. She wrapped her fuzzy blanket like a shawl and padded her way to answer the door. The door cracked open, and she peeked through the small space.

Ericka's whisper sounded more like a hiss. "You didn't look through the peephole or check the window. For all you know, I could be a serial killer."

"I knew it was you." Whitney lied.

"How? I covered the peephole with my finger."

"That's how." Whitney opened the door wider to let her sister in. "You're the only one who does that."

Inside the house, Ericka's gaze wandered around the room, stopping when she got back to Whitney. "I thought you might need some company."

"I'm doing okay," Whitney shut the door and shuffled back to the couch. The cheesecakes were gone, and they were hawking brownies. "I was about to buy a cheesecake. But my window of opportunity closed." She frowned. "That seems to be a common theme in my life lately."

"Yep, you shouldn't be alone."

"I'm fine." Whitney wrapped herself a little tighter in the blanket.

"You were about to buy baked goods from a telemarketer. I am here to tell you you're not okay, Whit." She plopped on the couch next to Whitney. "And that's a good thing."

Whitney craned her neck, pulling back from her sister.

"Really. It means you opened yourself to love. Sometimes. More times than most people will ever admit, we get hurt." Ericka said.

"Then why bother?" If Whitney wasn't in such a mood, she should be horrified at how much she sounded like Ivan, but she was doing a much better job than him at sounding like the professional cynic.

"Because, one time, we'll find something special like Mom and Dad, or Thom and Grace." Ericka settled on the couch. "But we'll never find it if we don't try."

"Says the woman who attends weddings as my plus one." Despite her bitterness, Whitney knew Ericka was right. She just wished her sister would follow her own advice.

Ericka shifted her weight and pulled her foot beneath her leg. "Says the woman who is here to tell you that you were right."

"About?" Whitney said a lot of things to her sister. Most of the time, because of her youngest sister status, the wisdom was ignored. Her curiosity was sincere.

Ericka couldn't help smiling. Her face flushed with color. "Dustin. We've been on a couple of dates. He's a nice guy. I could see things between us going somewhere."

Whitney felt her mood shift with something similar to hope. Things hadn't worked out for her, but it could for her sister. "Is that why I haven't seen much of you lately?"

"Yeah, I'm sorry about that." Ericka connected her gaze with Whitney's, amplifying the remorse.

In light of her fiasco, Whitney found it easy to forgive her sister. "Why didn't you say anything?" She asked, hoping Ericka didn't give an excuse like Conrad's "going public opens the relationship to drama" baloney.

"We wanted to grow organically. You know, without outside interference. Once we were comfortable with each other, we planned on going public." Ericka's answer consoled Whitney while adding a nail to the coffin of her relationship with Conrad. Dustin was a retired football player, and his only qualms were nurturing the relationship with Ericka so they could withstand the obstacles.

It was odd. Talking with Ericka about her love life made Whitney feel better. It didn't eliminate the pain. It shifted her focus, turning the heartbreak into annoying background noise. Her heart wasn't invested in the conversation. If it were, Whitney would have pointed out that outside interference, via her, helped Ericka and Dustin connect.

She suspected a lot of her days would be going through the motions. Making sure she said the right thing at the appropriate time.

"How long do you stay mad?" Ericka threw a glance toward the door.

"Why?" Whitney pushed into the back of the couch, using the firmness to steady herself. She'd hidden her phone in her nightstand. If she didn't see the calls or texts, or worse, the absence of them, she'd settle down, find her groove, and get back to normal.

Tap, tap, tap. The sisters looked at each other. Ericka's eyes were supportive. Whitney's searching for what to say or do.

"Call me tomorrow." Ericka skittered off the couch. "We'll plan something for this weekend." She opened the door. Her voice was lower than a murmur. Whitney couldn't hear what Ericka said, just the tone—apologetic and supportive.

It had only been a couple of hours, but Conrad had changed to how Whitney saw him that first day at Jamie's birthday party. They were on opposite sides. He was on the front stoop, and she was standing in front of the door. He was larger than life. Whitney's body prickled, sensing his attention.

"About what happened earlier." He glanced over his

shoulder like the past was standing behind him. "I may have overreacted."

Her father had always taught Whitney to listen, and she hadn't. From the beginning, Conrad admitted he was too busy to be in a relationship. He told her that he didn't have time for love. She had challenged him.

"You were working with the information you had." Whitney closed the door behind her. She had a blanket thrown over her shoulder to protect her from the chill in the air, but it also served as a shield. She leaned against the door frame.

"I'm sorry your surprise was ruined." That was all she had to offer him. She tried to make him happy and, in doing so, dug a wedge in the fragile line in their picture of happiness. Her resolve to do something special for him pried at the vulnerability. She'd pushed until it shattered into shards.

"Are things going to be okay between us?"

That was all he had? Are things going to be okay? Of course, they'd be okay. Whitney was always the one who took the high road. She thrived in working in the background, garnering as little attention as possible. Her shoulder tipped up and dropped. "It'll be awkward for a while, but it isn't anything that will get in the way of your progress."

"That's not what I'm asking, Whit." He motioned to move forward and withdrew into his space. "I don't know what to do to fix this."

"It'll be hard at first. But you'll move on, and you'll find someone better. She'll be more suited to your lifestyle."

"But that's you." He motioned to step forward and stopped when Whitney held up her hand.

"If it were me, it wouldn't have been so easy for you to dismiss me." All the advice her mother had given her rushed to the front of her mind. At the front was, "Take the chance at love. You'll be better for it." And Whitney was. She believed she was worthy of love. She believed she deserved to be treated like she was an equal. Most important, she deserved a guy who would be proud of being seen with her. She had Conrad to thank for the shift in her thinking. He was the one who had opened her eyes to all of it.

He rubbed his jaw, relaying his discomfort with being so wrong. "I'm used to changing the plays. Not the team members."

The steadiness returned to Whitney's voice. "This isn't football. I'm not some guy that gets knocked on his behind and recovers with a hand up and a slap on the behind."

"I never said—"

Whitney cut him off with an eyebrow raise and a stern glare. She'd use his language to help him understand. "You called the play. Now we see it to completion."

"I know what we have is worth fighting for. I'll prove it." He pivoted on his heel and slowly descended the stairs. On the landing of the third step, he turned his head over his shoulder. "This isn't the end of us, Whitney."

It would have been too hard to watch him drive away. Whitney backed into her door, and eased it shut. It would take some time, but Conrad would figure it out. Guys like him didn't belong with women like her.

Chapter 46

Fishing for Reconciliation

Conrad directed his attention to the speakers in the far corners of the room, the appointment book on the front desk, the handle on the front door–any place but the window that gave him a direct view of the empty space in the parking lot.

The space that was devoid of Whitney's car.

The space that poked at his insides and stirred the feelings that made him ask questions that lacked answers. Questions like where was Whitney parking her car? When would she go out the front door for a lunch run? And did the inclination to call him strike her as much as it had him?

He was so buried in his attempts to distract himself with his to-do list, he didn't notice that his father had entered the Sports Center until Austin Hayes stood in front of Conrad wearing a look of expectation.

His father wore his signature blue cap with USA embroidered on the front. A thin fabric hoodie covered most of his black t-shirt. The look was familiar to a different setting. "I stopped by to check out your place." He scanned the area around them. "You've done well."

It shouldn't have mattered to Conrad that his father approved. But it did. A welling of pride brightened his disposition. Not enough to erase the animosity Conrad used as a shield. His father had deceived him. Still, he was his father, and he deserved Conrad's respect. "Thanks. What brings you around?"

"You." Austin leaned his elbow on Rene's desk. "I wanted to see if you had time to go fishing with your old man. It'll be a father kidnapping his son on his birthday day."

Conrad had to hand it to his father. He knew how to play his cards. Presenting the invitation in front of people forced Conrad to consider the suggestion. He tipped his head toward the appointment book. "I'd love to, but my schedule is full."

Austin's face remained firm. His eyes held a gentle persistence. It had been years since Conrad had seen the expression. It said that no matter how hard he wrangled, Conrad wasn't escaping the situation. "I called. Your assistant said your schedule for today is free. She said something about you canceling meetings."

A soft exhalation danced over the groan lurking below Conrad's vocal cords. That's why Stephanie had run off.

When they were closer, Austin took Conrad and his brother on weekly fishing trips. Time sat still, and their problems didn't seem as large when they sat in that old canoe. It was as though the fishing lines bore the weight of their troubles.

It was their monthly routine. Out in that little boat or over a hole cut into the ice, Dad listened, and Conrad and his brother talked. A longing struck Conrad. He missed the simpler times. But that was beside the point.

"Why now?"

"So you don't repeat my mistake."

"Go. Please." Jess waved her hand in a shooing motion. She tilted her head to clarify that she was talking to Austin. "He's been a bear that needs to go into hibernation but refuses to enter the cave."

Stephanie circled from around the corner and took her place by Jess's side. Her one-tip nod added to her accusatory tone. "He ate all my caramel corn."

"I asked first," Conrad had to defend himself. He wasn't as grumpy as they were trying to make him seem.

His father crossed his arms in front of him and parted his legs like he was talking with the guys on the sideline of a game. "He stress eats."

"And he does that thing where he half closes one eye and frowns." Stephanie shuddered.

Why is she exaggerating? Conrad frowned and as quickly recovered before they used his expression to validate their arguments.

Jess nodded in agreement with Stephanie. "It is the worst pirate captain impersonation."

It was time to put an end to the mutiny. Conrad growled, "I can hear what you're saying. I'm right in front of you."

Jess said, "Then, you can hear our vote. Who thinks Conrad should take the afternoon off and go fishing with his father."

Hands went up. The guy on the leg lift machine paused at the standing position and lifted a finger to say I agree.

Conrad thought he would burst under the pressure of the aggravation. He shook his head, admitting defeat. He'd surrender to their wishes and go fishing, but not without protest. "We will talk about this when I get back."

"Gladly," Stephanie and Jess spoke in unison.

He threw a glance toward the chiropractic office. Had Whitney seen his father's pickup with the boat perched on the roof? The sun reflected off the glass, making it hard to tell who was in the front office.

At this point, there was no point in masking his feelings. Better yet, he had failed.

Everyone saw what Conrad wasn't willing to admit. Conrad wanted to talk to Whitney.

If he could talk to her, she'd sense the bottomless pit of sorrow that grew deeper by the hour. Then she'd give him the chance he didn't deserve, but he wanted so badly it was consuming him.

He wanted Whitney in his life.

He wanted to make her laugh, to see that curve at the corner of her lip when she considered something he said, to be the man that reminded her she didn't have to work so hard to be loved. At the time, he didn't know it, but Conrad fell in love with Whitney Stansfield when she tripped over the lawn chair at Jamie's birthday party.

Except, beyond pleasantries, she refused to talk to him. When she did, she was measured, speaking with a grace that pained both of them.

Conrad stiffened, stalling the feelings that threatened to overwhelm him. He climbed into the passenger side and closed the door behind him.

It was his father's pickup, but it was obvious Claire's hand had touched the vehicle. There were little coasters in the cup handles, and a monogrammed organizer hung off the back of the driver's seat. Seeing his father's car and how much his mother doted on him, Conrad asked himself. How had they made it this far?

He mined through memories for hints. Austin had always been supportive of Conrad. He'd work alongside Claire at the weekly football spaghetti dinners, doling out plates of noodles and joking with the guys. Once after a game, he walked in on them kissing in the kitchen. His dad always had charisma. Is that why he cheated on Claire? Is that how he learned to distort the truth?

He had ruined Conrad.

The buildings lining the side of the highway thinned, leaving the occasional sign to guide drivers. Trees aged over time, and surviving extreme weather, filled the gaps. They were fifteen minutes away from the dock.

"Go ahead. Ask." Austin's voice encouraged.

Self-righteous anger tethered Conrad's words to his vocal cords. He shook his head. He spat out, "How?"

That was all Conrad needed. The one word triggered the surge. *How could he have cheated?*

How could he live two lives?

Did he and Kevin have any other siblings?

The biggest one. Would he have said anything if circumstances hadn't demanded the truth be told?

Only one word passed through the rapid fire. "Why?" *Why did he let Conrad go through life believing the lie?*

The scent of pine drifted in with the breeze coming in the open window. "The answer to the first question is more complicated. I'll start with why."

The air in the cab stilled. It was as if nature knew a bomb was about to be dropped, and she prepared herself for the repercussions.

He said, "Your mother. I mean Claire,"

Conrad interrupted to correct his father. He was right the first time. "My mother."

He swallowed hard and tipped his head. "Right. Your mother worried you'd reject her once you knew the truth."

"This wasn't her fault." Conrad wasn't about to let his mother carry the blame for his father's sins.

"I never said it was. I told you why. I didn't say it was right. I didn't say it was the best option. I didn't say it was your mother's fault. I'm trying to say that we didn't want things to change."

His father shifted into his motivational speaker voice. It was the one he'd used before he let Conrad out of the car, releasing him to the locker room. He'd tell Conrad that, win or lose, he was proud of him. "You never doubted we loved you and would be there for you. That was all that mattered. How our family came together didn't matter."

Until Conrad almost died. And then it mattered.

Conrad had one family member with a blood type that matched his. The friend he always loved like a brother–because he was. Adrian.

Then, the truth mattered. The truth brought a trifecta of companions–questions, trust issues, and the stiff arm. The stiff arm Conrad used to push people away. But that wasn't as bad as the trust issues disguised within his questions. Were people telling him the truth or what he wanted to hear?

Except, Whitney told him the truth, and he stiff-armed her. Conrad wanted to slam his fist into the dashboard. To blame his father. However, this time, it wasn't his parent's fault.

And he was getting a taste of what he'd inflicted—being on the receiving end of forced distance hurt worse than being at the bottom of the tackle pile.

"We'll get through this, Conrad. I don't know when or how long it will take. Good times or bad. We will always be a family."

Kevin said as much. Claire never changed. Sitting in the pickup with his father, Conrad saw the quiet determination. The distance Conrad used to protect had turned into a poison pill.

Conrad swallowed his pride. It was the least deadly. "For

the sake of our family, I hope we catch some fish because I do not like anchovy pizza."

If Conrad wasn't paying attention, he'd have missed it. The gleam in the corner of his dad's eyes. It almost looked like a tear.

———

Conrad's father had come prepared. He gave Conrad a sharp assessing glare that dared him to attempt fishing in his polo shirt embroidered with the Sports Center logo and two hundred dollar cross trainers. "I have an extra pair of shorts and an old t-shirt you might want to borrow."

Just as Conrad glanced down at the shoes he was dreading ruining, his dad said, "Your mom packed a pair of water shoes for you."

Ah, his mother was in on the olive branch. Conrad should have known. His father passed the bag, releasing it when Conrad had a firm grip on the handle. "We talked. When you and Kevin were younger, I took you on these trips to get us in the habit of talking. Now that you're back home, we need to bring it back. It won't be so awkward." He turned around and circled back. "And I miss this."

Conrad dropped the bag by the rear tire of the pickup and got into position to help his father loosen the boat from the trailer. He easily fell into the routine of loosening the straps, folding them, and securing them in a bag his father stored in the back of the boat.

"You want to direct traffic or drive the boat into the water?"

Conrad rubbed his jaw to soften his laugh. "Direct traffic." He'd use the signals to tell his father which direction to turn. The only one Austin ever paid attention to was stop, and that was after he'd accidentally driven the pickup into the lake.

They'd depended on the kindness of a stranger to help tow it out.

His father had always been the kind of guy who did things his way. At least he made an effort to show that he wanted to hear what Conrad or his brother had to say. Austin Hayes's problem was listening. Once he knew the answer, he tuned everything out.

Conrad wagged his pointer finger to the right. The tires groaned with the shift in direction, and Austin drove backward with the boat aimed in the direction Conrad had told him to go.

His father called out. "Don't look so surprised. I'm not too old to learn."

Claire had said on more than one occasion that the rift had changed Austin. Conrad had seen it in subtle ways. His father asked more questions. At the time, Conrad interpreted it as manipulation to make him talk.

Now, he second-guessed himself.

Maybe, Claire was right. His father had changed and cared about what Conrad and Kevin thought.

The boat floated in the water, waiting for Conrad and his father. Conrad parked the car while his father waited for him alongside the dock. Midway through the parking lot, Conrad noticed the absence of the wall. It had been gone for some time. The last time he remembered feeling it was at the Sports Center.

His mind was silent, too.

The narrative was gone.

He wasn't telling himself to watch out for deception.

It was almost as if he trusted his father again. While it was freeing, the sensation was also unsettling, like he was on the water and could slip beneath the surface at any moment.

While he changed his clothes behind the open pickup doors

he used as protection, Conrad considered his stance. He had a choice. Be on guard, yet friendly, or give his father a chance.

Conrad's lungs filled, and his diaphragm expanded. If he wanted a chance, it was only fair he extended the courtesy to the man he may have unfairly blamed for all his character flaws.

Chapter 47

I Had Cupcakes

Jasmine and Adrian's bickering bled through the open screen door. "You didn't die."

"Years of my life are somewhere out there." Adrian pointed toward the road leading up to the house.

Their bickering validated what they'd admitted in the conference room amid the balloons and ribbons. They were a couple. Conrad's companions, amusement, angst, and awareness, were with him when he greeted them at the door. If he'd taken a minute to read the signs, his life would be on the same trajectory.

Adrian shook Conrad's hand. "Happy Birthday, Bro." He pointed with his thumb at Jasmine, "This one's feisty today."

His gaze scanned the room. Conrad guessed what he was looking for. He'd been doing the same thing. "She's not here."

"I'm sorry." Jasmine hugged Conrad, "She'll come around."

Would it be today? According to Thom, Whitney had never been one to hold onto anger.

With the chance of Whitney's forgiveness in mind, Conrad grabbed at every opportunity to slip away. He'd meander to the kitchen island and watch the front door, hoping Whitney would emerge from the other side.

It wasn't too far a reach. When he was in the kitchen at Jamie's birthday party, she showed up on the doorstep with Jasmine. And that pink box filled with cupcakes.

Every time, his mother appeared at his side and waved him away with the back of her hands facing up, like he was an intrusion in the kitchen. "It's your birthday. Go have some fun."

He'd have a valid excuse every time. He needed to refill a drink, fetch some napkins, or help refill a snack bowl. The last time she hugged him and whispered in his ear. "Give it time. She'll come around."

Time clawed at Conrad. Each scratch tattooed remorse deeper. He was going to have to do something. But what?

So far, his only answer had been to wait by the door. But what if she'd moved on?

Jamie dug into his slice of the strawberry-marbled sheet cake and shoveled the forkful of dessert into his mouth. Each rotation of his jaw taunted Conrad. He took a swig of tea and swallowed. "Whitney baked cupcakes for my birthday."

Conrad worried his father's youthful indiscretions would hamper his reputation. He'd never been so wrong. Assuming the worst about Whitney was an infinite degree worse. Since he'd been gone, every male within a twenty-mile radius had deemed themselves her protector, and Conrad's mess up was the perfect opportunity to assert their intention.

Seth called Conrad under the guise of birthday felicitation. "I know I'm supposed to say sorry about what happened between the two of you. But these cupcakes are worth waiting to give my condolences. Thanks, and Happy Birthday."

For the record, Seth didn't sound the least bit sorry.

Conrad was over his birthday. He was over being the bad guy. He was definitely over his friends acting like he was the only one who had ever messed up with a woman. At least Jamie had given Conrad something to work with. "Yet you had another woman sleep in your bed that night."

Jamie wretched until he surrendered to the coughing fit.

Conrad's response had hit the target. "Look, here's a man choking on his consequences."

Jamie croaked, "Because my sister would have killed me if it was Whitney."

"Wait. What?"

Jamie swallowed a large gulp of his drink. He cleared his throat. "She deserves better than you."

"You?"

"According to my sister, no."

"Ouch." The back of Conrad's neck pricked, and he glanced around to find the source. Jasmine was on the other side of the room. Could she sense that her brother was talking about Whitney?

Apparently, Jamie seemed indifferent. Conrad squirmed. Medusa could have taken some lessons from Jasmine on how to glare—or was it the other way around? Had the OG man-killer taught Jasmine? Adrian approached her with a drink. Just as quickly, her eyes softened, and the air around her almost shimmered. He turned back to his conversation with Jamie. "If it makes you feel any better, Jasmine feels the same way about me."

"Let's play some darts." Jamie didn't wait for an answer. He strolled to the garage like his request was a given. Conrad admired and resented his friend's confidence. What if he didn't want to play darts? Jamie just assumed.

It didn't stop there. He handed Conrad the blue and silver-streaked darts, keeping the red and black for himself. "What if I wanted that color?"

"Oh, no problem. I figured because blue is your favorite color."

"How did you know that?"

Jamie waved at Conrad's blue shirt. "Everything is blue, your pickup, the paint in the Sports Center. I bet your underwear is blue, too."

Conrad's head dropped, but he stopped short of pulling out his waistband to check. A tinge of sadness washed over him. "Am I that predictable?"

"Not on the football field, and that was what mattered." Jamie took his place behind the line. "What do you miss the most?"

"About?"

"Keep up. Whitney. What do you miss most about her?"

"She sings all the time." A soft smile stroked Conrad's lip. "One time, she was making stir fry and listening to an 80's playlist. The song 'It Takes Two' starts playing. She's singing. Some of it was on key. Most of it was off." A chuckle rose in his chest, sounding more like a soft cough. "Then she took the towel and started waving that thing like she was at a rock concert. Her braid was whipping around."

Jamie interrupted. "And you started dancing with her?"

"No."

"You didn't twerk?" Jamie threw his hands in the air the way a coach would when a player missed an easy play.

The disappointment in Jamie's voice pressed against the spot in Conrad's heart. He shook his head. Nothing was better than confessing what he had done. Conrad stood in front of the line and aimed his dart. It landed on the twenty-point spot, barely missing the bulls-eye.

"You pretended like it didn't happen." Jamie said it like he was a sports commentator.

Conrad scowled. "I'm not that bad. I asked if she added chili peppers to the stir fry, and said she was spicy."

She laughed.

He missed the laugh.

"Whitney has had a thing for you for as long as I can remember. Like before either of us had chest hair. And you thought Adrian would come between you?" Jamie gestured with his dart toward Jasmine and Adrian, who were one step away from removing their clothing with their eyes. "Okay, I can see where you may have been led astray."

He yelled, "Mess with my sister, and you mess with me."

Adrian backed away, but his eyes remained zoned in on Jasmine.

It seemed to be enough to satisfy Jamie. "Seriously though, why? What led you to the illogical conclusion that your girlfriend was sneaking behind your back with your best friend?"

"Have you seen his social media?" Conrad nudged his chin toward Adrian and Jasmine, who were taking a selfie with cake. "I couldn't have been the only one. "There are pictures of them together all over the internet."

"Look here, kids." Jamie curled his lip into a sarcastic half-grin. "A man hung himself with his own stupidity. Did it ever occur to you to do the same?"

This Conrad could work with. He said, "Whitney is a private person."

Jamie retrieved his phone from his pocket and slid through some screens. He held the phone up for Conrad to see a picture of Whitney, Ericka, and Ivan huddled close together with a lake behind them.

Conrad read the caption. "They're kayaking?"

Jamie scrolled through the screen. It was full of images of Whitney with her friends and family. Jamie, Adrian, and even Seth were in a couple of them. "Rumor has it you said you didn't want pictures of you two together. You asked for privacy. Then you turned around and penalized the person for following through with your ridiculous demands."

Jealousy sliced through Conrad, leaving a residue of anger in its wake. She was kayaking and smiling and having fun—without him. He would not let this get the best of him. He shrugged. "Cupcakes are overrated."

Jami shook his head in disgust. "Your pride is overrated."

Chapter 48

Race Day

Sleep taunted Whitney. It was close enough for her to want it but just out of reach. Then the moment she succumbed to the peace of slumber, her alarm signaled it was time for her to get ready for the day.

Whitney grumbled her negotiation with the universe to turn back the clock to give her more time. The universe used the sleep alarm as a response. *Get out of bed and get going.*

So she did. In the shower, she gave herself the best pep talk she could muster with the little sleep she'd tasted. The adrenaline from the excitement of the fun run would sustain her. Then she could fall into bed for a long, hard sleep session.

It worked. She was out the door by four a.m. with her travel mug filled with coffee sweetened with her favorite creamer.

The dose of dread over seeing Conrad most likely added to her wakefulness. Every time the inclination to hesitate or, even worse, give Conrad a piece of her mind, Whitney rehearsed how she'd act.

Paste on a smile.

And, if the urge to contradict Conrad gets too strong, refer to the first line of action. Grit your teeth and smile.

She rehearsed the plan on the drive to the run, stopping when she pulled up to the entrance of the parking lot. An older gentleman, the kind who looked like he only needed the energy of those around him to function, greeted her at the entrance of the VIP parking. "Can I get your name, ma'am?"

He held up the clipboard, making a show of his commitment to the task assigned him.

"Whitney Stansfield."

"Say no more. It's an honor to finally meet you. He tucked the clipboard under his arm, and a smile brightened his already pleasant-looking face. "My name's Roger, by the way."

"Nice to meet you, Roger." The familiarity Roger used unsettled Whitney. Conrad had been the face of the run, and she'd worked behind the scenes.

Unless—Whitney threw out her guess as to how he knew her. "Are you friends with Mark and Darcy?" Maybe he had been on one of their walks, and Whitney was distracted by the other walkers?

"Nah, I'm a friend of the Hayes family. Conrad thinks the world of you. You were all he talked about the last time we had dinner." Roger winked. "Now I know why." Then he stepped away, pointing at a space at the front of the lot. "Don't let me keep you. Your space is labeled."

Roger's statement seemed a little odd. The same Conrad, who didn't want a picture with her on social media, always talked about her?

The contradiction irked Whitney. Then she looked at the flagged chording around the park and decided the conversation had something to do with the fun run.

Whitney thanked Roger and parked where he told her. In the time it took for her to turn off the car and open the door, a girl in her early twenties waited at her bumper, greeting her with a wave. Like Roger, she had a clipboard and wore a royal blue volunteer t-shirt. Whitney straightened her t-shirt and met her where she was waiting. "Am I late?"

"You're just in time. Conrad wanted us to ensure you didn't get lost in the crowd." Whitney glanced around at the near-empty parking lot.

The sun had peeked over the horizon line, and the air was heavy with moisture from the dew on the grass. Music from what she assumed was the volunteer tent blended with the sounds of the birds. In the next hour, it would be a different scene. People of all shapes and sizes, amped by the activities, would be milling around.

"We're going over station assignments. I'm with you at the starting line. By the way, my name is Judy."

"Excuse me?" Whitney shook the cobwebs out of her head to hear more clearly.

Judy's sympathetic grin said she was as awkward as Whitney. "I know. It's early. I think Mark squinted the whole way to the tent."

Whitney knew she wouldn't need the plan. Mark and Darcy would be enough of a buffer for her to keep her composure, and unlike her traitorous, well-meaning brother, Mark would speak up for her instead of telling Conrad how to win Whitney over. Things just got better. It came out in her voice. "They're here?"

"Sure are. I'll take you to them." On the way to the tent, Judy diverted their flow several times to introduce Whitney to small clusters of people wearing either the blue volunteer shirts or the green water station volunteer shirts. It was Conrad's idea that they have different shirts for different tasks at the fun run.

At the time, Whitney thought it was something people would use to establish a pecking order. She'd always been at the bottom, so she wasn't keen on the idea. After seeing the number of volunteers, she understood the logic. It wouldn't be like shopping at Target, where people instinctively asked people with red shirts for help.

Whitney repeated people's names to help herself remember who they were. They all seemed to know who she was and were excited about their volunteer station.

The attention, like a strong gust of wind on dust bunnies hidden under the bed, blew away all the bravado Whitney built in those sleepless hours, leaving her with an uneasy feeling that swirled around her stomach.

She was supposed to be anonymous.

She had stayed in her lane.

She had relegated all the credit for the fun run to Conrad, and like they had done when they were younger, she worked behind the scenes.

People Judy hadn't introduced to Whitney waved. Some she recognized from runs in the years past, but most she hadn't ever seen. A mile from where they'd met, Judy led Whitney up the stairs into an open-air tent elevated with scaffolding.

Chairs with water bottles on the seats lined the back of the tent. Conrad, Seth, and Adrian stood in a semi-circle. They wore light gray fun run polo shirts embroidered with the logo Conrad had his public relations firm design. Mark, Darcy, Thom, and Grace stood across from them. Whitney looked down at her shirt. She wore the same swag bag t-shirt that all the runners would have received.

The metal riser creaked. Conrad's posture said he was focused on the conversation taking place. His gaze drifted toward Whitney and landed like a piece of metal to a magnet. She set her hand on her chest to soften the power of the pull. She saw remorse flicker across his eyes. His jaw hardened, and he returned his gaze to the group. That's how it was with Conrad. Appearances mattered. As quickly as he could want her, he could forget her.

Her heartbeat scolded her with each tap against her ribcage. She had not adequately prepared herself for this, but she'd do her best. The chatter through the walkie-talkie came in one clear voice. "We need an assist. The speakers at the second-mile refreshment station just cut out."

Judy spoke into the microphone. "I'm on it." Then she called out to the small group, "Mind if I take your golf cart?"

"Yeah, sure." Adrian waved her away with a friendly smile. His eyes connected with Whitney's. His brows waved slightly as if to say, "It's game day."

She glanced behind him to the starting line. As far as the eye could see, people were milling in the middle of Main Street. By the time the race started, the line would be at least three blocks long.

A bright humility melted the dregs of resentment. Conrad and his team had done much more than Whitney could have ever imagined. Sure, he was a pretentious piece of work, but he was an effective one.

The circle widened, making room for Whitney to join the conversation. "You want to go through the routine, or are you good?" Conrad asked.

"I'm good." Whitney had read through the itinerary so many times that she could recite it down to the minute by memory. Conrad would greet the crowd. He'd introduce Mark and Darcy and Thom and Grace. Just before the starting siren sounded, she'd go to the front of the line closest to the sidewalk, where her brothers would accompany her. Mark and Darcy would go into the pace car for the runners. Thom and Grace would talk with Conrad, Adrian, and Seth would call out the time and congratulate the runners as they crossed the finish line.

Darcy waved at Ruby and Pauline on the sidewalk in front of the Morning Grind. "Can we go talk with people until the race starts?"

"Sure, we'll have a countdown, so you'll know how much time you have to get back."

"Great." Mark ushered Darcy to the stairs. Whitney followed behind them.

"Ah, Whit," Thom called after her before she could touch the railing. "Do you mind hanging out with Grace for a minute? I need to go talk to Dad."

Grace threw an apologetic smile. That meant one thing. This was a setup, and she was the decoy. It couldn't be worse than what she'd endured the past week. There were a lot of meetings, and she was pretty sure the issues in a couple of them could have been resolved with a quick email. Whitney said, "Sure. We can catch up." Since they had just spoken yesterday, there wasn't much for Whitney and Grace to catch up on. But it saved face.

The chairs seemed like just as good a place as any to wait, so they wandered in that direction.

Thom looked back, "Whit."

"Yeah." She expected Thom to ask if she wanted a sports drink or if she wanted him to bring back a snack.

He glanced at the crowd that had doubled since the sun had cast yellow and gold lines across the horizon line. "I'm glad I didn't trade you for Rusty Walker's G.I. Joe in third grade."

"What?" She couldn't believe her ears. Rusty Walker was a scrawny kid who followed Thom and Ivan like a puppy. He'd hinted at wanting a sibling. "My mom says I'm enough kid for her and my dad."

Tom tipped his head like he was reading the memory. "Yeah, you'd made me mad, and I asked Mom why she brought you home. Right in front of Mom, he asked if he could trade all of his G.I. Joes for you. And he had some of the cool ones."

Whitney laughed. "And Mom wouldn't let you."

"Yeah, I'm glad about that too. If I'd traded you, all of this might never have happened." Thom gestured with his chin to the crowd behind him.

Thom had said kind things in the past. He said he was proud of Whitney when she'd graduated college. He'd called her a good friend when she supported Grace through Geoff's passing. He'd even said she looked nice every once in a while.

Whitney didn't mind. That's how brothers were. They kept their feelings close to their chest. He could mess with her, but heaven help the poor idiot who messed with Whitney.

She allowed herself to take in what her brother had said. The words rolled around her mind as she looked at the crowd that was larger than anything she'd ever seen. As though he was reading her mind, he said, "An oak tree starts with a seed smaller than the palm of our hands."

Movement in the crowd drew Whitney's attention. People parted and came back together like waves in a pond. She strained her eyes to see what would be the cause of it.

She saw a flicker of brown on the ground.

It couldn't be.

Then when the crowd dispersed again. Whitney focused just ahead of the wave.

It was.

"Riley," she gasped. "I'll be back as soon as I can."

The metal stairs clacked against the weight of Whitney's feet, colliding with them. Mixed in with the noise, she heard Thom call after her, "Make sure you're here in time for the race to start."

She pushed through the crowd, heading in the direction of where she last saw Mrs. Abernathy's dog. The poor woman would be distraught. There were too many people, and the likelihood of Riley getting hurt or stolen would add to her anxiety.

Whitney lowered her body to the waist level of those around her. Whitney called out, "Riley! Here, boy."

She ignored some rude guy's comment, "Lady, you should have your dog on a leash."

The terrier pranced to Whitney and danced in a circle. She held out her arms, and the dog jumped into her chest.

Whitney baby-talked to the dog. "Your mama is going to be so worried about you."

Riley lapped her chin with doggy kisses, leaving Whitney to walk with an obscured view through the crowd. She thought she'd never reach a clearing but finally made it to the road leading to Mrs. Abernathy's house.

It wasn't that far a walk, especially with the noise gauging the distance. By the time Whitney reached the end of Mrs. Abernathy's block, the music was muffled. The occasional high tone bled over. Otherwise, it was fairly silent.

The sun was up, and birds flitted in the trees. Whitney checked the time on her step checker. She had a little more than a half hour to get to the starting line. It had taken her ten minutes to get this far. So it would be easy to make it back without being missed. She strolled by the neatly cut lawns, the houses with doors open, stopping in front of the gate leading to Mrs. Abernathy's porch.

Whitney opened the gate, rubbed the space between Riley's ears, and set him on the ground. "Promise me you won't run away."

The dog whimpered and ran circles around Whitney's legs. She backed away, and he howled and barked. The hairs on Whitney's arms turned into antennae, trying to find the source of the dog's unusual behavior. She'd walk him to the door. Mrs. Abernathy would understand when Whitney hurried away.

She knocked, and the door gave way. Mrs. Abernathy was on the ground with her face resting on her arm. "I've tried for hours but can't get up."

Chapter 49

This is Not Like Her

Conrad scoured the crowd, looking for a brown ponytail. It wasn't much, but that was all he had to work with to differentiate Whitney from the hundreds of people wearing blue race shirts in front of the stands.

Upbeat music blared through the sound system. The scent of sunscreen wafted from the crowd, competing with the lilacs in the nearby bushes. Sirens passing through town roared in the undertones of the music.

Conrad had made sure everyone knew Whitney Stansfield was the race founder and preferred blending in with the crowd. The previous race's volunteers vouched for what he said. One had gone as far as mentioning a time Whitney heard the port-a-potties were low on toilet paper and personally restocked every one of them.

One guy said, "So what I'm hearing is she's one of those undercover boss types." The "I gotta meet her" glint in his eyes got him stationed to manning the dunk tank.

Then everybody caught on to the tone behind Conrad's words. Whitney was high priority and off-limits.

A woman in a visor and short shorts waved. She looked familiar but not enough for Conrad to associate her face with a name. She pushed through the crowd and disappeared into the sea of faces. Since she wasn't who he was looking for, Conrad dismissed her from his thoughts and returned to what he was doing. "I don't see Whitney anywhere."

"I knew these would come in handy." Darcy dug into her purse and extracted a pair of birdwatching binoculars. Her voice sounded like one of the people on the National Geographic Channel. "She shouldn't be that hard to find. She was there a minute ago."

Mark had his hand pressed against his brow. "When Erick gets here, he'll find her in a second. The man has a superpower. He can find his daughters within seconds. Remember that time when Whitney and Ericka didn't want to go home after a concert at the state fair? She was a couple of months short of turning eighteen."

"That's right. She tried hiding in the middle of the crowd." Darcy pointed her binoculars to the center of the group in front of them.

Mark's chest rose in a soft chuckle. "Erick walked straight up to her like he was supposed to meet her at the exact point."

Before things went awry, Conrad had the gift. He could sense when Whitney woke up in the morning and when her eyes gave way to sleep. It was also what triggered his suspicions. He knew something was off that night.

His insecurities sabotaged his confidence. Adrian asked if eight was okay. Whitney would have been with Conrad at the restaurant at eight. If Conrad had kept his cool, he'd have read the signs pointing toward an office surprise party.

Now she was polite, distant, unreadable. Conrad would do anything to get that closeness with her back.

Erick and three of Whitney's brothers and Ericka walked

along the curb. They wore matching jackets with the stripe down the sleeve, looking like those cartoon families, prepared for a major competition. All were lean, healthy, and had serious expressions that said if it were a race, they'd win.

"This is not like her to disappear," Grace said. "Whitney usually checks in."

This was not the time to panic.

Conrad sent a text to Whitney. "Where are you?"

There were no dots.

She wasn't reading her phone, which meant plan B.

He approached the microphone. "Whitney Stansfield, can you return to the stands?"

"He's had a hard time keeping up with her from day one." Conrad recognized Nathan's voice. He would have laughed with the crowd if he weren't so concerned. That first day they were together without Jasmine or Adrian, Whitney tried ditching Conrad. It didn't work. She put up quite the fight, but he wore her down.

Conrad's gaze darted over the crowd despite the feeling in his gut that she wasn't anywhere he'd be able to see her. "Do we need to get the police involved?"

Thom opened his phone. "Whitney made us sign up for the Find My Friend app last year. At the time, I thought it was stupid." His expression shifted from curious to focused. "The app shows that she is in the neighborhood." He slid his pointer finger and thumb, expanding the screen. "Oh, two blocks away."

The race was scheduled to start in five minutes.

Beads of sweat formed on Conrad's back. Otherwise, he kept his cool, scaling the panic to a manageable level. "Why is she all the way over there?"

"I don't know. The dot is bouncing but doesn't move. Could she have lost her phone there?"

Conrad's phone vibrated with the message, "Start without

me. Mrs. Abernathy fell. I'm waiting for the ambulance with her."

"What should we do?" Darcy looked to Mark. "We've never started without her."

"It sounds like she'll be a while," Mark said.

"She'll catch up," Thom said. "Whitney always finishes what she starts."

Mark and Darcy went to the corner of the stage to take their place at the front of the crowd.

A sinking feeling pushed at Conrad's stomach. Who knew how long she'd be with Mrs. Abernathy? Odds were the race would delay the first responders. He nodded to Seth to start the race.

Seth introduced Mark and Darcy and gave the backstory for the race.

There was still no Whitney.

Seth asked the audience to give a round of applause to the volunteers.

There was still no Whitney.

They counted down the race. "Three, two, one," and a buzzer sounded. The golf cart with Mark and Darcy rolled into motion, and the crowd followed.

Thom held up the phone screen so Grace could see it. "I didn't know my sister could move that fast."

Everything moved in slow motion. Conrad hadn't experienced this level of focus since he'd been on the football field.

An out-of-breath Whitney was on the other side of the street. A sea of heads passed her on their way to the starting line. Whitney's gaze landed on Conrad, and for a brief second, the wall she'd been peering from behind was gone. She seemed happy to see him. Her eyes shifted toward something on the other side of the stands, and her facial expression hardened to resolve. A woman he'd met at Jamie's birthday party pulled her along with the crowd.

Conrad saw it.

His breath caught in the area in the middle of his chest.

She was happy to see him.

As quickly as the moment happened, it passed. Whitney's face said that something had changed.

A woman in shorty shorts and a slit cut in the front of her run shirt was beside Conrad. She crossed her arms beneath her cleavage and tipped her head. "You are a hard person to get a hold of."

"I feel like I should know you." Conrad was polite despite the "be careful" vibe his gut sent off like a sonar through his body.

"Probably because we have a history." She coyly dipped her head. "I was on the sidelines cheering for you for five years."

It clicked.

She was the woman who asked for the picture when he and Whitney were on their date.

Conrad looked back to where Whitney had been waiting and then back at the woman.

Whitney changed as soon as the woman was by Conrad's side. And then it clicked. Samantha was Whitney's weapon. She was the tool she'd used to decide Conrad could do better?

Well, she was wrong.

"Excuse me" Conrad reached into his back pocket, retrieved his phone, and typed, "I'll have your avocado smoothie at the finish line." He punctuated it with a wink face emoji.

The first time Whitney tried to blow him off, they wound up at his house, having a lively discussion about avocados being a breakfast food. He was banking on it happening again.

Chapter 50

Not Today

At first, the crowd moved at a snail's pace, and they were so close together it was hard to see beyond the people directly ahead and behind Whitney. Now that she was in the mix, she saw the flaw in her plan of getting to the starting line, finding her friends, and enjoying the walk.

Back in the day. She cut off the stream of thought. People closer to retirement age started their complaints with "when I was your age" or "back in the day."

Whitney didn't want to criticize progress, but things were a lot simpler in the days when she didn't have to worry about being trampled by a woman wearing a tutu pushing a baby carriage.

She was surrounded by people yet felt all alone. Some wore headphones. Most talked among themselves. None included her in their conversations. Being the youngest of six children left Whitney unprepared for the loneliness that clawed at her.

"Where are you?" She texted Jasmine.

"We just passed the shoe store."

Near the beginning. The one place the moving crowd obstructed her from going, but she got there in time to meet up with Jasmine and Adrian. Whitney, more worried about being trampled than keeping up, lost them just as quickly.

The change in the signs over the storefronts and variations in the treetops marked the distance. The hardware store. Manuel's Mexican food. By the time they reached the dress boutique, the crowd had thinned, allowing her to see pavement.

Gap by gap, Whitney eased her way to the sidewalk. Ruby and Pauline, wearing matching pink caps embroidered with the fun run logo, walked by. Their elbows were bent, and their arms pumped in a slower version of a walker competing for a set time. From what Whitney could tell, one was happier about their progress. The other was looking for an excuse to slow down, and she was glad to have been found by Whitney.

"Thank you for saving me." Ruby tilted her head toward Pauline and frowned to say somebody didn't get the memo. "I'm here to check out the guys in running shorts."

"If you'd have been here a minute later, you'd have missed us," Pauline said. She had the eye on the prize look on her face. "We're almost at full momentum."

A gray-haired man that looked like he was fit from the day he was born jogged by.

"See. I knew I wouldn't be disappointed." Ruby fell in line with Whitney and matched her pace as though they were meant to be a group of three.

"Adding Conrad to the team was a great idea. There are more people to meet."

"It's also harder to find the people I'm looking for." Conrad was used to standing out in a crowd. Large groups reminded Whitney how easy it was to get lost.

"That's when you know who's looking out for you," Pauline replied.

"It works out," Ruby said. "Remember back in the day when it was just a handful of us? You had to tag team with the other event coordinators." She scanned the area around Whitney, noticing that she was alone. "Oh, I suppose you still do that."

Whitney had worked with the committee for most of the year. Now it was race day, and the communication with Whitney seemed superficial. From what she had seen, the teams from different stations coordinated their flow.

The space between the three friends and the other walkers increased, eliminating the claustrophobic feeling of others pressing in on them. "Thousands of people couldn't break us apart. That's what happens with good friends. We always find each other."

True to form, Pauline and Ruby talked Whitney through the benefits of the changes in her situation. If she didn't know any better, Whitney would have thought that life had plunked her into that moment for an attitude adjustment.

"Speaking of." Pauline pointed at the sidewalk in front of the Sweet Treats Cafe. Nathan and Jack, with necks craned like baby birds searching for food, walked by the door.

"The cinnamon rolls come after the walk." Whitney had taken Ruby's wisdom to heart and found her sense of humor.

"What if they sell them all before we get there? It's not like we're the fastest walkers in the pack." Nathan's gaze lingered on the door as though the extra attention would entice the owner to come out and say, "I've saved some for you."

"It's a good thing they have a table at the vendor's station." That was one of the perks of Conrad joining the team. He convinced local businesses to contribute samples to guide people to their stores. Whitney intentionally left out the part about the portions being smaller. There were so many goodies at the finish line Nathan wouldn't have time to worry about how much he got.

Two fit people that looked to be in their twenties came up alongside the group. "Are you Whitney?"

Their enthusiasm at recognizing Whitney didn't feel natural, but then she remembered that Conrad's team had added the story of the race's beginnings to the website. The couple must have been among the few who read all the details of a race. She replied, "The one and only."

"Do you mind if we take a picture with you?"

It was a weird request, but Whitney didn't see a problem with it. She said, "Sure."

The group spread to make room for the photo.

With the enthusiasm of a soccer mom, the woman waved for them to move closer. "We want all of you. It'll fit better with the vibe."

They all pulled in. The woman's partner held up the phone and tilted it so they'd all fit on the screen. After a few clicks, he said, "One of these will work."

They joined the group. The one with the camera kept pace while fiddling with the screen. "We're the first to get a selfie."

"No way!" The taller of the two friends said, "My name is Bridget, and he's Weston. We're from Ashbrook."

Whitney said, "Nice to meet you. We're the Lilac Lane Walkers."

Bridget asked, "Why don't you have t-shirts?"

Weston said, "Then it would be easier for people to find them."

"Find us?" Nathan's voice said he had picked up on the feeling that they were left out of a conversation.

Bridget replied, "A blogger wrote about the fun run. She noticed that the promo material focused on Geoff's family and Conrad Hayes."

The Lilac Lane Walkers shared a glance that expressed that they were impressed. Someone had made an effort to notice the people who rarely got attention. Not that any of them wanted it, but it was nice to be seen.

"And that website promoting the run barely mentioned the person who started it all. So she wrote your story."

Whitney's heart stalled. Her story?

"About twenty minutes ago, she posted on social media that you had gotten lost in the crowd and asked for help finding you. Where's Whitney became a trending hashtag. People have been posting pictures of you at the race."

The chatter in Whitney's mind stole her ability to respond. A hashtag?

"I think that's called stalking," Ruby said.

"It happens to famous people all the time," Bridgett said.

"But I'm just Whitney."

"The voice that reminds people to take care of their hearts so they can have a full life." Bridgett corrected.

Weston sounded like he'd meant it when he said, "We're giving attention to someone saying something people need to hear."

They were saying kind things, but the sense of intrusion alarmed Whitney. She was an occupational therapist in small-town Montana. The race would pass, and people would forget she existed. Yet, it was a small taste of Conrad and Adrian's life. Was this what they felt like at lunch when they visited the chocolate factory?

Ruby and Pauline picked up the conversation, leaving Whitney to spin in the cycle of what she should do. Whitney's shoes felt too tight, and the heat her body generated was a degree higher than she would have liked. Worries pounded her. Was her hair okay? Had she said or done anything that would embarrass herself? Her family? The fun run?

An aching feeling clouded her enjoyment of the walk. *Was this what Conrad felt all the time? Everything he did was under scrutiny. No wonder he was so sensitive about the picture at lunch.*

She noticed people on the sidewalks were taking pictures. Had they done that in years past, or was this something new?

A small crowd had formed at the water station at the two-mile mark, slowing the flow of foot traffic.

"We can go around," Nathan suggested. "There's cinnamon rolls at the finish line."

"Hey, Whit! Wait up." Ivan stepped off the curb, signaling for the rest of Whitney's family to follow.

Seeing her parents and siblings lightened the mental load Whitney had been carrying. Being the youngest girl in a family with six children often had its complications. Every friend and potential date was met with exponential scrutiny. Her family was her wall of protection. Whenever Whitney would get upset with her brothers or father, they'd accept her anger and say, "This too shall pass." It was their way of saying that their family ties were stronger than the problems.

Even though it was well-intentioned, being the subject of a hashtag was stressful. Her family waiting for her put it into perspective. It was temporary, and she may have been making a bigger deal of it than she realized.

When they circled around her, Whitney noticed that Bridgett and Weston, in their matching athletic wear, fit more with her family than Whitney did.

Her dad patted her on the shoulder. "What's that look on your face?"

"I get to walk with the most handsome man in the crowd," Whitney said.

Her dad talked to her mom. "She thought we'd forgotten her."

"One time." Her mother threw her hands in the air. "You forget a child at the grocery store one time, and you never get to live it down."

The banter was back. Whitney sighed with the breaking of the adrenaline's hold on her.

Ericka leaned in to talk to Whitney. "Did you know there's a Where's Whitney hashtag?"

"Yeah, it's weird," Whitney said.

"And people are sending online donations to support the scholarship?"

"It's hard to be upset when you frame it like that," Whitney replied. Did she like the attention? No. Would she endure it? Yes. When the day was done, Whitney would have to thank Conrad for taking over the fun run.

Chapter 51

Happily Ever After

The tides had turned powerfully, and Conrad had less than an hour to tame them. He had failed and had done so miserably.

Noisemakers rattled, and the blare of bullhorns announced Whitney's arrival at the finish line.

A crowd of people.

Wait.

Conrad focused on faces.

Whitney's family and Ruby and Pauline...all the people who had been with Whitney from the origins of the Healthy Heart Fun Run were together to finish the race.

True to form, Whitney was the dot of color in the middle. The rest of her family had worn dark jogging suits.

Conrad's pocket vibrated with yet another notification. It was another reminder of his counterintuitive attempts to control the stream of information about his personal life. This time it was administered with slivers of guilt.

Samantha

She and everyone in front of the starting tent heard his conversation with Nathan. While Conrad, Thom, and everyone else underneath the awning were scratching their heads, Samantha posted a picture of the crowd with a thoughtful request for information about Whitney's whereabouts.

Hey! Whitney is low-key awesome. She's always doing something behind the scenes to make sure your day is the best. And we lost her in the crowd. If you see her, can you share a pic and label it #whereswhitney so we can keep track of her?

Within seconds someone posted a picture of Whitney walking toward Main Street.

Within minutes there was a conversation going about protecting the race's founder.

In less time than that, the hashtag #whereswhitney had grown into a game and fundraiser. People who couldn't make the event wanted to contribute to the cause.

Conrad had to get to Whitney. To explain that beyond friendly banter, Samantha had no interest in him. To tell Whitney that it was obvious to Samantha and anyone that had seen them together that she was his inspiration. To tell her that he didn't want another day to go by without her knowing that he was in love with her.

Seth waved the clipboard in his hand. "You go ahead. We have things covered."

They were on the downslide. People, waiting for results, snacked on bananas and samples. Grills had been fired up, and the smell of roasting hot dogs and hamburgers overpowered the nose-pinching scent of sports creams.

Conrad trotted down the steps to meet them. He was halfway down when Seth said, "Don't blow it this time."

"I don't plan on it."

"Really?" Seth held out the smoothie Conrad was supposed to hand to Whitney. "Then you might want to bring this with you."

He met Conrad at the top of the stairs. "It's Whitney."

The words meant to encourage tightened their grip around Conrad's chest.

Exactly. It was Whitney. The woman he'd taken for granted. When he finally saw her for who she was, a ray of pure light in his world contaminated with suspicions, he shielded himself when he should have basked in her presence. He should have held on to her and declared to the world that there was something good in it—and this goodness in the form of a beautiful woman had found and loved him.

Instead, he tried to hide her, and then blamed her when she tried to fit in his mold.

She deserved every bit of the attention she was getting, thanks to Samantha.

Whitney used to make fun of Conrad and his fans. "C'mon now, you know you dug having all those people waiting for you after a game outside the locker room."

Conrad asked, "Why didn't I ever see you?"

She replied, "Because I'd get lost in the crowd."

Whitney had gotten lost in the crowd, but it was because they were protecting her.

The crowd around him competed for his attention, for an autograph, for a photo op, and Whitney thought she'd get brushed to the side.

It was time to change the narrative.

Multicolored ribbons narrowed the path making it easier to keep track of times and the order that people finished. Erick's hands, softly gripped on Whitney's shoulders, guided her through the chute, straight to Conrad.

Conrad held his arms open wide for her to walk into his embrace.

When she was secure in his arms, he breathed in her scent. She still smelled like strawberry shampoo. "Losing you was the scariest thing to have ever happened." Conrad kept his tone light. Anyone outside their core group would think he meant before the event started. The mist in his eyes promised he'd right his wrong and be the man she deserved.

Whitney froze. She gestured with raised brows and a quick darting of her eyes. There were cameras, people, they had an audience.

That didn't matter anymore. He only cared about her.

Conrad dangled an event's promotional cup in front of her. "I'm sorry to disappoint you. It's a mango pineapple smoothie. Apparently, our love of avocado isn't a mutual experience."

"If you're not drinking it, I will." Ivan pushed around Whitney, but didn't get far.

She playfully nudged him with her shoulder. "Get your own."

Her mother took the smoothie. "I'll hold this for you." Then she nudged her chin toward Conrad. "What do we say to men who give us smoothies?"

Whitney shook her head like she was behaving out of obligation. Then she stepped in and hugged Conrad again.

Conrad whispered in her ear, "I'm so proud of you." He wrapped his free arm around her waist, picked her up, and kissed her.

She didn't hesitate or stiffen or give signs of resistance. She wrapped her arms over his shoulders and kissed him back.

The clicks of camera shutters around them marked the moment. Conrad Hayes was in love with Whitney Stansfield, and if the grin on her face was any indication, she was on the road to forgiving him for failing to say so sooner.

Chapter 52

Does This Mean?

She'd expected a smoothie. A high five. Maybe a comment about making a good time, considering she started late. Something professional.

Conrad standing at the finish with his arms wide open.

Her father whispering in her ear, *go to him*.

Ivan antagonizing her to make her claim.

None of those were in Whitney's morning visualization of her day. Her heart danced one step ahead of her. Conrad's embrace pushed it into beating double-time. She may have lost consciousness when he kissed her.

Whitney's legs turned to jelly, and she swooned when Conrad released her. He quickly wrapped his arms around her shoulder and guided her and her family to the staging tent.

The rest of the day was a blur filled with visits to the different venues around the park and talking to walkers.

When the tents were packed and put away, the debris cleared by the cleaning crew, and the crowd dwindled to kids playing soccer in the park, Whitney and Jasmine retreated to the gazebo.

Jasmine tipped her toe into the heel of her sneaker and slid it off. "What a day."

Adrian and Conrad trotted up the stairs. Adrian slapped Conrad's chest with the back of his hand. "I told you they'd be here."

Conrad didn't sound impressed. "It was the last place we looked."

He filled the space beside Whitney. "Have you checked your notifications lately?"

"I couldn't keep up, so I stopped trying," Whitney admitted. Being popular was more work than she'd realized.

"There's one I think you'll want to see." His hand flap egged her to take a look.

Whitney scrolled. They all looked the same to her, and she was one swipe away from giving up when she saw one from Conrad. She squinted. What did it mean?

She read the comment where she was tagged.

ConradHayes: @whits_end, can you answer @luvtoliv's question?

The post was a picture of Conrad with his arm around Whitney. They were looking into each other's eyes. The comment said, "Today couldn't have happened without these two people."

Whitney returned to the comment section. Conrad's post was a reply to the question from a Luvtoliv.

LuvtoLiv: Does this mean @ConradHayes is off the market?

ConradHayes: @ whits_end, can you answer @luvtoliv's question?

Whitney looked at Conrad. What was he expecting her to say?

"I've been miserable for the past week. When things aren't

right between us, it feels like something catastrophic is waiting for me around the corner."

Whitney reflected on the day. Whenever an issue came up, it was handled before it became a problem. All the volunteers had just as much, if not more, fun as the people who paid to attend the event. Several of them planned a cookout for the following weekend. Conrad had united a community.

"It's not the same without you by my side," Conrad confessed. "Ever since I've been back, I've been working to prove that your help in high school mattered. I think. No, I know. I was trying too hard. And in doing so, I hurt the person I was trying to impress."

"You were trying to impress me?"

"At first, no. I was trying to fit in. But as we got deeper into the project, it was obvious that you set a solid foundation. I could do bigger, but not better than what you'd already accomplished. It was like when we were kids and had visions of what we would do when it was our time to leave our mark on the world. You'd already made yours, Whit. You didn't need me."

Adrian and Jasmine had moved to the other side of the gazebo, pretending that something on the other side of the park had their attention.

"You're right. I didn't need you, Conrad. I wanted you. When someone is done needing you, they can throw you away. When they want you, they know you're important, so they hold on to you as best as they can."

And that is why she couldn't accept his apology that night. They were on the cusp of the run. She'd never know if he was more worried about losing her or her connections.

"Well, Whitney. I want you. I want to go on hikes, and I want to take selfies, and I want to buy ice cream, and I want to take romantic trips....I want to catch up on all the things I missed."

His chest rose and fell beneath his breathing, and his gaze begged her to believe him.

Whitney joined the comment stream beneath the picture and typed her reply. Then, she showed her phone screen to Conrad.

whits_end: @luvtoliv @conradhayes is off the market.

Conrad's shoulders slumped. He exhaled and kissed Whitney on the forehead. "I love you, Whitney."

"It's about time," Adrian said.

"Seriously," Jasmine agreed. "They acted like we were the ones that were stubborn."

"The nerve of some people." Adrian shook his head in mock disgust.

Jasmine replied, "Which is why we will graciously accept the invitation to have pizza at Conrad's house."

"We'll see you there in an hour." Adrian and Jasmine walked out of the gazebo, leaving Whitney and Conrad watching behind them.

Whitney said, "They didn't wait for me to tell you that I loved you, too."

Jasmine peeked her head through the opening. "Because everybody already knew that." She tiptoed to where she left her shoes and picked them up and backed away. "Don't pay me any mind. You two can pick up where you left off."

Conrad cupped Whitney's cheek and kissed her. "You can tell me you love me on the way to pick up avocados for the salad."

"You knew?"

"Looking back at all you've done for me. I should have known." Conrad pressed his forehead onto Whitney's and grinned. "I'm in love with you."

Whitney replied, "And you're off the market."

Chapter 53

Award Night

Whitney sat in the front row of the stadium—close enough for Conrad to see her but far enough to give him room to bask in his glory. He had done everything he said he would. For days, the town was filled with people who had left Cottage Cove and returned to reconnect with their past.

Another player from the high school football team that had gone on to be a civil engineer in Atlanta was working with the city council to add commemorative benches and sculptures on the Lilac Lane walking trail.

Geoff's parents, the high school principal, and the athletic director sat to the right of Conrad, who was leaning forward at his waist, pressing his elbow into his knee. Whitney willed him to pull away from the discussion he was having with Seth and the football coach. It didn't work.

She couldn't blame him. With the upbeat music and the stadium filling with people, excitement in the air was palpable, making it hard to focus on anything that wasn't directly in front of him.

A silver tarp had been laid on the basketball court to protect the wood. All the fun run coordination team sat in chairs on the floor facing the court. The other spectators sat in the navy blue bleachers.

At first, it didn't register to Whitney that the man in the pressed khaki dress pants that passed by her was Adrian. He settled into the seat beside her.

"Where's Jasmine?" Whitney looked in the direction from where he had entered the row, hoping to see her.

"She cornered the Booster Club president in the lobby to talk about a fundraiser at the summer carnival. When I heard the word dunk tank, I took it as a cue to leave."

A bubble of laughter escaped from Whitney. "You are doomed, my friend."

The gentle man-in-love glow brightened his face. "Thank you."

"You're welcome," Whitney's chest warmed with pride about being right. Adrian and Jasmine belonged together.

"Isn't it crazy? How we get in our own way." Adrian's cheeks flushed to a shade of pink.

Adrian's chest rose with pride that was contagious. "Yeah, but you can't blame a guy for playing it safe."

Whitney felt the warmth of a man who had run from love but had been caught. All his talk about being too damaged was fear of rejection.

Jasmine's voice startled Whitney. "I'll give you points for trying to hide, Adrian. But we know you'll get more when people line up to give you a good soaking."

While Adrian shook his head in mock defeat, Whitney stood in a motion for Jasmine to trade her places.

Just as they were situated, the music died down, and the principal tapped the microphone. A screech echoed through the auditoriums, and people cringed.

His radio host's smooth voice came through the sound

system, "Sorry about that. Sometimes I don't know my strength." People groaned at his joke, and he released a rich, deep laugh.

"I know we're here to talk about someone. Someone influential in the sports community. This someone then brought that gift home."

Even though Whitney knew the story by heart and could add some details the principal omitted, she hung onto every word. She liked the part where the principal talked about Conrad connecting with the high school football team and talking with them about being healthy physically and mentally.

Conrad's attention was centered on the principal. He smiled when the principal talked about them playing pee wee football together. And, his lips stiffened into a straight line of reverence when the principal talked about how Conrad honored Geoff's memory by joining efforts with the fun run.

Two women who were cheerleaders when Conrad played football walked out holding either side of a plaque. They rotated beside the podium so everyone could see Conrad's jersey.

"From this point forward, football number thirty-five is retired."

The stands erupted with applause and cheers. The principal waved Conrad to the podium to speak. Conrad rose, and people clapped louder and pounded their feet in the stands.

Conrad croaked, clearing his throat, and they quieted.

"I am blown away." Conrad gestured with the t-shirt. "I thought we were here to present the scholarships."

The stands aww'd.

"I have one of those big checks in the back."

The two cheerleaders hurried to the side of the stands and returned with a check.

"Next year, several Cottage Cove Hawkeyes won't have to worry about how their college textbooks will be paid for."

The cheerleaders presented the check for twenty-eight thousand dollars. "This is an accumulation of money from the fun run and donations from the Where's Whitney social media conversation."

Athletes dressed in Cottage Cove gear stood and whistled. Conrad stood with his palms pressed against the podium. When the volume dropped to a level where he could be heard, he cleared his voice into the microphone.

"There are several people we need to recognize. There's Mark and Darcy Hill. Geoff may not have had as much game time as the rest of us, but his time here was powerful."

People clapped. Grace hugged her mom. Mark nodded and waved, acknowledging the recognition.

"I also want to share something that isn't on the agenda." He turned his gaze toward the principal. "If that's okay with you."

The principal bobbed his head, encouraging Conrad to continue.

"First, the fun run is coordinated by a committee of people."

Whitney leaned forward to smile at Seth. He, along with Thom, had onboarded Conrad.

"When I returned to Cottage Cove, I didn't know how to step back into the community. I am a lucky man because Whitney Stansfield shared her dream. Protecting hearts." He pointed toward the crowd. "Your hearts. Everything she has done was to give you a chance for a future."

Prickles followed the rush of blood that streamed through Whitney's body. She tensed against her muscles twitching in preparation to run from the surge of heat that was sure to follow.

Conrad smiled softly. His gaze landed on Whitney. "We are lucky enough to be ignorant of how different our lives would be without someone like her."

Jess and Ericka approached the podium. Jess set a plaque on

the stand. Ericka smiled at Whitney, and they took their place behind Conrad.

"Cottage Cove's beacon of hope, Whitney Stansfield, has won the Women Making A Difference Award. Can all of you join me in congratulating her?"

Applause echoed throughout the gymnasium. Adrian patted Whitney on the back. Jasmine pulled Whitney up into a hug. "I'm so happy for you."

Whitney didn't know where her parents had come from. Her father picked her up into a hug and twirled her around. "Look at what my youngest daughter has done." Her mother kissed her on the cheek. Whitney's mind buzzed.

The principal met Conrad at the podium and attached a lapel microphone to his collar.

Whitney's family backed away, and Conrad walked away from the podium, to the stands, until he was directly in front of her. "But, wait, there's more."

Everyone laughed because he sounded like one of those home-shopping telemarketers.

When the laughter settled, Conrad said. "I wouldn't be here today if Whitney hadn't helped me when I was a senior in high school. I suffered a concussion and couldn't retain information. She stuck by my side, helping me pass my classes. I want to ask her today if she'd stay by my side for the rest of our lives."

Whitney blinked. Had she heard correctly?

The crowd fell silent.

Conrad reached into his pocket and knelt on one knee. "I am asking if you would do me the honor of being by my side for the rest of our lives as my wife. If you say yes, I promise to do my best to honor and support you with the same tenacity you have shown me."

"Me?" Whitney thought for sure she was dreaming.

"Yes, you." Conrad's eyes were bright with love.

Whitney's voice was stuck somewhere in the back of her throat. She pressed her hands against her lips and nodded.

Conrad tilted his head, facing his ear toward Whitney. His voice was infused with hope. "Yes?"

She squeaked out, "Yes."

The crowd erupted in cheers.

Conrad slid the ring on her finger and hugged her. "I love you."

Whitney wrapped her arms around his waist and squeezed, glad for the embrace. How many times had she dreamed this moment, thinking it would never come true? She was glad to be wrong. "I love you too."

Then he kissed her. Right there in front of everyone. Their classmates, friends, family—her father, who probably was smiling wider than everyone in the room.

Life had taken a turn neither of them had seen coming. Conrad Hayes did go for girls like her. She had not one, but two pictures on the front page of Cottage Cove Weekly, and a ring on her finger to prove it.

Epilogue

Whitney's face was inches away from Conrad's. His eyes were pools of color, reflecting what she would have guessed was bliss. She felt the same way, dancing in his arms at their wedding reception.

"We did it." His attention flitted to the people around them. "All the people who have brought us to this point. In one room. Celebrating the best decision I've ever made." He pressed his lips onto her forehead, kissing her gently. "We will be together for the rest of our lives."

The last part sounded like a promise to himself and a declaration to Whitney. The music that had been a gate between the two of them and the room of people softened to a stop. "Now, it's time for the parents to join the bride and groom on the dance floor."

Whitney and Conrad looked up. Her head spun, shifting her focus from one person to the entire room. The first notes to Copacabana, and her brow shot up. That was all Whitney had time to see. She was in a line with her father and mother to her right. Claire and Austin were to Conrad's left. Their arms moved in rhythm with the music, and they took one step at the same time, giving away that they had synchronized a dance. With the transition to the next song, their line dance morphed into a juke dance. From there, it turned into the Electric Slide.

That was the signal for the DJ to invite everyone to join.

Thom and Ben were the first to join in, starting what became a dance battle to see who had the best moves. The ladies cheered and hollered.

Off on the corner of the dance floor, Ivan talked his dance partner, a twelve-year-old girl, wearing a navy blue chiffon dress, through the steps. The hard lines of focus amplified every hesitant step she took. Her younger brother, an eight-year-old dressed in a vest that matched the groomsmen, missed just as many steps. He compensated with improvised finger raises or twirls. One time he did a little bit of the twist. Ivan encouraged and smiled at the girl until halfway through the song, when she found her footing and her confidence.

The we-did-it feeling filled Whitney to the point of surprise. Every time she thought she had achieved the pinnacle of happiness, the feeling would come along and prove her wrong.

They'd organized two more fun runs and built two non-profit organizations. One was for athletes to monitor their physical and mental health. The other was to support students' study habits. Now, she and Conrad were partners in life.

Whitney stopped by the wedding party's table for a glass of water. Again, awe filled her. The flowers, woven in a pattern and wrapped with burlap ribbon, still smelled amazing.

Jasmine squeezed her hand. "I love this. You pulled all of our family and friends together." Jasmine's father and mother, older versions of Jamie and Jasmine, were seated at the table nearest the bridal party, talking with Adrian's mother and her boyfriend.

Whitney said, "I bet they're planning your wedding."

Jasmine's blush said she hoped so but didn't want to think

about it until Adrian had formally proposed. So she took a note out of Whitney's manual "Did you see Ivan with Jess's kids? They were so adorable." She raised her drink to direct Whitney's attention to Ivan, who had a group of teenage girls in line to dance with him. He twirled Jess's daughter. She gave him one of her rare smiles and giggled mid-spin.

"My brother is the dance whisperer." Ivan and Whitney practiced dancing in middle school. He wanted to look good for all the girls. She didn't want to trip and fall on her face. He'd resurrected the practice. Whitney glanced around the room, looking for Jess. Ivan had a thing for her, but wouldn't follow through with the interest. "Too bad he can't convince their mothers to join in the fun."

She found Jess, off in the corner with a very pregnant Grace, Sammy, and a couple of other women. They talked and laughed and snacked on foods from the snack buffet.

Whitney wanted to join them, but every time she thought about sitting down, someone pulled her into a conversation or a dance or something just as fun.

So much had changed since that picture of her kissing Conrad hit the highlights of the sports section in every newspaper around the country. She had become interesting, and the gift of retreating to the corner had become less frequent.

"I know what you mean." Jasmine tapped her perfectly manicured nail on her lips. "I have an idea." She smoothed the front of her dress and headed toward the table.

Whitney pulled on the front of her dress and hustled to catch up to her friend. "What's the idea?"

"I can't say," Jasmine said. "It'll give you plausible deniability."

Ben approached Whitney. "Mom wants a picture of all of us in front of the cake for the Christmas card picture ."

Whitney grimaced. Her mother loved the nontraditional

Christmas card pictures—the ones where the family was chaotic, messy, real. They were the cards everyone posted on their refrigerators and kept there for half the year.

The Stansfield siblings in front of Whitney's wedding cake made of stacked cupcakes sounded like a very bad idea. Saving her cake became Whitney's number one priority, forcing her to trust that Jasmine wouldn't do something foolish like locking Ivan and Jess in the janitor's closet.

She glanced back. It was too late anyway. Jasmine was at the table with the other women. Dan and Ivan were at the cake table. Thom and Conrad were halfway across the dance floor on their way to meet them.

Whitney saw her window of opportunity to suggest a different idea for the family Christmas card. Grace had to be in the picture, too. The group would be too large, and her mother would have to find an alternative location for the impromptu Christmas card picture.

She pulled away from her brothers. "Let me get Grace." Before they had a chance to deter Whitney, Grace turned. Every woman at the table had their eyes on the partially assembled Stansfield family. Grace had her hand over her mouth, shielding her laugh. Jess's wide eyes and red face told the story. Jasmine had struck.

Thom had the advantage of flat shoes and pants, beating Whitney in the race to get Grace. Not that Whitney minded. He slowed to turn into the perfect gentleman. Holding the chair steady for Grace. Keeping one arm out for her to hold for balance, and the other resting gently on her lower back.

They had just made it to the table when Grace gasped. Everyone's gaze darted toward her. Grace said, "My water."

Then the camera flashed.

She backed away. Thom supported her. "Where are my keys?"

"My purse is in the car," Grace said.

Dan and Ben held the table steady while people moved to action.

Conrad kissed Whitney on the forehead. "We should go distract our guests."

Ivan or Jess or both had beaten them to it. They were in the middle of the dance floor in one of those dance circles. Jess's son was in the middle doing the best, John Travolta, Staying Alive hand motion while shuffling.

And Whitney's heart swelled to the point of bringing tears to her eyes. She had her cake intact, her family was growing, and Conrad Hayes was her partner in keeping it all together.

Here we are at the end of Conrad and Whitney's story. This is where I have to thank several people.

Paula (insert heart emoji) She's been with me from the beginning. I started this story in 2021 and got stuck after a series of school-related illnesses. Paula, thank you for being the heart on the other side of the book cover.

Stevie and Kim, you were there hearing me work through Conrad and Whitney's challenges. Stevie won't read this book because it's sweet, and she's a thriller reader. Kim called me regularly, asking for launch updates. Imagine her disappointment when Rona caught me not once, or twice, but three times in one year.

Mary Ellen, you have the gift of sending me notes at the perfect time.

My husband, Randy. He's the one who made me healthy brain snacks, said my meal contribution, peanut butter and jelly sandwiches, were the best he'd eaten, and has figured out the recipe for the best cup of coffee.

My editor, Tiffany Shand. Thank you for pushing me to be a better storyteller.

Last but not least, you, my reader friends. Every time I write a story, you are in the cozy chair across from me, laughing at the funny parts, cringing in the uncomfortable moments, and gushing at the sweet scenes. You make storytelling so much fun.

Thank you.

This is where I'll ask you to leave a review of *Cottage Cove Homecoming*. Let people know what you like about the Cottage Cove characters, or how the story made you feel. It gives people a better idea if the story will suit their needs.

Or, if you're still at a loss for words, can you leave some stars? I love stars.

And with all that, I'll close here sending you off with happily ever after wishes.

Bookish hugs

Merri

Author's Note

If you want some short stories to tide you over until the next book launches, I have published Small Town Spring. You can download the book. There is the option of joining my reader newsletter. Once to twice a month, I share reviews of books, updates to what I'm writing, and links to other books you can download for free.

Because we live in a remote area, I love social media. If you want to keep in touch, I have a variety of ways of talking with people. The links are below.

Until the next book,

Merri

facebook.com/merrimaywether

instagram.com/merrimaywether

pinterest.com/merrimaywether

What's Next?

Cottage Cove New Beginnings

In the picturesque town of Cottage Cove, Jess embarks on a fresh chapter of life with her two children, determined to rebuild and rediscover happiness. As a guiding light for others to regain confidence, she's an expert in empowering others, yet her ex-husband's betrayal has left her questioning her own worth.

Enter Ivan, captivated by Jess's charm from the moment they met. While managing an after-school program brings him fulfillment, he can't help but feel inadequate compared to the influential figures in Jess's life. Recognizing her need for genuine companionship, Ivan becomes steadfast in his commitment to being the friend she deserves.

Meanwhile, Jess's children astutely observe the strained dynamics among the adults and take it upon themselves to show them the pure joy of play and unity. Through their innocent gestures, they unwittingly bridge the gaps, becoming catalysts for connection and healing.

How will Jess find the strength to trust her heart again? Can

Ivan prove that his genuine care and support transcend flashy careers and influential connections?

Immerse yourself in Merri Maywether's heartwarming tale where love, healing, and self-discovery intertwine, reminding us that the simplest acts of love can lead to the most profound transformations.

Other Stories Like Cottage Cove Homecoming

For more brother's best friend stories, try:

Welcome Home in the Three Creeks, Montana Series

Home Is Where The Heart Is in the Three Creeks, Montana Series

202 *Canterbury Lane* in the Ashbrook, Montana Series

For more second chance at life, second chance at love stories, try:

Welcome Home in the Three Creeks, Montana series

Home Sweet Home in the Three Creeks, Montana series

Home For Good in the Three Creeks, Montana series

Honey, I'm Home in the Three Creeks, Montana series

222 *Redemption* Lane in the Ashbrook, Montana series

323 *Love Lane* in the Ashbrook Montana series

Paradise Hills Summer in the Paradise Hills, Montana series

Piece of Cake in the Small Town Stories Series

For a Visit in the Small Town Stories Series

More Titles by Merri Maywether

The Ashbrook, Montana Series

While navigating through real-world problems, the friends and family in Ashbrook find second chances at love.

537 Redemption Lane

324 Hope Road

222 Redemption Lane

121 Patience Place

323 Love Lane

452 Memory Lane

202 Canterbury Lane

The Small-Town Stories Series

Light-hearted quick reads for characters within the Ashbrook and Three Creek's, Montana series.

Piece of Cake

Get Well Soon

Just A Friend

For a Visit

The Three Creeks, Montana Series

For a friends to happily ever after romance story, visit Three Creeks, Montana.

Welcome Home

Home Sweet Home

Honey, I'm Home

Home for Good

Home Is Where The Heart Is

The Paradise Hills, Montana Series

In a cozy town nestled at the foothills of a mountain, love touches the heart of those who seek it.

Meet Me by the Christmas Tree

Paradise Hills Summer

Paradise Hills Trick or Treat

Paradise Hills Thanksgiving

Christmas Wishes

Holiday Kisses

*

One Fake Boyfriend

Hope Springs Series

Sweet Holiday Romance Novellas

Hope Springs Harvest Days

Winter Wonderland Inn

Mistletoe Mischief

Cottage Cove Small Town Sweet Stories

Cottage Cove Homecoming

Cottage Cove New Beginnings (launches 9-2024)

Made in the USA
Coppell, TX
13 August 2024